The Wonder Clock

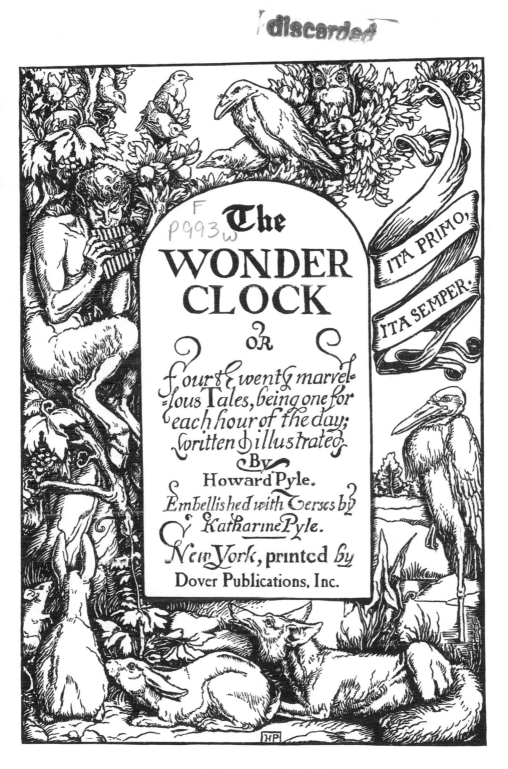

The WONDER CLOCK

OR

Four & Twenty marvel-lous Tales, being one for each hour of the day; written & illustrated By Howard Pyle. Embellished with Verses by Katharine Pyle. New York, printed by Dover Publications, Inc.

ITA PRIMO, ITA SEMPER.

Published in Canada by General Publishing
Company, Ltd., 30 Lesmill Road, Don Mills,
Toronto, Ontario.
Published in the United Kingdom by Constable
and Company, Ltd., 10 Orange Street, 'London
WC 2.

This Dover edition, first published in 1965, is an
unabridged and unaltered republication of the
work first published by Harper & Brothers in 1887.

Standard Book Number: 486-21446-X
Library of Congress Catalog Card Number: 65-26023

Manufactured in the United States of America

Dover Publications, Inc.
180 Varick Street
New York, N. Y. 10014

PREFACE.

 PUT on my dream-cap one day and stepped into Wonderland.

Along the road I jogged and never dusted my shoes, and all the time the pleasant sun shone and never burned my back, and the little white clouds floated across the blue sky and never let fall a drop of rain to wet my jacket. And by and by I came to a steep hill.

I climbed the hill, though I had more than one tumble in doing it, and there, on the tip-top, I found a house as old as the world itself.

That was where Father Time lived; and who should sit in the sun at the door, spinning away for dear life, but Time's Grandmother herself; and if you would like to know how old she is you will have to climb to the top of the church steeple and ask the wind as he sits upon the weather-cock, humming the tune of Over-yonder song to himself.

"Good-morning," says Time's Grandmother to me.

"Good-morning," says I to her.

"And what do you seek here?" says she to me.

"I come to look for odds and ends," says I to her.

"Very well," says she; "just climb the stairs to the garret, and there you will find more than ten men can think about."

"Thank you," says I, and up the stairs I went. There I found all manner of queer forgotten things which had been laid away, nobody but Time and his Grandmother could tell where.

Over in the corner was a great, tall clock, that had stood there silently with never a tick or a ting since men began to grow too wise for toys and trinkets.

But I knew very well that the old clock was the
Wonder Clock;
so down I took the key and wound it—gurr! gurr! gurr!

Click! buzz! went the wheels, and then—tick-tock! tick-tock! for the Wonder Clock is of that kind that it will never wear out, no matter how long it may stand in Time's garret.

Down I sat and watched it, for every time it struck it played a pretty song, and when the song was ended — click! click! — out stepped the drollest little puppet-figures and went through with a dance, and I saw it all (with my dream-cap upon my head).

But the Wonder Clock had grown rusty from long standing, and though now and then the puppet-figures danced a dance that I knew as well as I know my bread-and-butter, at other times they jigged a step I had never seen before, and it came into my head that maybe a dozen or more puppet-plays had become jumbled together among the wheels back of the clock-face.

So there I sat in the dust watching the Wonder Clock, and when it had run down and the tunes and the puppet-show had come to an end, I took off my dream-cap, and—whisk!—there I was back home again among my books, with nothing brought away with me from that country but a little dust which I found sticking to my coat, and which I have never brushed away to this day.

Now if you also would like to go into Wonderland, you have only to hunt up your dream-cap (for everybody has one somewhere about the house), and to come to me, and I will show you the way to Time's garret.

That is right! Pull the cap well down about your ears.

*   *   *   *   *   *   *

Here we are! And now I will wind the clock. Gurr! gurr! gurr!
Tick-tock! tick-tock!

———————

So Life Begins.

Table of Contents.

List of Illustrations.

One O'clock.

One of the *Clock*, and silence deep
Then up the *Stairway*, black and steep
The old *House–Cat* comes creepy-creep
With soft feet goes from room to room
Her green eyes shining through the *
And finds all fast asleep.(gloom,)

K.
P.

K.P.

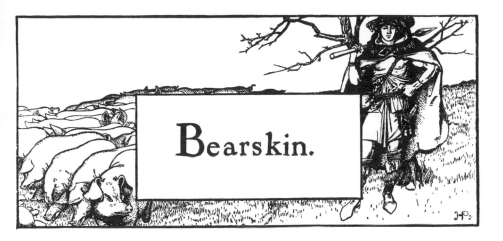

Bearskin.

I.

THERE was a king travelling through the country, and he and those with him were so far away from home that darkness caught them by the heels, and they had to stop at a stone mill for the night, because there was no other place handy.

While they sat at supper they heard a sound in the next room, and it was a baby crying.

The miller stood in the corner, back of the stove, with his hat in his hand. "What is that noise?" said the king to him.

"Oh! it is nothing but another baby that the good storks have brought into the house to-day," said the miller.

Now there was a wise man travelling along with the king, who could read the stars and everything that they told as easily as one can read one's A B C's in a book after one knows them, and the king, for a bit of a jest, would have him find out what the stars had to foretell of the miller's baby. So the wise man went out and took a peep up in the sky, and by and by he came in again.

"Well," said the king, "and what did the stars tell you?"

"The stars tell me," said the wise man, "that you shall have a daughter, and that the miller's baby, in the room yonder, shall marry her when they are old enough to think of such things."

"What!" said the king, "and is a miller's baby to marry the princess that is to come! We will see about that." So the next day he took the miller aside and talked and bargained, and bargained and talked, until the upshot of the matter was that the miller was paid two hundred dollars, and the king rode off with the baby.

As soon as he came home to the castle he called his chief forester to him. "Here," says he, "take this baby and do thus and so with it, and when you have killed it bring its heart to me, that I may know that you have really done as you have been told."

So off marched the forester with the baby; but on his way he stopped at home, and there was his good wife working about the house.

"Well, Henry," said she, "what do you do with the baby?"

"Oh!" said he, "I am just taking it off to the forest to do thus and so with it."

"Come," said she, "it would be a pity to harm the little innocent, and to have its blood on your hands. Yonder hangs the rabbit that you shot this morning, and its heart will please the king just as well as the other."

Thus the wife talked, and the end of the business was that she and the man smeared a basket all over with pitch and set the baby adrift in it on the river, and the king was just as well satisfied with the rabbit's heart as he would have been with the baby's.

But the basket with the baby in it drifted on and on down the river, until it lodged at last among the high reeds that stood along the bank. By and by there came a great she-bear to the water to drink, and there she found it.

Now the huntsmen in the forest had robbed the she-bear of her cubs, so that her heart yearned over the little baby, and she carried it home with her to fill the place of her own young ones. There the baby throve until he grew to a great strong lad, and as he had fed upon nothing but bear's milk for all that time, he was ten times stronger than the strongest man in the land.

One day, as he was walking through the forest, he came across a wood-man chopping the trees into billets of wood, and that was the first time he had ever seen a body like himself. Back he went to the bear as fast as he could travel, and told her what he had seen. "That," said the bear, "is the most wicked and most cruel of all the beasts."

"Yes," says the lad, "that may be so, all the same I love beasts like that

he Baby drifts in the basket down the river to the reeds beside the bank where the she-bear finds it.):(

as I love the food I eat, and I long for nothing so much as to go out into the wide world, where I may find others of the same kind."

At this the bear saw very well how the geese flew, and that the lad would soon be flitting.

"See," said she, "if you must go out into the wide world you must. But you will be wanting help before long; for the ways of the world are not peaceful and simple as they are here in the woods, and before you have lived there long you will have more needs than there are flies in summer. See, here is a little crooked horn, and when your wants grow many, just come to the forest and blow a blast on it, and I will not be too far away to help you."

So off went the lad away from the forest, and all the coat he had upon his back was the skin of a bear dressed with the hair on it, and that was why folk called him "Bearskin."

He trudged along the high-road, until he came to the king's castle, and it was the same king who thought he had put Bearskin safe out of the way years and years ago.

Now, the king's swineherd was in want of a lad, and as there was nothing better to do in that town, Bearskin took the place and went every morning to help drive the pigs into the forest, where they might eat the acorns and grow fat.

One day there was a mighty stir throughout the town; folk crying, and making a great hubbub. "What is it all about?" says Bearskin to the swineherd.

What! and did he not know what the trouble was? Where had he been for all of his life, that he had heard nothing of what was going on in the world? Had he never heard of the great fiery dragon with three heads that had threatened to lay waste all of that land, unless the pretty princess were given up to him? This was the very day that the dragon was to come for her, and she was to be sent up on the hill back of the town; that was why all the folk were crying and making such a stir.

"So!" says Bearskin, "and is there never a lad in the whole country that is man enough to face the beast? Then I will go myself if nobody better is to be found." And off he went, though the swineherd laughed and laughed, and thought it all a bit of a jest. By and by Bearskin came to the forest, and there he blew a blast upon the little crooked horn that the bear had given him.

Presently came the bear through the bushes, so fast that the little twigs flew behind her. "And what is it that you want?" said she.

"I should like," said Bearskin, "to have a horse, a suit of gold and silver armor that nothing can pierce, and a sword that shall cut through iron and steel; for I would like to go up on the hill to fight the dragon and free the pretty princess at the king's town over yonder."

"Very well," said the bear, "look back of the tree yonder, and you will find just what you want."

Yes; sure enough, there they were back of the tree: a grand white horse that champed his bit and pawed the ground till the gravel flew, and a suit of gold and silver armor such as a king might wear. Bearskin put on the armor and mounted the horse, and off he rode to the high hill back of the town.

By and by came the princess and the steward of the castle, for it was he that was to bring her to the dragon. But the steward stayed at the bottom of the hill, for he was afraid, and the princess had to climb it alone, though she could hardly see the road before her for the tears that fell from her eyes. But when she reached the top of the hill she found instead of the dragon a fine tall fellow dressed all in gold and silver armor. And it did not take Bearskin long to comfort the princess, I can tell you. "Come, come," says he, "dry your eyes and cry no more; all the cakes in the oven are not burned yet; just go back of the bushes yonder, and leave it with me to talk the matter over with Master Dragon."

The princess was glad enough to do that. Back of the bushes she went, and Bearskin waited for the dragon to come. He had not long to wait either; for presently it came flying through the air, so that the wind rattled under his wings.

Dear, dear! if one could but have been there to see that fight between Bearskin and the dragon, for it was well worth the seeing, and that you may believe. The dragon spit out flames and smoke like a house afire. But he could do no hurt to Bearskin, for the gold and silver armor sheltered him so well that not so much as one single hair of his head was singed. So Bearskin just rattled away the blows at the dragon—slish, slash, snip, clip—until all three heads were off, and there was an end of it.

After that he cut out the tongues from the three heads of the dragon, and tied them up in his pocket-handkerchief.

Then the princess came out from behind the bushes where she had lain hidden, and begged Bearskin to go back with her to the king's castle, for the king had said that if any one killed the dragon he should have her for his wife. But no; Bearskin would not go to the castle just now, for the time was not yet ripe; but, if the princess would give them to him, he would like to have the ring from her finger, the kerchief from her bosom, and the necklace of golden beads from her neck.

The princess gave him what he asked for, and a sweet kiss into the bargain, and then Bearskin mounted upon his grand white horse and rode away to the forest. "Here are your horse and armor," said he to the bear, "and they have done good service to-day, I can tell you." Then he tramped back again to the king's castle with the old bear's skin over his shoulders.

"Well," says the swineherd, "and did you kill the dragon?"

"Oh, yes," says Bearskin, "I did that, but it was no such great thing to do after all."

At that the swineherd laughed and laughed, for he did not believe a word of it.

And now listen to what happened to the princess after Bearskin had left her. The steward came sneaking up to see how matters had turned out, and there he found her safe and sound, and the dragon dead. "Whoever did this left his luck behind him," said he, and he drew his sword and told the princess that he would kill her if she did not swear to say nothing of what had happened. Then he gathered up the dragon's three heads, and he and the princess went back to the castle again.

"There!" said he, when they had come before the king, and he flung down the three heads upon the floor, "I have killed the dragon and I have brought back the princess, and now if anything is to be had for the labor I would like to have it." As for the princess, she wept and wept, but she could say nothing, and so it was fixed that she was to marry the steward, for that was what the king had promised.

At last came the wedding-day, and the smoke went up from the chimneys in clouds, for there was to be a grand wedding-feast, and there was no end of good things cooking for those who were to come.

"See now," says Bearskin to the swineherd where they were feeding their pigs together, out in the woods, "as I killed the dragon over yonder, I ought at least to have some of the good things from the king's kitchen; you shall go and ask for some of the fine white bread and meat, such as the king and princess are to eat to-day."

Dear, dear, but you should have seen how the swineherd stared at this and how he laughed, for he thought the other must have gone out of his

Bearskin slayeth ẙ Dragon but will not go with ẙ Princess to ẙ castle.

Thus the Princess sits and weeps and weeps.

wits; but as for going to the castle—no, he would not go a step, and that
was the long and the short of it.

"So! well, we will see about that," says Bearskin, and he stepped to a
thicket and cut a good stout stick, and without another word caught the
swineherd by the collar, and began dusting his jacket for him until it
smoked again.

"Stop, stop!" bawled the swineherd.

"Very well," says Bearskin; "and now will you go over to the castle for
me, and ask for some of the same bread and meat that the king and
princess are to have for their dinner?"

Yes, yes; the swineherd would do anything that Bearskin wanted him.

"So! good," says Bearskin; "then just take this ring and see that the princess gets it; and say that the lad who sent it would like to have some of the bread and meat that she is to have for her dinner."

So the swineherd took the ring, and off he started to do as he had been told. Rap! tap! tap! he knocked at the door. Well, and what did he want?

Oh! there was a lad over in the woods yonder who had sent him to ask for some of the same bread and meat that the king and princess were to have for their dinner, and he had brought this ring to the princess as a token.

But how the princess opened her eyes when she saw the ring which she had given to Bearskin up on the hill! For she saw, as plain as the nose on her face, that he who had saved her from the dragon was not so far away as she had thought. Down she went into the kitchen herself to see that the very best bread and meat were sent, and the swineherd marched off with a great basket full.

"Yes," says Bearskin, "that is very well so far, but I am for having some of the red and white wine that they are to drink. Just take this kerchief over to the castle yonder, and let the princess know that the lad to whom she gave it upon the hill back of the town would like to have a taste of the wine that she and the king are to have at the feast to-day."

Well, the swineherd was for saying "no" to this as he had to the other, but Bearskin just reached his hand over toward the stout stick that he had used before, and the other started off as though the ground was hot under his feet. And what was the swineherd wanting this time—that was what they said over at the castle.

"The lad with the pigs in the woods yonder," says the swineherd, "must have gone crazy, for he has sent this kerchief to the princess and says that he should like to have a bottle or two of the wine that she and the king are to drink to-day."

When the princess saw her kerchief again her heart leaped for joy. She made no two words about the wine, but went down into the cellar and brought it up with her own hands, and the swineherd marched off with it tucked under his coat.

"Yes, that was all very well," said Bearskin, "I am satisfied so far as the wine is concerned, but now I would like to have some of the sweetmeats that they are to eat at the castle to-day. See, here is a necklace of golden

ℬearskin and þͤ swineherd have a grand feast.

beads; just take it to the princess and ask for some of those sweetmeats, for I will have them," and this time he had only to look towards the stick, and the other started off as fast as he could travel.

The swineherd had no more trouble with this asking than with the others, for the princess went down-stairs and brought the sweetmeats from the pantry with her own hands, and the swineherd carried them to Bearskin where he sat out in the woods with the pigs.

Then Bearskin spread out the good things, and he and the swineherd sat down to the feast together, and a fine one it was, I can tell you.

" And now," says Bearskin, when they had eaten all that they could, " it is time for me to leave you, for I must go and marry the princess." So off he started, and the swineherd did nothing but stand and gape after him, with his mouth open, as though he were set to catch flies. But Bearskin went straight to the woods, and there he blew upon his horn, and the bear was with him as quickly this time as the last.

" Well, what do you want now," said she.

" This time," said Bearskin, " I want a fine suit of clothes made of gold-and-silver cloth, and a horse to ride on up to the king's house, for I am going to marry the princess."

Very well; there was what he wanted back of the tree yonder; and it was a suit of clothes fit for a great king to wear, and a splendid dapple-gray horse with a golden saddle and bridle studded all over with precious stones. So Bearskin put on the clothes and rode away, and a fine sight he was to see, I can tell you.

And how the folks stared when he rode up to the king's castle. Out came the king along with the rest, for he thought that Bearskin was some great lord. But the princess knew him the moment she set eyes upon him, for she was not likely to forget him so soon as all that.

The king brought Bearskin into where they were feasting, and had a place set for him alongside of himself.

The steward was there along with the rest. " See," said Bearskin to him, " I have a question to put. One killed a dragon and saved a princess, but another came and swore falsely that he did it. Now, what should be done to such a one?"

" Why this," said the steward, speaking up as bold as brass, for he thought to face the matter down, " he should be put in a cask stuck all round with nails, and dragged behind three wild horses."

" Very well," said Bearskin, " you have spoken for yourself. For I killed the dragon up on the hill behind the town, and you stole the glory of the doing."

" That is not so," said the steward, " for it was I who brought home the three heads of the dragon in my own hand, and how can that be with the rest?"

Then Bearskin stepped to the wall, where hung the three heads of the dragon. He opened the mouth of each. " And where are the tongues?" said he.

At this the steward grew as pale as death, nevertheless he still spoke up as boldly as ever: " Dragons have no tongues," said he. But Bearskin only laughed; he untied his handkerchief before them all, and there were the three tongues. He put one in each mouth, and they fitted exactly, and after that no one could doubt that he was the hero who had really killed the dragon. So when the wedding came it was Bearskin, and not the steward, who married the princess; what was done to him you may guess for yourselves.

And so they had a grand wedding, but in the very midst of the feast one came running in and said there was a great brown bear without, who would come in, willy-nilly. Yes, and you have guessed it right, it *was* the great she-bear, and if nobody else was made much of at that wedding you can depend upon it that she was.

As for the king, he was satisfied that the princess had married a great hero. So she had, only he was the miller's son after all, though the king knew no more of that than my grandfather's little dog, and no more did anybody but the wise man for the matter of that, and he said nothing of it, for wise folk don't tell all they know.

Tvvo O'clock·

The *Black Cock* crowed;
The *Moon* was bright;
The *Red Cock* answered
Through the night.

Big *Gretchen*, sleeping,
Turned in bed,
And tossed her arms
Above her head.

The old *Hound* stretched.
And, breathing deep,
He settled down
Again to sleep.

The Water of Life.

II.

NCE upon a time there was an old king who had a faithful servant. There was nobody in the whole world like him, and this was why: around his wrist he wore an armlet that fitted as close as the skin. There were words on the golden band; on one side they said:

"WHO THINKS TO WEAR ME ON HIS ARM
MUST LACK BOTH GUILE AND THOUGHT OF HARM."

And on the other side they said:

"I AM FOR ONLY ONE AND HE
SHALL BE AS STRONG AS TEN CAN BE."

At last the old king felt that his end was near, and he called the faithful servant to him and besought him to serve and aid the young king who was to come as he had served and aided the old king who was to go. The faithful servant promised that which was asked, and then the old king closed his eyes and folded his hands and went the way that those had travelled who had gone before him.

Well, one day a stranger came to that town from over the hills and far away. With him he brought a painted picture, but it was all covered with a curtain so that nobody could see what it was.

He drew aside the curtain and showed the picture to the young king, and it was a likeness of the most beautiful princess in the whole world; for her eyes were as black as a crow's wing, her cheeks were as red as apples, and her skin as white as snow. Moreover, the picture was so natural that it seemed as though it had nothing to do but to open its lips and speak.

The young king just sat and looked and looked. "Oh me!" said he, "I will never rest content until I have such a one as that for my own."

"Then listen!" said the stranger, "this is a likeness of the princess that lives over beyond the three rivers. A while ago she had a wise bird on which she doted, for it knew everything that happened in the world, so that it could tell the princess whatever she wanted to know. But now the bird is dead, and the princess does nothing but grieve for it day and night. She keeps the dead bird in a glass casket, and has promised to marry whoever will bring a cup of water from the Fountain of Life, so that the bird may be brought back to life again." That was the story the stranger told, and then he jogged on the way he was going, and I, for one, do not know whither it led.

But the young king had no peace or comfort in life for thinking of the princess who lived over beyond the three rivers. At last he called the faithful servant to him. "And can you not," said he, "get me a cup of the Water of Life?"

"I know not, but I will try," said the faithful servant, for he bore in mind what he had promised to the old king.

So out he went into the wide world, to seek for what the young king wanted, though the way there is both rough and thorny. On he went and on, until his shoes were dusty, and his feet were sore, and after a while he came to the end of the earth, and there was nothing more over the hill. There he found a little tumbled-down hut, and within the hut sat an old, old woman with a distaff, spinning a lump of flax.

"Good-morning, mother," said the faithful servant.

"Good-morning, son," says the old woman, "and where are you travelling that you have come so far?"

"Oh!" says the faithful servant, "I am hunting for the Water of Life, and have come as far as this without finding a drop of it."

"Hoity, toity," says the old woman, "if that is what you are after, you have a long way to go yet. The fountain is in the country that lies east of the Sun and west of the Moon, and it is few that have gone there and come back again, I can tell you. Besides that there is a great dragon that keeps watch over the water, and you will have to get the better of him before you can touch a drop of it. All the same, if you have made up your mind to

he young king looks upon ẏ beautiful
picture which the stranger sheweth him.

go you may stay here until my sons come home, and perhaps they can put you in the way of getting there, for I am the Mother of the Four Winds of Heaven, and it is few places that they have not seen."

So the faithful servant came in and sat down by the fire to wait till the Winds came home.

The first that came was the East Wind; but he knew nothing of the Water of Life and the land that lay east of the Sun and west of the Moon; he had heard folks talk of them both now and then, but he had never seen them with his own eyes.

The next that came was the South Wind, but he knew no more of it than his brother, and neither did the West Wind for the matter of that.

Last of all came the North Wind, and dear, dear, what a hubbub he made outside of the door, stamping the dust off of his feet before he came into the house.

"And do you know where the Fountain of Life is, and the country that lies east of the Sun and west of the Moon?" said the old woman.

Oh, yes, the North Wind knew where it was. He had been there once upon a time, but it was a long, long distance away.

"So; good! then perhaps you will give this lad a lift over there to-morrow," said the old woman.

At this the North Wind grumbled and shook his head; but at last he said "yes," for he is a good-hearted fellow at bottom, is the North Wind, though his ways are a trifle rough perhaps.

So the next morning he took the faithful servant on his back, and away he flew till the man's hair whistled behind him. On they went and on they went and on they went, until at last they came to the country that lay east of the Sun and west of the Moon; and they were none too soon getting there either, I can tell you, for when the North Wind tumbled the faithful servant off his back he was so weak that he could not have lifted a feather.

"Thank you," said the faithful servant, and then he was for starting away to find what he came for.

"Stop a bit," says the North Wind, "you will be wanting to come away again after a while. I cannot wait here, for I have other business to look after. But here is a feather; when you want me, cast it into the air, and I will not be long in coming."

Then away he bustled, for he had caught his breath again, and time was none too long for him.

The faithful servant walked along a great distance until, by and by, he

came to a field covered all over with sharp rocks and white bones, for he was not the first by many who had been that way for a cup of the Water of Life.

There lay the great fiery dragon in the sun, sound asleep, and so the faithful servant had time to look about him. Not far away was a great deep trench like a drain in a swampy field; that was a path that the dragon had made by going to the river for a drink of water every day. The faithful servant dug a hole in the bottom of this trench, and there he hid

himself as snugly as a cricket in the crack in the kitchen floor. By and by
the dragon awoke and found that he was thirsty, and then started down to
the river to get a drink. The faithful servant lay as still as a mouse until
the dragon was just above where he was hidden ; then he thrust his sword
through its heart, and there it lay, after a turn or two, as dead as a stone.

After that he had only to fill the cup at the fountain, for there was
nobody to say nay to him. Then he cast the feather into the air, and there
was the North Wind, as fresh and as sound as ever. The North Wind
took him upon its back, and away it flew until it came home again.

The faithful servant thanked them all around — the Four Winds and
the old woman—and as they would take nothing else, he gave them a few
drops of the Water of Life, and that is the reason that the Four Winds
and their mother are as fresh and young now as they were when the world
began.

Then the faithful servant set off home again, right foot foremost, and
he was not as long in getting there as in coming.

As soon as the king saw the cup of the Water of Life he had the horses
saddled, and off he and the faithful servant rode to find the princess who
lived over beyond the three rivers. By and by they came to the town, and
there was the princess mourning and grieving over her bird just as she had
done from the first. But when she heard that the king had brought the
Water of Life she welcomed him as though he were a flower in March.

They sprinkled a few drops upon the dead bird, and up it sprang as
lively and as well as ever.

But now, before the princess would marry the king she must have a
talk with the bird, and there came the hitch, for the Wise Bird knew as well
as you and I that it was not the king who had brought the Water of Life.
" Go and tell him," said the Wise Bird, " that you are ready to marry him
as soon as he saddles and bridles the Wild Black Horse in the forest over
yonder, for if he is the hero who found the Water of Life he can do that and
more easily enough."

The princess did as the bird told her, and so the king missed getting
what he wanted after all. But off he went to the faithful servant. " And
can you not saddle and bridle the Wild Black Horse for me ?" said he.

" I do not know," said the faithful servant, " but I will try."

So off he went to the forest to hunt up the Wild Black Horse, the
saddle over his shoulder and the bridle over his arm. By and by came the
Wild Black Horse galloping through the woods like a thunder gust in

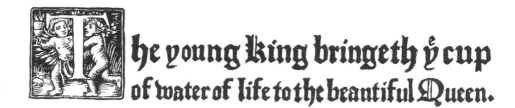

The young king bringeth ỹ cup of water of life to the beautiful Queen.

summer, so that the ground shook under his feet. But the faithful servant was ready for him; he caught him by the mane and forelock, and the Wild Black Horse had never had such a one to catch hold of him before.

But how they did stamp and wrestle! Up and down and here and there, until the fire flew from the stones under their feet. But the Wild Black Horse could not stand against the strength of ten men, such as the faithful servant had, so by and by he fell on his knees, and the faithful servant clapped the saddle on his back and slipped the bridle over his ears.

" Listen now," says he; " to-morrow my master, the king, will ride you up to the princess's house, and if you do not do just as I tell you, it will be the worse for you; when the king mounts upon your back you must stagger and groan, as though you carried a mountain."

The horse promised to do as the other bade, and then the faithful servant jumped on his back and away to the king, who had been waiting at home for all this time.

The next day the king rode up to the princess's castle, and the Wild Black Horse did just as the faithful servant told him to do; he staggered and groaned, so that everybody cried out, " Look at the great hero riding upon the Wild Black Horse!"

And when the princess saw him she also thought that he was a great hero. But the Wise Bird was of a different mind from her, for when the princess came to talk to him about marrying the king he shook his head. " No, no," said he, " there is something wrong here, and the king has baked his cake in somebody else's oven. He never saddled and bridled the Wild Black Horse by himself. Listen, you must say to him that you will marry nobody but the man who wears such and such a golden armlet with this and that written on it."

So the princess told the king what the Wise Bird had bidden her to say, and the king went straightway to the faithful servant.

" You must let me have your armlet," said he.

" Alas, master," said the faithful servant, " that is a woful thing for me, for the one and only way to take the armlet off of my wrist is to cut my hand from off my body."

" So!" says the king, " that is a great pity, but the princess will not have me without the armlet."

" Then you shall have it," says the faithful servant; but the king had to cut the hand off, for the faithful servant could not do it himself.

But, bless your heart! the armlet was ever so much too large for the

The Faithful Servant gives ỹ young king ỹ golden bracelet from his wrist as the other desires. ℭ

king to wear! Nevertheless he tied it to his wrist with a bit of ribbon, and off he marched to the princess's castle.

"Here is the armlet of gold," said he, "and now will you marry me!"

But the Wise Bird sat on the princess's chair. "Hut! tut!" says he, "it does not fit the man."

Yes, that was so; everybody who was there could see it easily enough; and as for marrying him, the princess would marry nobody but the man who could wear the armlet.

What a hubbub there was then! Every one who was there was sure that the armlet would fit him if it fitted nobody else. But no; it was far too large for the best of them. The faithful servant was very sad, and stood back of the rest, over by the wall, with his arm tied up in a napkin. "You shall try it too," says the princess; but the faithful servant only shook his head, for he could not try it on as the rest had done, because he had no hand. But the Wise Bird was there and knew what he was about; "See now," says he, "maybe the Water of Life will cure one thing as well as another."

Yes, that was true, and one was sent to fetch the cup. They sprinkled it on the faithful servant's arm, and it was not twice they had to do it, for there was another hand as good and better than the old.

Then they gave him the armlet; he slipped it over his hand, and it fitted him like his own skin.

"This is the man for me," says the princess, "and I will have none other;" for she could see with half an eye that he was the hero who had been doing all the wonderful things that had happened, because he said nothing about himself.

As for the king—why, all that was left for him to do was to pack off home again; and I, for one, am glad of it.

And this is true; the best packages are not always wrapped up in blue paper and tied with a gay string, and there are better men in the world than kings and princes, fine as they seem to be.

Three O'clock.

The *Rooms* were cold, the *Hearth* was grey:
Asleep in the ashes the *Kobold* lay.
 The *Board-Floor* creaked,
 The *Grey-Mouse* squeaked,
And the *Kobold* dreamed its ear he tweaked.

K Ω P;
 ❨ Υ;des.

 He wrinkled up
 His *Forehead* and *Nose*,
 And smiled in his sleep,
 And curled his *Toes*.

III.

HERE was a soldier marching along the road —
left, right! left, right! He had been to the wars
for five years, so that he was very brave, and
now he was coming home again. In his knap-
sack were two farthings, and that was everything
that he had in the world. All the same, he had a
rich brother at home, and that was something to
say.

So on he tramped until he had come to his rich brother's house.

"Good-day, brother," said he, "and how does the old world treat you."

But the rich brother screwed up his face and rubbed his nose, for he
was none too glad to see the other. "What!" said he, "and is the Pewter
Penny back again?" That was the way that he welcomed the other to his
house.

"Tut! tut!" says the brave soldier." and is not this a pretty way to
welcome a brother home to be sure! All that I want is just a crust of bread
and a chance to rest the soles of my feet back of the stove a little while.

Oh, well! if that was all that he wanted, he might have his supper and a
bed for the night, but he must not ask for any more, and he must jog on in
the morning and never come that way again.

Well, as no more broth was to be had from that dish, the soldier said
that he would be satisfied with what he could get; so into the house he
came.

Over by the fire was a bench, and on the bench was a basket, and in the basket were seven young ducks that waited where it was warm until the rest were hatched. The soldier saw nothing of these; down he sat, and the little young ducks said "peep!" and died all at once. Up jumped the soldier and over went the beer mug that sat by the fire so that the beer ran all around and put out the blaze.

At this the rich brother fell into a mighty rage. "See!" said he, "you never go anywhere but you bring Trouble with you. Out of the house before I make this broom rattle about your ears!"

And so the brave soldier had to go out under the blessed sky again. "Well! well!" said he, "the cream is all sour over yonder for sure and certain! All the same it will better nothing to be in the dumps, so we'll just sing a bit of a song to keep our spirits up." So the soldier began to sing, and by and by he heard that somebody was singing along with him.

"Halloa, comrade!" said he, "who is there?"

"Oh!" said a voice beside him, "it is only Trouble."

"And what are you doing there, Trouble?" said the soldier.

Oh! Trouble was only jogging along with him. They had been friends and comrades for this many a bright day, for when had the soldier ever gone anywhere that Trouble had not gone along with him?

The brave soldier scratched his head. "Yes, yes," says he; "that is all very fine; but there must be an end of the business. See! yonder is one road and here is another; you may go that road and I will go this, for I want no Trouble for a comrade."

"Oh, no!" says Trouble, "I will never leave you now; you and I have been comrades too long for that!"

Very well! the soldier would see about that. They should go to the king, for things had come to a pretty pass if one could not choose one's own comrades in this broad world, but must, willy-nilly, have Trouble always jogging at one's heels.

So off they went—the soldier and Trouble—and by and by they came to the great town and there they found the king.

"Well, and what is the trouble now?" said the king.

Trouble indeed! Why, it was thus and so, here was that same Trouble tramping around at the soldier's heels and would go wherever he went. Now, the soldier would like to know whether one had no right to choose one's own comrades—that was the business that had brought him to the king!

Well, the king thought and thought and puzzled and puzzled, but that

The Brave Soldier bringeth his Trouble to ẏ town along with him.

nut was too hard for him to crack, so he sent off for all of his wise councillors to see what they had to say about the matter.

So, when they had all come together the king told them that things were thus and so, and thus and so, and now he would like to know what they all thought about it.

Then the wise councillors began to talk and talk, and one said one thing and another another. After a while they fell to arguing with loud voices, and then they grew angry and began talking all at once, and last of all they came to fisticuffs. Then you should have heard what a racket they made! for they buffeted and cuffed one another until the hair flew as thick as dust in the mill.

That was the kind of prank that Trouble played them.

Now the king had a daughter, and the princess was as pretty a lass as one could find were he to hunt for seven summer days. When she heard all the hubbub she came to see what it was about, for that is the way with all of us, and of women folk more than any. And the king told her all about it; how the soldier had come to that town to get rid of Trouble, and how he had done nothing but bring it with him.

"Perhaps," said she, "Trouble might leave him if he were married."

At this the king fell into a mighty fume, for no man likes to have a woman tell him to do thus and so when things are in a pickle. He should like to know what the princess meant by coming and pouring her broth into their pot! If that was her notion she might help the soldier herself. Married he should be, and *she* should be his wife—that was what the king said.

So the soldier and the princess were married, and then the king had them both put into a great chest and thrown into the sea—but there was room in the chest for Trouble, and he went along with them.

Well, they floated on and on and on for a great long time, until, at last, the chest came ashore at a place where three giants lived.

The three giants were sitting on the shore fishing. "See, brothers," said the first one of them, "yonder is a great chest washed up on the shore." So they went over to where it was, and then the second giant took it on his shoulder and carried it home. After that they all three sat down to supper.

Just then the soldier's nose began to itch and tickle, so that, for the life of him, he could not help sneezing.

"At-tchew!"—and there it was.

**H**ere † the Brave Soldier brings his trouble before the King to find if it shall follow him wherever he goes.

3

"Hark, brothers!" said the third giant, "yonder is somebody in the chest!"

So the three giants came and opened the chest, and there were the soldier and the princess. Trouble was there too, but the giants saw nothing of him.

They bound the soldier with strong cords so that they might have him to eat for breakfast in the morning.

And now what was to be done with the princess?

"See, brothers," said the first giant, "I am thinking that a wife will about fit my needs. This lass will do as well as any, and, as I found her, I will just keep her."

"Prut! how you talk!" said the second giant, "do you think that nobody is to marry in the wide world but you? Who was it brought the lass to the house I should like to know! No, I will marry her myself."

"Stop!" said the third giant. "You are both going too fast on that road. I thought of a wife long before either of you. Who was it found that the lass was in the house, I should like to know!"

And so they talked and talked until they fell to quarrelling, and then to blows. Over they rolled, cuffing and slapping, until each one killed the other two, so that they all lay as dead as fishes. And that was an end of them.

"See, now," said Trouble to the soldier, "who can say that I have done nothing for you? I tell you, comrade, that I am a good friend of yours, and love you as though you were my born brother. Listen! over yonder in the field is a great stone under which the giants have hidden stacks and stacks of money. Go and borrow a cart and two horses, and I will go with you and show you where it is."

Well, you may guess that that was a song that pleased the soldier. Off he went and borrowed a cart and two horses. Then he and Trouble went into the field together, and Trouble showed him where the stone was where the treasure lay.

The soldier rolled the stone over, and there, sure enough, lay bags and bags, all full of gold and silver money.

Down he went into the pit and began bringing up the money and loading it into the cart. After a while he had brought it all but one bag full.

"See, Trouble," said he, "my back is nearly broken with carrying the

The three Giants fight one another like fury.

money. There is still one bag down there yet; go down like a good lad and bring it up for me."

Oh, yes! Trouble would do that much for the soldier, for had they not been comrades for many and one bright, blessed days? Down he went into the pit, and then you may believe that the soldier was not long in rolling the stone into its place. So there was Trouble as tight as a fly in a bottle.

After that the soldier went back home again with great contentment— as I would have done had I ridden home upon a cart full of gold and silver, all of which belonged to me. He had left one bag of money, but then it was worth that much to be rid of Trouble.

After that the soldier built a ship and loaded it with the money. Then he and the princess sailed away to the king's house, for they thought that maybe the king would like them better now that Trouble had left them and money had come.

When the king saw what a great boatload of gold and silver the soldier had brought home with him he was as pleased as pleased could be. He could not make enough of the brave soldier; he called him son, and walked about the streets with him arm in arm, so that the folks might see how fond he was of his son-in-law. Besides that he gave him half of the kingdom to rule over, so that the soldier and the princess lived together as snugly as a couple of mice in the barn when threshing is going on.

Well, one day a neighbor came to the rich brother and said, "Dear! dear! but the world is easy with your brother, the soldier!"

At this the rich brother pricked up his ears. "How is that?" said he— "my brother, the soldier? How comes the world to be easy with him, I should like to know?"

Oh, the neighbor could not tell him that; all that he knew was that the soldier was living over yonder with a princess for his wife, and more gold and silver money than a body could count in a week.

Well, well, this would never do! The rich brother must pick up acquaintance with the soldier again, now that he was rising in the world. So he put on his blue Sunday coat and his best hat, and away he went to the soldier's house.

Well, the soldier was a good-natured fellow, and bore grudges against nobody, so he shook hands with his brother, and they sat down together by the stove. Then the rich brother wanted to know all about everything —how came it that the other was so well off in the world?

Oh, there was no secret about that; it happened thus and so. And then the soldier told all about it. After that the other went home, but there was a great buzzing in his head, I can tell you!

"Now," says he to himself, "I will go over yonder to the giants' house, and will let Trouble out from under the stone. Then he will come here to my brother and will turn things topsy-turvy, and I will get the bag of money that was left there."

So, off he went until he came to the place where Trouble lay under the stone. He rolled the stone over, and—whisk! clip!—out popped Trouble from the hole. "And so you were leaving me here to be starved, were you?" said he.

"Oh, dear friend Trouble! it was not I, it was my brother, the soldier!"

Oh, well, that was all one to Trouble; now that he was out he would

The rich man takes home money and trouble.

stay with the man who let him out, and there was an end of it. "So bring along the bag of gold," says he, "for it is high time that we were going home."

So the rich brother took the bag of gold over his shoulder, and the two went home together; and if anybody was down in the mouth, it was the rich brother.

And now everything went wrong with him, for Trouble dogged his heels wherever he went. At last his patience could hold out no longer, and he began to cudgel his brains to find some way to get rid of the other. So one day he says,

"Come, Trouble, we will go out into the forest this morning and cut some wood."

Well, that suited Trouble as well as anything else, so off they went together, arm in arm. By and by they came to the forest, and there the man cut down a great tree. Then he split open the stump, and drove a wedge into it. So it came dinner-time, and then Trouble and he ate together.

" See now, Trouble," said the man, " they tell me that you can go any-where in all of the world."

" Yes," said Trouble, " that is so."

" And could you go into that tree that I have split yonder?"

Oh, yes ; Trouble could do that well enough.

If that was so the man would like to see him do it, that he would.

Oh, Trouble would do that and more, too, for a friend's asking. So he made himself small and smaller, and so crept into the cleft in the log as easily as though he had been a mouse. But, no sooner was he snugly there than the man seized his axe and knocked out the wedge, and there was Trouble as safe as safe could be. He might beg and beg, but no, the man was deaf in that ear. He shouldered his axe and off he went, leaving Trouble where he was.

Dear me ! that was a long time ago ; or else some busybody must have let Trouble out of that log, for I know very well that he is stumping about the world nowadays.

KΩP.
II des.

Four O'clock·

The *Air* grew chill, the *Sky* was grey;
The *Black Cock* crowed, and far away
Another answered. In a dream
The *Kobold* drank thick clotted *Cream*,
And chased *Roast-Goose*. He woke and *
And turned upon his other side.⁽ˢⁱᵍʰᵉᵈ,⁾

How three went out into the Wide World.

IV.

THERE was a woman who owned a fine grey goose. "To-morrow," said she, "I will pluck the goose for live feathers, so that I may take them to market and sell them for good hard money."

This the goose heard, and liked it not. "Why should I grow live feathers for other folks to pluck?" said she to herself. So off she went into the wide world with nothing upon her back but what belonged to her.

By and by she came up with a sausage.

"Whither away, friend?" said the Grey Goose.

"Out into the wide world," said the Sausage.

"Why do you travel that road?" said the Grey Goose.

"Why should I stay at home?" said the Sausage. "They stuff me with good meat and barley-meal over yonder, but they only do it for other folk's feasting. That is the way with the world."

"Yes, that is true," said the Grey Goose; "and I too am going out into the world, for why should I grow live feathers for other folk's plucking? So let us travel together, as we are both of a mind."

Well, that suited the Sausage well enough, so off they went, arm in arm.

By and by they came up with a cock.

"Whither away, friend?" said the Grey Goose and the Sausage.

"Out into the wide world," said the Cock.

"Why do you travel that road?" said the Grey Goose and the Sausage.

"Why should I stay at home?" said the Cock. "Every day they feed me with barley-corn, but it is only that I may split my throat in the mornings, calling the lads to the fields and the maids to the milking. That is the way with the world."

"Yes, that is true," said the Grey Goose; "why should I grow live feathers for other folk's picking?"

And—

"Yes, that is true," said the Sausage, "why should I be stuffed with meat and barley-meal for other folk's feasting?"

So the three being all of a mind, they settled to travel the same road together.

Well, they went on and on and on, until, at last, they came to a deep forest, and, by and by, whom should they meet but a great red fox.

"Whither away, friends?" said he.

"Oh, we are going out into the wide world," said the Grey Goose, the Sausage, and the Cock.

"And why do you travel that road?" said the Fox.

Oh, there was nothing but tangled yarn at home: the Grey Goose grew live feathers for other folk's picking, the Sausage was stuffed for other folk's feasting, and the Cock crowed in the morn for other folk's waking. That was the way of the world over yonder, and so they had left it.

"Yes," said the Fox, "that is true; so come with me into the deep forest, for there every one can live for himself! and nobody else.

So they all went into the forest together, for the Fox's words pleased them very much.

"And now," said the Fox to the Grey Goose, "you shall be my wife," for he had never had a sweetheart before, and even a Grey Goose is better than none.

"And what is to become of us?" said the Sausage and the Cock.

"You and I shall be dear friends," said the Great Red Fox. Thereat the Cock and the Sausage were content, for it took but little to satisfy them.

Well, everything was just as the Great Red Fox had said it should be: the Goose kept her own feathers, the Sausage was stuffed for its own good, the Cock crowed for its own ears, and everything was as smooth as rich cream. Moreover, the Great Red Fox and the Grey Goose were husband

he Grey Goose goes out into the wide world, where she and a discontented Sausage meet the Cock and the Fox. **C**

and wife, and the Great Red Fox and the Sausage and the Cock were dear friends.

One morning says the Great Red Fox to the Grey Goose, " Neighbor Cock makes a mighty hubbub with his crowing !"

" Yes, that is so," said the Grey Goose ; for she always sang the same tune as the Great Red Fox, as a good wife should.

" Then," said the Great Red Fox, " I will go over and have a talk with him."

So off he packed, and by and by he came to Neighbor Cock's house. Rap ! tap ! tap ! he knocked at the door, and who should look out of the window but the Cock himself.

" See, Neighbor Cock," said the Great Red Fox, "you make a mighty hubbub with that crowing of yours."

" That may be so, and that may not be so," said the Cock ; " all the same, the hubbub is in my own house."

" That is good," said the Great Red Fox, " but one should not trouble one's neighbors, even in one's own house ; so, if it suits you, we will have no more crowing."

" I was made for crowing, and crow I must," said the Cock.

" You must crow no more," said the Great Red Fox.

" I must crow," said the Cock.

" You must not crow," said the Great Red Fox.

" I must crow," said the Cock.   And that was the last of it for—snip !— off went its head, and it crowed no more. Nevertheless, he had the last word, and that was some comfort. After that the Great Red Fox ate up the Cock, body and bones, and then he went home again.

" Will Neighbor Cock crow again ?" said the Grey Goose.

" No ; he will crow no more," said the Fox ; and that was true.

By and by came hungry times, with little or nothing in the house to eat. " Look !" said the Great Red Fox, " yonder is Neighbor Sausage, and he has plenty."

" Yes, that is true," said the Grey Goose.

" And one's friend should help one when one is in need," said the great Red Fox.

" Yes, that is true," said the Grey Goose again.

So off went the Great Red Fox to Neighbor Sausage's house.   Rap ! tap ! tap ! he knocked at the door, and it was the Sausage himself who came.

" See," said the Fox, " there are hungry times over at our house."

he Great Red Fox goes
to call on neighbour Cock at his
house because he will crow in the
morn.

The Great Red Fox calls upon the Sausage.

"I am sorry for that," said the Sausage; "but hungry times will come to the best of us."

"That is so," said the Great Red Fox, "but, all the same, you must help me through this crack. One would be in a bad pass without a friend to turn to."

"But see," said the Sausage, "all that I have is mine, and it is inside of me at that."

"Nevertheless, I must have some of it," said the Great Red Fox.

"But you can't have it," said the Sausage.

"But I must have it," said the Great Red Fox.

"But you can't have it," said the Sausage.

And so they talked and talked and talked, but the end came at last, for one cannot talk forever to an empty stomach. Snip! snap! and the Sausage was down the Great Red Fox's throat, and there was an end of it. And now the Fox had all that his friend had to give him, and so he went back home again.

The Great Red Fox rests softly at home.

"Did Neighbor Sausage give you anything?" said the Grey Goose.

"Oh, yes; he gave me all that he had with him," said the Great Red Fox; and that also was very true.

After that the world went around for a while as easily as a greased wheel. But one day the Great Red Fox said to the Grey Goose: "See now, my bones grow sore by lying on the hard stones."

"That is a great pity," said the Grey Goose; "and if the hard stones were only soft, I, for one, would be glad."

"Yes," said the Great Red Fox, "that is good; but soft talking makes them none the easier to lie upon. Could you not spare me a few of your feathers?"

"A few feathers indeed!" said the Grey Goose, "it was not for this that I left the ways of the world over yonder. If you must have feathers you must pluck them from your own back."

"Prut!" said the Great Red Fox, "how you speak! A wife should do all that she can to make the world soft for her husband."

Then you should have heard the Grey Goose talk and talk.   But it was no use; when times are hard with one, one's wife should help to feather the nest—that was what the Great Red Fox said.

Snip! snap! crunch! cranch! and off went the Grey Goose's head. After that the Fox ate her up, body and bones, and there was an end of her.   Then he lay upon soft feathers and slept easily.

Now this is true that I tell you: when a great red fox and a grey goose marry, and hard times come, one must make it soft for the other— mostly it is the grey goose who does that.

Also I would have you listen to this: some folks say that it is not so, but *I* tell you that the ways of the world are the ways of the world, even in the deep forest.

Five O'clock·

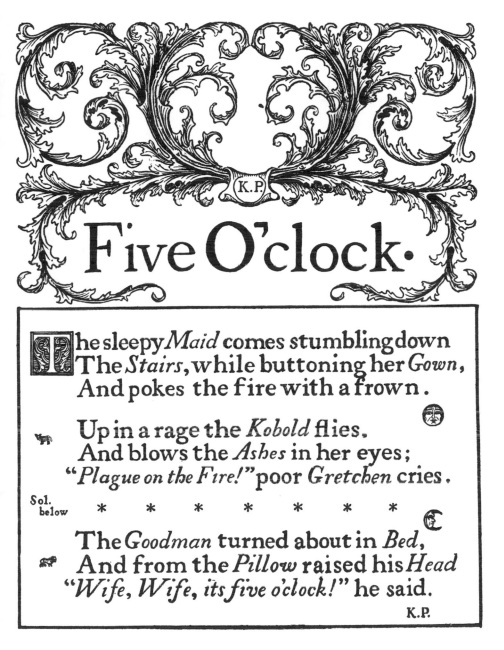

The sleepy *Maid* comes stumbling down
The *Stairs*, while buttoning her *Gown*,
And pokes the fire with a frown.

Up in a rage the *Kobold* flies,
And blows the *Ashes* in her eyes;
"*Plague on the Fire!*" poor *Gretchen* cries.

Sol.
below   *   *   *   *   *   *   *

The *Goodman* turned about in *Bed*,
And from the *Pillow* raised his *Head*
"*Wife, Wife, its five o'clock!*" he said.

K.P.

4

The Clever Student and the Master of Black Arts.

C:

HP:

V.

THE wood-chopper's son was not content to follow in the steps of his father, and to do nothing better than make fagots all the days of his life. So off he went to the great school at the capital, and there he studied and studied until he became the cleverest student in all of the world. But of this his father thought nothing, for he had no care to know more than he could see in front of his nose.

"I can speak sixteen languages," said the Clever Student, "I am a master-hand at geometry and astronomy, and I know quite as much of black art as the Great Master himself."

"But can you chop wood?" said the wood-chopper, "and can you bind the fagots?"

No; the Clever Student knew nothing of that trade, but there were better eggs in Luck's nest than wood-chopping. He knew enough of the black art to be able to change himself into a fine, dapple-gray nag whenever he chose, and by no more than the turning of a word or two. That he would do, and the old wood-chopper should take him to the town and sell him for fifty dollars.

"But there is one thing you must remember," said the Clever Student, "you must take the bridle from off my head when you sell me, for so long as it is on me I must, willy-nilly, remain a horse. The Great Master of Black Arts would like nothing better than to catch me in such a trap as that, for his books tell him that he is to have bad luck through me, and he has been after me for this many a day."

The wood-chopper promised to remember all that the Clever Student told him, and then the other went around back of the house and changed himself into a fine, dapple-gray horse. The wood-chopper slipped a bridle over the nag's nose and a leg over his back, and then off he rode towards the town.

On and on they jogged till they came to where two roads crossed, and there stood one who looked no better than he should. This was the Great Master of Black Arts himself; but of that the wood-chopper knew nothing at all.

"How do you find yourself, friend?" said the Master of Black Arts to the wood-chopper; "that is a fine horse that you have there, to be sure. Is he for sale now?"

"Yes," said the wood-chopper, "the nag is for sale, and fifty dollars will buy him—only the bridle does not go along with the horse."

Good! The wood-chopper might keep the bridle and welcome; but palm to palm for a true sale, and here was the money.

So they shook hands, and then the Master of Black Arts counted out the money, and the wood-chopper pocketed it, and he had never rubbed his fingers over so much in all of his life before.

Then, as quick as a wink, the Master of Black Arts drew a bridle out of his pocket. It was as thin as a wire and as light as silk, yet I tell you the truth when I say that if he had ever slipped it over the nose of the Clever Student it would have been an ill thing for him.

But the Student had his eyes open, and his wits about him. No sooner had his father taken the bridle off of him than—whisk! pop!—he changed himself into a pigeon and away he flew till the wind whistled behind him.

But the Master of Black Arts knew a trick as good as that, that he did. Whisk! pop!—and he became a hawk, and away he flew after the pigeon, and all that the wood-chopper could do was to stand and look after them— But he had the fifty dollars in his pocket, and that was something and more or less.

On and on flew the two, and if the pigeon flew fast, why, the hawk flew faster.

By and by they came to the shore of a great sea. And that was a good

thing for the Clever Student, for, just as the hawk was about to grip him, he dropped to the water and became a little fish, and away he swam.

But the Master of Black Arts knew a trick as good as that. Down to the water he dropped and became a pike, and after the little fish he swam till the water boiled behind him.

On and on they swam, and if the little fish swam fast, why, the great pike swam faster. On and on they swam till they came to a place where a beautiful princess, as white and as red as milk and rose leaves, was walking along beside the shore gathering pretty shells into a little basket. And that was a good thing for the Clever Student, for just as the Master of Black Arts was about to catch him he changed himself into a ruby ring and jumped out of the sea and into the basket of the princess, and there he was safe and sound.

Presently the princess looked down into the basket, and there lay the ring. "What a pretty ring!" said she. "And how came it here?"

She slipped it upon her finger, and it fitted as though it had been made for nobody in the world but her. As for the Clever Student, he liked to be there, I can tell you, for he thought that he had never seen such a pretty lass.

Well, by and by the princess had gathered all of the shells that she wanted, and then she went back home again.

When she had come there and to her own little room, all of a sudden a tall, good-looking young fellow stood before her. That was the Clever Student, who had changed himself back into his own true shape again. At first the princess was ever so frightened, but the Student talked to her so pleasantly that she began after a while to think that she had never seen such a nice, clever young fellow. So they passed the time very pleasantly together until evening drew near, and then the Student had to go.

But the Master of Black Arts was not at the end of his tricks yet.

And the Clever Student knew that as well as he knew anything.

"See, now," said he to the princess, "the Master will be coming after me before long. When he comes he will ask for the ruby ring, and he must have it, but I have a trick in my head to meet that."

He cut off a lock of his hair and then pricked his arm till it bled. With the blood he wet the hair, and by his arts he made of it a ruby ring so like what he himself had been that even the princess herself could not have told the one from the other. After that he changed himself into a necklace of carbuncles, and the princess was just as fond of it as she had been of the ring.

he Clever Scholar remains a Ruby Ring no longer, having regained his own true shape.

Sure enough, it happened just as the Clever Student had foretold. Before a great while the Master of Black Arts came along and on his arm he carried a basket. Rap! tap! tap! he knocked at the door of the king's house. Down went one and asked him what he wanted.

Oh! he only wanted to see the king; he had something for him here in the basket. So he was shown up to where the king was, and then he opened the basket and in it was a little black hen.

"Only a little black hen!" you say? Wait; you should hear all before you speak!

The Master of Black Arts stood the little black hen on the table. "Hickety-pickety!" said he, and before the king knew what to think of it the little black hen had laid an egg all of pure silver. And that hen *was* worth the having.

As for the king, bless me! but he was glad to have such a hen as that. If the master wanted anything that the king could give him, he had only to ask for it and it was as good as his.

"So; good!" says the Black Master, "then there is a little ruby ring that the princess wears and that I have taken a fancy to; if I may have that it will be all that I ask for."

Oh! if that was all that he wanted he should have it and welcome, that was what the king said. So the pretty princess was sent for, and the king asked her if she would give the Master of Black Arts the ruby ring that she wore.

"Oh, yes!" says the princess, "he shall have that and welcome, for I have grown tired of it long ago." So she gave it to him, and off he went on the same path that he had come.

As soon as he had reached home, he put the ring into a mortar and ground it up until it was as fine as flour in the mill.

"There!" said he to himself, "that is an end of the Clever Student at any rate."

After that he went back to his books again and began to read them, and then he soon found how he had been tricked by the Clever Student.

The princess and the Clever Student were sitting together. "See, now," said the Student, "the Master of Black Arts will be coming this way again in a little while. He will be wanting the necklace of carbuncles, and you will have to let him have it. But I have a trick for his trick yet, so that perhaps we will get the better of him in the end."

So the Clever Student did as he had done before; he pricked his arm

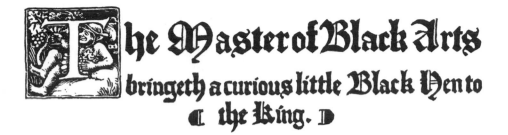

The Master of Black Arts

bringeth a curious little Black Hen to the King.

till it bled, and with the blood he wet a lock of his hair.   Then by his arts he changed the lock of hair into just such a necklace of carbuncles as he himself had been.   After that he changed himself into a pearl ear-drop, and the princess hung him in her ear, and there he dangled.

Sure enough; by and by came along the Master of Black Arts with another basket.   And you may believe that they did not let him cool his toes by long standing outside the door.   He opened his basket, and in it was a white drake.

"Only a white drake!" you say?   Yes, yes; but just wait for a little!

The Master of Black Arts stood the drake on the table and said, "Spickety-lickety!"

"Quack! quack!" said the drake, and every time it said "quack" a gold piece dropped from its mouth.

Hui! if the king was pleased with the little black hen, you can guess how glad he was to have such a drake as that!   All that the Master of Black Arts had to do was to ask for what he wanted, and he might have it if the king had it to give.

"Good!" says the Master of Black Arts; "then the princess has a necklace of carbuncles that I have taken a fancy to; if I may have that I will be satisfied."

So the princess was sent for without waiting any longer, and would she let the Master have the necklace of carbuncles that she wore around her neck?

"Yes, indeed!" says the princess, "that I will!   I have grown sick and tired of it long ago."   So she took it off of her neck and gave it to the Master of Black Arts, and off he went with it.

When he came home he put the necklace into the mortar, just as he had done the ring, and ground it up and ground it up until it was as fine as the dust on the shelf.   There! he thought, that is an end of the Clever Student at any rate.

Then he went back to his books, and it was not long before he found that he had been tricked again.

"I can make no more changes," said the Student, "for I am nearly at the end of my arts.   The Black Master will be wanting your ear-drop when he comes, but, instead of giving it to him, throw it against the wall as hard as you can.   After that we shall have to trust to good Mother Luck."

It was not long before the Master of Black Arts came with his basket on his arm, just as he had done twice before; he opened the basket, and there was a grey goose.

"Only a grey goose!" you say? Wait a moment, and you shall see that it was not like any grey goose in our town!

The Master of Black Arts stood the grey goose on the table; "Flickety-whickety!" said he.

"Cackle! cackle!" said the grey goose, and every time it said "cackle" a bright diamond dropped on the table.

When the king saw that he rubbed his hands and rubbed his hands, and could not say enough of thanks to the Master of Black Arts. And what would the Master have now? He had only to ask and it was his.

"Oh!" says the Master of Black Arts, "the princess has a pearl ear-drop that I have taken a liking to, if I may have that I will be quite satisfied."

So the princess was sent for, and this time she was not so willing to let the Master have what he wanted. She wept and begged, and begged and wept; but it was all to no purpose; the Master of Black Arts wanted the pearl ear-drop, and the Master of Black Arts must have it—that was what the king said. So at last the princess took the pearl ear-drop out of her ear, but, instead of giving it to the Master, she threw it against the wall as hard as she was able, just as the Clever Student had told her to do.

And then what do you think happened? Why, the Student turned himself into a ripe melon, so that when it struck the wall it burst open and the seeds that were inside were scattered all over the floor.

But the Master of Black Arts knew a trick as good as that. He changed himself into a great red cock, and began pecking away at the seeds, gobbling them up as fast as he could. By and by he looked around, and not another seed could he see, whereupon he hopped up on a chair and, shutting his eyes and flapping his wings, he crowed "cock-a-doodle-do!"

But listen! One melon-seed had rolled into a crack in the floor, and the cock had not seen it. That was a bad thing for him, for while his eyes were shut and he was crowing "cock-a-doodle-do!" the Clever Student changed himself from the melon-seed into a great fox. Up he jumped —snip! snap!—and off flew the cock's head, and there was an end of it and of the Master of Black Arts.

After that the Student turned himself into his own true shape again. Then he and the princess told the king all about the business, and when the king heard how fond the princess was of the lad, he said that there was only one thing to be done, and that was to call in the minister.

What happened to the Master of Black Arts after all his tricks.

So the Student was married to his dear princess, and that is what comes of book-learning.

After the wedding was all over, and the fiddlers had gone home, the Clever Student set out for his father's house in a fine coach drawn by six beautiful horses. There was the old man, making fagots in the forest back of the house, just as he had always done. At first he would not believe that the great lord in the coach was his own son. "No, no," says he; "and is it becoming in a fine spark from the great town to come here and make sport of a poor old wood-chopper. I know very well that my son is nothing but a poor student." But at last he got the whole matter through his head, and then he was so glad that he kissed his son on both cheeks, and asked him whether he had not always said that it was better for his boy to study books than to make fagots. For this is true: everything happens for the best when Luck strokes one the right way.

So the fagot-maker went back with his son to the fine house that the lad lived in, now that he had married a princess.

There everything was made easy for him, and he always had a warm corner to sit in back of the stove.

And that is the end of this story.

Six O'clock.

K&P.

The *Door* is open,   Sol above.
   The *Dew* is bright;
Forgotten now
   Is the lonesome *Night*,
And the *Starling* whistles,
   "*All is right*".

The *House-wife* moves
   With her briskest tread
The *Chairs* are set,
   And the *Table* spread
With *Honey* and *Eggs*
   And *Cream* and *Bread*.

K&P.

The Princess Golden-Hair and the Great Black Raven.

VI.

ONCE upon a time there was a king who had three daughters, the two elder were handsome enough, but the youngest, whose name was Golden-Hair, was the prettiest maiden to be found within the four ends of the earth.

One day the king went out hunting with all his people. Towards evening he found himself in the forest at a place where he had never been before, and where he was not able to tell the north from the south, nor the east from the west, for he was lost. He wandered up and down and here and there, but the farther he went the less able he was to find the road home again. As he wandered thus he came to a place where a great raven, as black as the soot in the chimney, and with eyes that glowed like two coals of fire, sat in the middle of the path in front of him.

"Whither away, king?" said the Great Black Raven.

"That I cannot tell," said the king, "for I am lost."

"See now," said the Raven, "I will show you the way out of the forest, if you will give me your youngest daughter to be my wife."

"Oh, no," said the king, "I can never do such a thing as that, for my daughter is as dear to me as the apple of my eye."

"Very well, then," said the Raven, "off I go, and then there will be no getting out of the forest for you, but here you will have to stay as long as you live."

5

Now one will do much before one will stay in a dark forest forever, and though it was a bad piece of business to be sure, the king promised at last that if the Raven would show him the way home again, it should have the Princess Golden-Hair for its wife, though it was a pity for the girl, and that was the truth. So the Raven flapped on ahead of the king, and showed him the way out of the forest.

"To-morrow," it said, "I will come for my bride."

Sure enough, when the next morning came, there was the Great Black Raven sitting outside of the castle gateway waiting for the Princess Golden-Hair to be sent to him.

But it was not the princess whom he got after all; for the king had bade them dress the swineherd's daughter in the princess's dress, and it was she who went to the Great Black Raven. "A Great Black Raven," said the king to himself, "will never be able to tell a swineherd's daughter from a real princess."

Well, the Raven took the swineherd's daughter on its back and away it flew over woods and meadows, hills and valleys, until by and by it came to a rude little hut that stood on the tip top of a great bleak hill. And not a living soul was there, only a great number of birds of different kinds.

In the hut was a table, and on the table stood a golden goblet of red wine, a silver cup of white wine, and an earthenware jug full of bitter beer.

"This is our home," said the Raven; "and now will my dear one drink refreshment after her long journey?"

Yes, indeed; the swineherd's daughter would do that, for she was weary after her ride through the air. So she went to the table and took a good drink of the beer, "for," said she to herself, "the golden goblet and the silver cup are too fine for the likes of me."

Then the Raven knew that she was no true princess to be contented with bitter beer out of an earthenware jug when she could have good red wine from a golden goblet. "Come," said he, "home we go again, for you are not the bride I seek!" Therewith he took her upon his back once more, and away they flew over hill and valley till they had come back to the king's castle again.

"See," said the Raven, "this is not the one I want. Let me have my true bride or you will suffer for it."

At this the king was frightened. "Very well," said he, "come to-morrow and you shall have your true bride."

Well, when the next morning came, there was the Raven waiting outside

 he King being lost in yͤ Forest meets with the Great Black Raven.

of the castle gateway.   But, after all, it was not the princess that he got, for the king had ordered that the steward's daughter should be dressed in the princess's dress, " for surely," said he to himself, " she is a good enough bride for a Great Black Raven."

So the Raven took her on his back and away he flew till he had come to the little hut on top of the bleak hill.   There stood the golden goblet, the silver cup, and the earthenware jug just as they had done before.   And now would not the dear maiden drink a drop after her long journey?

Yes, indeed, that she would; so she took a good, hearty drink of the white wine in the silver cup, " for," said she to herself, " silver is none too good for a steward's daughter."

But the Raven saw very well that she was no true princess, or she would never have been contented with the silver cup.   " Come," said he, " home we go again, for you are not the bride I seek."   So he took her on his back once more and away he flew to the king's castle.   " See how you treat me," said he to the king, " you promise me one bride and give me another. To-morrow morning I will come for the true one again, and if I do not get her this time you will suffer for it, for I will pick out your eyes and tear down your castle about your ears!"   And away he flew.

And now the king was terribly frightened, and saw that there must be no trickery this time.   So the next morning when the Raven came it was the Princess Golden-Hair herself whom he got and none other.   Up he took her on his back and away he flew with her.   As for the princess, she did nothing but weep and weep, so that when they came to the little hut on top of the bleak hill, she was glad enough to drink a drop for refreshment's sake.   She never looked at the earthen jug or the silver cup, but going straight to the golden goblet she wet her lips with the good red wine.

And then what do you think happened?   Why, the hut grew and grew until it changed into a splendid castle all built of pure silver and gold, and all of the many birds outside changed into men and women servants.   As for the Great Black Raven, it was a Raven no longer, but the handsomest prince in all of the world, and the only thing black about him was the long curling locks of his hair.   He kissed the Princess Golden-Hair and said: " Now, indeed, have I found my true bride and none other.   You have freed me and my castle and all of my people from enchantment, which no one but a real princess could do.   For my wicked stepmother laid spells upon us which could only be broken when a real princess drank out of the golden goblet."

 **rincess Golden Hair, being** a true princess, drinketh from the golden cup & touches neither ẏ silver noȝ ẏ clay.

Then they were married, and a fine wedding they had of it, I can tell you.

Well, a year passed by, and the princess was as happy as the days were long; but at the end of the twelve months she began to long to see her father and her sisters again. So she spoke of her longing to the Raven prince, but he only shook his head. No; he would not hear of her going, for he felt that nothing but misfortune would come of it.

But the princess begged and begged so prettily that at last the prince said she might go if she would be contented to stay only three days. Then he gave her a napkin of the finest linen, and told her that whenever she wanted anything, she had only to spread the napkin and wish and it would be there. But there was one thing she must not wish for, and that was for him himself, for of that misfortune would come for sure and certain.

So off the princess went to her father's house, and a fine sight she made of it, I can tell you; for she rode in a golden coach drawn by four milk-white horses, so that every one she passed stopped and looked after her, and the little boys cried " Hi!" and ran along beside.

Her father and her sisters wondered what fine lady it was that was coming to the castle, and when the coach stopped they came out to look. Dear, dear, but the king was glad to see her; as for her two sisters, they grew as green as grass with envy, for when they heard where she dwelt, and what a fine castle it was, all built of pure gold and silver, and what a handsome prince it was that she had for a husband, they were ready to burst with spite, for each felt that she might have had all this for herself if the Raven prince had only chosen her instead of Golden-Hair. So when the princess had told them all about what had happened, they only nodded and winked at one another as though they did not believe a word of it.

"Yes, yes," said they, "it is all very well to talk about your handsome prince; but why did he not come along with you, we should like to know?"

The princess could not tell them that; but she could bring him quickly enough whenever she chose, for all that she had to do was to spread her napkin and wish and he would be there. She would show them that what she had said was true, had her prince not forbidden her.

But the envious sisters only jeered and laughed as though all that the princess said was the best jest in the world.

Now one can bear anything better than laughter. So the end of the matter was that the princess spread the linen napkin on the floor and wished that the Raven prince might be with them.

 **rincess Golden Hair cometh to Death's door where sits Death's aged Grandmother spinning flax within.**

No sooner had she wished it than there he stood; but he looked at no one but her. " Did I not tell you that misfortune would come of it if you wished for me?" said he. " Now, I must leave you and go where you are not likely ever to see me again."

Then the princess would have spoken, but he gave her no time for that. He snatched up the napkin, and, becoming a Raven once more, he flew through the open window and across the tree-tops and was gone. At the same time her golden coach vanished, and, the coachman and footmen became so many birds and flew away, so that not one of her fine things was left.

The poor princess wept and cried for a whole day and a whole night. But at the end of that time she dried her eyes, and, putting the three golden apples in her pocket, and tucking up her skirts, started off into the wide world to find her dear prince again.

Well, she travelled on and on and on for more days than she could count, and till she had been over nearly all of the world, but in all that time she could learn no news of the prince nor of whither he had gone. At last one day, about nightfall, she came to a little hut in a deep forest, and in the hut sat an old woman with hair as white as snow.

" What do you want, child?" said the old woman; " do you not know that this is Death's house, and that if he returns and finds you here he will kill you? I tell you that he spares neither the young nor the old, the plain nor the handsome. As for me, I am his grandmother."

But all this was one to the princess, and went in at one ear and out of the other; she could no longer drag one foot after the other, so there she must stay even if Death should find her when he came home.

Then she told Death's grandmother all that had happened to her, and Death's grandmother took pity on her because she was so pretty and so tired. She gave the princess something to eat and then hid her in the tall clock that stood in the corner, so that Death might not find her when he came home.

By and by in came Death and hung up his great scythe behind the door. " Hu-u-u-u!" cried he, " I smell Christian blood in the house for sure."

" Christian blood, indeed!" said his grandmother, " as though a Christian would come to this house if he had anywhere else to go! But now I think of it, a crow flew overhead to-day, and dropped a bone down the chimney. I threw it out as soon as I could, but perhaps that is what you smell."

So Death said nothing more, but sat down to supper and ate heartily, for he had had a long journey that day.

"See," said his grandmother, "I had a dream to-day. A princess is out in the world hunting for her Raven sweetheart, and cannot tell where to find him."

"That is easy enough to tell," said Death; "he lives in a great castle that stands at the end of the earth on a high hill of smooth glass."

"That is good," said Death's grandmother, "but I dreamed that after she found where he lived, she was too weary to journey thither."

"That is easy enough, too," said Death; "out in the forest yonder stands my pale horse tied to an oak-tree. If she could only find the horse and loose the bridle and mount his back he would take her there quickly enough, for he can travel more rapidly than the north wind."

"Yes, yes, that is all very well," said Death's grandmother, "but I had a third dream; I thought that when she came to the smooth hill of glass she did not know how to climb to the top; what is the answer to that?"

"Prut!" said Death, "that is easy to tell. Over by the glass hill are seven birds fighting in the tree-top for an old hat. If she will throw a stone in the midst of them they will drop the hat and fly away. It is Wish's own hat, and if she will put it on her head and wish herself at the top of the hill, she will be there quickly enough, I can tell you."

After that Death put on his cloak and took up his scythe and was off like a whirlwind, for he has little time to spare for talking, folks say. Then Death's grandmother opened the clock, and the princess came out and thanked her and went her way.

She hunted here and there through the forest until, sure enough, she found Death's great pale horse tied to an oak-tree. She loosened the bridle and mounted upon his back, and away they went till the chips and the stones flew behind them. So they soon came to the high hill of smooth glass that stood at the end of the earth, and there, on top of it, was the castle of the prince.

The princess dismounted from the pale horse, and away he galloped home again.

Then the princess hunted for the birds that Death said fought for Wish's hat, and presently she heard them making a great hubbub, and, looking up, saw them in the tree-top above her, fighting for the old hat, just as Death said they would be doing. She picked up a stone and threw it in the midst of them, and they dropped the hat and flew away screaming.

Then she put on the hat and wished herself at the top of the hill, and there she was as quick as a wink.

Now, her shoes were worn into holes by long journeying, and her clothes were torn to threads and tatters by the brambles through which she had passed, and hung fluttering all about her, and she looked for all the world like nothing else than a common beggar-maid, except for her golden hair. So it was that when she knocked at the door of the prince's castle, and the porter came and opened it and heard that she wanted to see the prince, he snapped his fingers and laughed. All the same he told her that the cook wanted a serving wench in the kitchen, and that she might have the place if she liked; if that did not suit her she might be jogging the way that she had come.

Well, there was nothing for it but for the princess to serve in the kitchen or to go away again. So she bound up her hair in a tattered kerchief so that the beautiful golden tresses might not be seen, and down she went to serve the cook.

The prince's dinner was cooking at the fire, and the princess was to watch it so that it might not be burned. So she watched it, and as she watched it she wept.

" Why do you weep, hussy?" said the cook.

" Ah me !" said the princess, " once I ate with my love and drank with my love and lived by his side. If he did but know to what I have come how his heart would ache !"

After that the dinner was served, but, while nobody was looking, the princess plucked a strand of her golden hair and laid it upon a white napkin and the napkin upon an empty plate. Over all she placed a silver cover, and when the Raven prince lifted it there lay the strand of golden hair. " Where did this come from?" said he. But nobody could tell him that.

The next day the same thing happened; the princess watched the dinner, and as she watched she wept.

" Why do you weep, hussy?" said the cook. And thereto the princess answered as she had done before: " Ah me ! once I ate with my love and drank with my love and lived by his side. If he did but know to what I have come, how his heart would ache !"

Then, while nobody was looking, she plucked another strand of golden hair and the prince found it as he had done the other, and no one could tell him whence it came.

The third day the same thing happened as had happened twice before:

The Princess finds her Prince.

the princess watched and wept, and when nobody was looking plucked a third strand of golden hair and sent it to the prince as she had the others.

Then the prince sent for the cook. "Who has been serving this and that with my dinner?" said he.

The cook shook his head, for he knew nothing, but perhaps the new serving wench could tell, for she wept and said things that none of them understood. When the prince heard this he sent for her, and the princess came and stood before him. He looked at her and knew her, for her golden hair shone through a hole in the ugly head-dress that she wore. Then he reached out his hand and snatched it off of her head, and her golden hair fell down all about her shoulders until it reached the floor. Then he took her in his arms and kissed her, and that was the end of all of her troubles.

After that they had a grand time at the castle; every one who came had all that he could eat, and wine and beer flowed like water. I, too, was there, but I brought nothing away with me in my pockets.

Seven O'clock·

Around about, ⊙☌⊕E3°26'.
Around about,
The *Kobold* played and in and out;
He peeped in every *Pot* and *Pail*,
And grinned, and pulled the *Pussy's* tail.

Clear.
pleasant.

Big clumsy *Gretchen*, washing up
The *Breakfast-dishes*, dropped a *Cup*;
It fell upon the *Kobold's Toe*,
And made him hop it hurt him so.

K.P.
del.

VII.

IN those days the Great Red Fox and Cousin Greylegs, the wolf, were great cronies, and whenever you would see one you might be sure the other was not far away. The Great Red Fox was a master-hand at roguery, and Cousin Greylegs, the wolf, came close behind him. That was how they made their living.

By and by they fell out, so that they were never good friends again, and this was how it happened.

There was to be a great fair, and the world and his wife and the little dog behind the stove were to be there.

"We will go too," says the pair of scamps; so off they went.

By and by they came to an inn where the windows were red with the good things cooking in the kitchen—green geese and ducks and chickens, and sausages, and cabbage, and onions, and all the nice things you can think of. But the two rogues had no money, and one cannot buy something with nothing out in the wide world. But they found a ladder against the side of the wall, and climbed up into the loft above and lay in the hay.

Dear, dear, how nice the good things did smell down in the kitchen! "My goodness!" says Cousin Greylegs, "but I would like to have a taste of them."

As for the Great Red Fox, he had been nursing his wits all the time, and now he had a trick hatched. So down he climbed from the loft the same way he had climbed up; and nobody saw him, for he took good care of that. Over he went to the stables where the horses stood munching away at the corn in the mangers. He loosened a bridle here and a bridle there until not one of the nags was fastened where he belonged; then he slipped back into the loft once more. By and by began the kicking and the squealing over at the stable; out ran the landlord and all the other folks with him, and not a soul was left in the kitchen. Then brother Greylegs and the Great Red Fox came down and helped themselves, and while they were about it the Great Red Fox stuffed a fistful of hazel-nuts into his pocket.

After a while the landlord and the rest of them came from the stable; but nothing was left for them of the good things but the leavings.

As for Cousin Greylegs and the Great Red Fox, why, they lay up in the loft among the straw, and ate and ate until they could eat no more.

By and by there came along somebody else on his way to the fair, and it was a rich corn-factor who made his money by buying corn cheap, and selling it dear to poor folks, so that he was as great a rogue as the two scamps up yonder in the loft. With him he brought a whole bag of money; but it bought him no supper that night, for all the good things had been stolen, and the corn-factor had to be contented with what pickings he could get. As for the bag of money, he put that in a great chest in the corner, and there he left it for safe-keeping.

Now up in the loft where the two rogues lay was a cowhide, which the landlord used for making straps and thongs and such like things. What does the Great Red Fox do but whip out his needle and thread and sew the cowhide fast to Cousin Greylegs' Jacket, though Cousin Greylegs knew no more of that than a mouse in a barrel. Then by and by the Great Red Fox was up to another of his tricks. "See," says he, "here I have a pocket-ful of hazel-nuts, and I am for cracking one."

"Tut, tut, brother," says Cousin Greylegs, "you must crack no nuts here."

"But I must crack a nut," says the Great Red Fox.

"But you must not," says Cousin Greylegs.

"But I must," says the Great Red Fox, and so he did.

"Hark!" says the landlord; "yonder is somebody up in the loft cracking the nuts that we were to have had for supper; it is a good beating he shall have for the trick he has been playing upon us."

When Cousin Greylegs heard this he did not stop to tarry or to think;

ousin Greylegs and the Great Red Fox go together to $\tilde{y}$ fair.

down he jumped from the loft, and away he scampered as fast as he could lay foot to the ground; but with him went the cowhide which the Great Red Fox had sewed fast to his jacket.

"Hi!" bawled the landlord, "there is the thief who stole our supper, and he is taking my cowhide into the bargain."

Off they all scampered after Cousin Greylegs and the cowhide. The corn-factor first of all.

As for Cousin Greylegs, why, he laid down to the running as though he had never been born for anything else. But it is hard work running with a cowhide flapping about one's legs, so they caught him just over the hill, and then, dear, dear, what a drubbing they gave him.

But as soon as everybody was safe away after Cousin Greylegs and the cowhide, the Great Red Fox came down from the loft, and marched off with the corn-factor's money without anybody being about to say "No" to him.

Off he went as happy as a cricket, until he came to the cross-roads over the hill and back of the woods, and who should he see sitting there but Cousin Greylegs rubbing the places that smarted the most.

"Hi!" says the Great Red Fox, "and is that you, Cousin Greylegs? Why, I have been looking up and down, over hill and over hollow for you. Here is a whole bag of money that I found at the inn over yonder, and if it wasn't for the trick that I played you, there was never a penny of it that would have come into our pockets."

"So!" says Cousin Greylegs. "Well, that was a different matter;" and he swallowed the drubbing he had had, for it was to be share and share alike with the money, and that was a salve for sore bones. So off they went together arm in arm.

By and by they came to another inn. "We'll stop here," says Cousin Greylegs, "and have another bite to eat before we go any farther." And that suited the Great Red Fox well enough, so in they went, and gave the bag of money into the landlord's keeping, and Cousin Greylegs ordered a supper fit for a lord.

But the Great Red Fox had his wits about him all this time, for he was not one to be caught napping when the sun was up. "Yes, yes," says he to himself, "Cousin Greylegs is up to some of his tricks, sure enough; we'll put a stopper in the bottle before the luck has dribbled out." So while Cousin Greylegs was pottering about in the kitchen down-stairs, seeing that the cooking was done to his mind, the Great Red Fox took a bag like the

ousin Greylegs steals away from the inn, carrying off a bag full of this & that with him.

one they brought with them, and filled it full of old rusty nails and bits of iron. Off he marched with it to the landlord. "See," says he, "Cousin Greylegs will come asking for a bag by and by; here it is, give it to him and he will be satisfied."

Sure enough, when the supper was over and the Great Red Fox was snoring in front of the fire, for all the world as though he were sound asleep, off packed Cousin Greylegs to the landlord. "Look," says he, "that bag that the Great Red Fox left here, just hand it over to me, will you? for I must be jogging. As for the Great Red Fox, you may let him have his sleep out."

Yes, that was all right, and the landlord knew nothing about the tricks of the two rogues, so he handed over the bag of rusty nails and bits of iron. And Cousin Greylegs never once thought of looking to see, for the bits of iron jingled, and the sound was enough for him, for that is the way with folks out in the world.

As for the Great Red Fox, he waited until Cousin Greylegs was well away on his own business, then off he stepped along the road that led the other way, and it was the bag of gold and silver money he carried with him.

But that is not all of the story; for listen: There was a poor old blind mole who lived in the ground because he had nowhere else to go, and that was his home. But the Great Red Fox thought nothing of him. On he came—tramp! tramp! tramp!—and would have trodden right on the roof of the mole's house. "Brother Fox," cried Grandfather Mole, "look where you are treading, or you will have the roof down about my ears."

"Pooh!" says the Great Red Fox, "when one has been sharp enough to trick such a keen blade as Cousin Greylegs, one is not going to step out of one's way for a little gray mole as blind as charity:" and so he was for going straight ahead.

But up jumped Grandfather Mole and caught hold of him, and then he felt the bag of gold and silver money the Great Red Fox carried. "Hi!" says he, "and here is a new card in the game." So he held on to the Great Red Fox and began to bawl with all his might and main, "Help, good folks! help! here is the Great Red Fox stealing my bag of gold and silver money!"

"Hush! hush!" said the Great Red Fox, for he was for having as little

The Great Red Fox meets ẏ old, blind Mole.

said about the bag of money as need be, "let me go and I will promise to tread on nobody's house." But no, it was easier to get into that hole than it was to get out again, for Grandfather Mole held on and bawled for help louder than ever. "Help! help! here is one robbing a poor blind mole of all he has in the world!" That was the way he kept up the song, and he made such a hubbub that the folks came running and hauled them both up before the Master Judge to see what he had to say about the business.

"The bag of money is mine," said the Great Red Fox.

"Yes, good! but where did you get it?" says the judge, and that was a question easier asked than answered.

"See now," says Grandfather Mole, "it is easy enough to talk, for breath is cheap in this town, but the thing is to put it to trial and find out who is telling the truth. We'll build a fire and try who can stand it the longest, and that will show the right in this matter as clear as a morning in hay-season."

Well, that suited the fox well enough, " for," says he to himself, " it is a pretty business if I can't stand a scorching as long as an old blind mole ;" and so that business was settled.

Out they all went, and it was Grandfather Mole who was to try the burning first of all. So they fetched sticks and twigs and covered him all over with them, and then set fire to them.

Dear, dear, but it was a fine blaze that went up, but the mole had his wits about him ; for as soon as he felt the heat of the fire he began digging down into the ground with all his might and main, so that not a spark touched him.

" Do you burn, Grandfather Mole?" says the Great Red Fox.

" No !" bawled Grandfather Mole. So they just threw on another armful of twigs.

By and by the Great Red Fox says again : " Do you burn, Grandfather Mole ?" for he thought by this time that the mole must be as scorched as an old shoe under the stove.

But Grandfather Mole was ready for him. " *No ! !*" he bawled, louder than ever.

Dear, dear, but here was a strange happening ; all the same, the Great Red Fox threw on wood and threw on wood, until the blaze went up like a chimney afire. " And *now* do you burn, Grandfather Mole ?" says he.

" NO !!!" bawled Grandfather Mole until you might have thought his throat would have split with the noise he made.

So they let the fire go out, and up came Grandfather Mole out of the ground looking as fresh and as sharp as a green gooseberry.

And now it was the Great Red Fox's turn ; and they heaped the sticks and twigs over him as they had done over Grandfather Mole, and then set fire to them.

" Do you burn?" says Grandfather Mole after a bit.

" NO !!!" bawled the Great Red Fox, as though his throat was made of leather.

So they threw on more sticks and twigs, but the Great Red Fox just shut his teeth and grinned, for he was bound that he would stand as much of a burning as an old blind mole.

The Great Red Fox beareth all that he can.

"Do you burn now?" says Grandfather Mole.

"No," says the Great Red Fox, but his voice was as small as peas in March. So they threw on another armful of wood, and the fire grew hotter and hotter.

"And do you burn now?" says Grandfather Mole.

"*Thunder and lightning, yes!*" bawled the Great Red Fox, and out he jumped and away he scampered, smoking like a charcoal kiln.

So all he gained by his roguery was a burnt skin and nothing to show for it; and that has happened more than once to rogues whose wits are so sharp that they cut their own fingers with them.

Now in our town we do not make puddings without plums, or tell a story without rhyme or reason, but if you wish to find any meaning in these words, you must put on your spectacles and look for it for yourself, even though the tale stands all legs and no head, as the man-in-the-moon said about his grandmother's tongs.

Eight O'clock.

The *Sun* in the *Sky*   *Grows warmer*
Is not yet high,
And the *Grasses* are wet by the *Pool*.
With hop and jump,
By *Hedge* and *Stump*,
The *Children* are going to *School*.

K.P.

K.P.

One Good Turn Deserves Another.

VIII.

NCE upon a time there was a lad who was a fisher-man, and every morning he shouldered his net, and went down to the river to catch fish to sell in the town.

One morning as he walked beside the edge of the water, he came upon a great tall stork caught in a trap that had been set for the water-rats.

It was a tender heart that the young fisherman had under his jacket, so when he saw Father Longlegs in such a pickle he waded out into the water, among the reeds and arrowheads to where the other was, and loosened the noose from about his leg.

The storks bring good-luck to folks some people say, and that was what happened to the young fisherman.

"One good turn deserves another," says Father Longlegs; "cross your heart three times, cast your net into the water yonder, and see what you catch." So the lad did as he was told, and when he drew his net to the shore, there was just one fish in it.

Yes; just one fish, but that was worth the catching, I can tell you, for the scales were all of pure silver and gold, so that it glistened like the moon on smooth ice, and it was most wonderful to see.

"There," says the stork; "and now if you have your wits about you, it is your fortune that you have caught out of the water. Take the fish up to the king's castle and show it to nobody but the king. When he sees it he will want to have it for his own and will be for buying it, but there is only one price you must ask for it, and that is to have the princess for your wife." That was what the stork said, and then he spread his wings and flew away over the house-tops.

So the lad wrapped the fish up in a clean white napkin and laid it in a wicker basket, and then off he marched to the king's castle to try his luck there, as the stork had said.

Rap! tap! tap! he knocked at the door.

Well, and what did he want?

Oh, he had brought a fish that he had caught over at the river yonder, but he would show it to nobody but the king himself.

No, it did no good for them to ask and to question and to talk; what he had said he had said. So at last they had to take him up-stairs, and there was the king sitting upon a golden throne with a golden crown upon his head and a golden sceptre in his hand.

"Well, and why do you wish to see me?" That was what the king said.

It was no word that the lad spoke with his tongue, but he just unfolded the napkin, and showed the king what he had brought in the wicker basket.

When the king saw the gold-and-silver fish, he thought he had never seen anything so wonderful in all of his life before. Then it was just as the stork had said. He must and would have the fish, no matter what it cost; and what would the lad take for it?

Why, the body over at the river yonder, who had put the lad up to catching the fish, had told him that there was only one price to be asked for it. Now, if the king would let him have the princess for his wife, he might have the fish and welcome; for *that* was the price, and the long and the short of it.

Well, the king hemmed and hawed, but he did not speak the little word "no;" and after a while he said he would send for the princess, and see what she had to say about it. So the princess came, and she was a beauty I can tell you, for the very sight of her was enough to make one's heart melt inside of one, like a lump of butter in the oven. And as for the wits of her, why, she was just as smart as she was pretty (which is saying much and a little over), and that is why the king had sent for her, for he wanted to get the gold-and-silver fish without paying the price for it.

"Yes," says the princess when the king had told her all. "I am ready enough to marry the lad, only he must promise to do one thing first."

Dear, dear, how the lad's heart jumped inside of him at that. He was

ather Longlegs, the Stork, puts the Fisher Lad in ye way of catching a strange fish in his nets. C

willing enough to promise whatever was asked, for he would do anything to marry the princess, now that he had seen how pretty she was.

"Very well, then," said the princess, "just bring me the key of wish-house and I will marry you."

"There," said the king, "that is a bargain; go and bring the key of wish-house and you shall marry the princess; and you may just leave the fish here until you come back again. And don't show your face about here without the key, if you wish to keep your head upon your shoulders."

So off went the lad from the king's castle, with nothing at all in his pocket and ill-luck astride of his back. Down he went to the river as straight as he could walk, and there stood Father Stork gazing down into the water and looking as wise as our minister on Sunday. See now, thus and so and thus and so had happened, and the stork had gotten him into a pretty scrape over at the castle by putting him up to asking such a price for his herring; that was what the lad said.

"Prut!" says the stork, "break no bones over that furrow; ill-luck always comes before good-luck, and rain before the little flowers; what is worth having is worth working for. Just get upon my back and I will carry you to where the queen of the birds lives; if anybody can put you in the way of finding the key of wish-house she will be the one." So the stork bent his red legs and up the lad got upon his back. Then Father Long-legs spread his wings and away he flew, and on and on, over field and fallow, over valley and mountain, over forest and over stream.

After they had gone so far that the lad thought the end of the world could not be a great way off, they came to a grand house, all built of red brick, that stood on a high hill, and that was where the queen of the birds lived. The stork flew straight to the house, and there was the queen of the birds walking in the garden.

The stork told everything from first to last, and that now what they wanted to know was, whether the queen of the birds could tell them where the key of wish-house was to be found.

No, the queen did not know that herself, but she would call all of the birds of the heavens and of the earth, and perhaps there would be some one among them that could tell.

A little silver whistle hung about her neck; she put it to her lips and blew upon it so shrilly that it made a body's ear ring to listen to it, and the birds of the heavens and of the earth came flying from far and near until the air was as full of them as a sunbeam is full of motes on sweeping-day.

The queen of the birds asked them one and all, from tom-tit to the wild swan, if they could tell where the key of wish-house was to be found; but not a single one of them knew.

After all the rest had spoken there came flying an old eagle, so old that he was as grey as the ashes upon the hearth, and he was six times as big as any of the rest. He had come from the other end of nowhere, and that is a long way off, as even simple Jack can tell you; that was what had kept him such a time in the coming.

And was it the key of wish-house that they were talking about? Oh, yes; the old eagle knew where the key of wish-house was as well as he knew his bread-and-butter, for the old Grey Master that lives on the iron mountain had it hanging back of the kitchen door, and the eagle had seen it there more than once.

"Very well," says the queen of the birds; "then here is a lad who has come out into the world hunting for that key, a good-hearted fellow who helped Father Stork out of a tight place over at the river yonder, where he had been caught in a trap set for the water-rats. Now can you not help him to find what he wants?"

Well, the old eagle did not say no, for one good turn deserves another ; so he took the lad on his back at the root of his wings and away he flew.

One would have thought that the red-legged stork had flown far, but it was nothing at all to the journey that the eagle took. On and on he flew for such a long way that I, for one, could never find words to tell you how far away it was.

All the same, every journey must have an ending. And at last they came to a great iron mountain the sides of which were as smooth as the face of a looking-glass; so it was a good thing for the lad that he had a great grey eagle to carry him up to the top, and that is the truth.

There on the top of the mountain lay a green meadow, so wide that the eye could not see to the other end of it. And in the middle of the meadow stood a tall castle; that was where the Grey Master lived who kept the key of wish-house back of the kitchen door.

"This is all the farther I can carry you just now," says the eagle; "but here is a feather, when you are ready to come away just throw it up into the air, and I will not be long in coming."

The lad thanked the eagle for the help he had had, and then he put the feather in the lining of his hat.

After that the eagle went one way and the lad went the other, and that was towards the castle where the Grey Master lived.

Off he stepped right foot foremost, and by and by he came to a little stream of water that ran along through the meadow. But just in the middle of the brook lay a great stone, that choked the stream so that it could hardly crawl around it.

"Here is a body in trouble as well as myself," said the lad, and he stooped and rolled away the great round stone so that the brook might flow smoothly and freely.

"One good turn deserves another," said the brook. "Look in the place where the great round stone lay and you will find a little red pebble; so long as you keep that pebble in your mouth you will be as strong as ten common men."

Well, the lad hunted until he found the pebble, and then he thanked the brook and jogged along the way he was going.

By and by he came to an apple-tree, and it was so loaded down with apples that the branches were bent to the very ground.

"Here is another body weighed down by the cares of the world," said the lad. So he shook some of the apples off and cut props to put under the branches, that they might not be broken by the load.

"One good turn deserves another," said the apple-tree. "Look under my roots and you will find a golden apple; while you keep that in your bosom neither fire nor water can harm you, for it is an apple from the tree of life."

Well, the lad found the apple under the roots of the tree, and then he said "thank you," and went on his way.

By and by he came to a place where he heard a great hubbub over the hedge; he looked and there he saw that it was a black cock and a red cock fighting for dear life, and the red cock was having the worst of it, for it was nearly dead already.

"Here is another who is having the worst of the fight," said the lad, and he jumped over the hedge, and drove away the black cock with the staff he held in his hand.

"One good turn deserves another," said the red cock. "I know what you have come hither to find, and I will give you a bit of advice that will be worth the having. When the Grey Master asks you what you want, tell him it is to watch his black cattle for one night. If you do that he must give you whatsoever you ask for. And listen; this is what

he Fisher Lad cometh to the Grey Master's house.

you must do to watch the cattle. When you open the stable door there
will come out three-and-twenty black cows, and after them a black bull
breathing fire and smoke. Him you must catch by the horns and must
hold him fast until the cock crows in the morning. But you must have
the strength of ten men to do that."

Well, the lad thanked the cock for the advice he had given, and then
he went on his way and up to the castle where the Grey Master lived.

He knocked at the door, and it was the Grey Master himself who came
and opened it. He was a head and shoulders taller than other men, was
the Grey Master, and he had but one eye, which gleamed and glistened
like the dog-star in January. Beside him flew two black ravens with eyes
as red as coals of fire.

"And what is it that you want?" said the Grey Master.

"Oh!" said the lad, "I have come from over in the brown world yonder, and I want to watch your black cattle for one night, that is all I am
after."

When the Grey Master heard what the lad said, he frowned until his
one eye shone like lightning. "Very well," said he, "you shall have a
chance and a try at what you want, but if you fail your head shall be cut off
and hung up over the gate yonder."

"That is not so pleasant to think of," said the lad; "all the same, I will
have a try and see what I can do." So in he came, and he and the Grey
Master sat down to supper together.

By and by, when the lad had eaten all that he wanted the Grey Master
told him it was time to go about the business he had come for. So off
went the lad to the stable where the four-and-twenty black cattle stood all
in a row. He opened the door, and out they ran helter-skelter and as fast
as they could push, and—whisk! pop!—soon as they came out of the door
each cow changed into a black crow and flew around and around the lad's
head as though it would beat his eyes out. Last of all came the black
bull, and the lad was ready and waiting for him.

He clapped the red pebble into his mouth, and then he was as strong as
ten common men. He caught the bull by the horns, and it might puff out
fire and smoke, as it chose, for it could do him no harm because of the apple
of life which he carried in his bosom.

How the bull did pitch and toss, and bellow and roar, to be sure, but
it was all for no use, the lad held on like hunger, until by and by the bull
stopped struggling and stood as quiet as a lamb. But the lad held fast to

the bull's horns, and all the time the black crows flew about his head, but never once so much as touched him.

At last a cock crew, and then they all changed again into cows, and the lad drove them back into the stable once more, and there they were.

By and by came the Grey Master. "Well," said he, "and did you watch the black cattle?"

Oh, yes, the lad had watched them, and it was no such hard task to do; there they were in the stable yonder, safe and sound.

Then you should have seen what a sour face the Master pulled over the business! All the same, he had to pay the lad; so what did he want for his wages?

"Oh!" said the lad, "it is little that I want. If you will let me have the key that hangs back of the kitchen door I will be satisfied." So the Grey Master had to go and get it for him, though he would rather have given him one of his eye-teeth.

Off marched the lad with what he had come for, and that is more than most of us get. But the Grey Master was not for letting him off so easy as all that, I can tell you, for the more he thought over the business the less he liked to give up the key of wish-house.

So after a while he took down the Sword of Sharpness which hung against the wall, slipped his feet into the Shoes of Speed that stood in the corner, took a peep into the Book of Knowledge which lay upon the shelf, to see which way the lad had gone, and then set off after him hot-foot, to get back what he had given away.

Just as the lad got to where the apple-tree stood he looked over his shoulder, and there he saw the Grey Master coming over the hills.

"And where shall I go now," says he.

"One good turn deserves another," said the apple-tree; "just come under my branches."

The lad did as he was told, and the apple-tree drooped its branches about him, until one could see neither hide nor hair of him.

By and by up came the Grey Master puffing and blowing. "Apple-tree," says he, "did you see the fisher-lad come by this way?"

No, the apple-tree had seen nobody go past that place. So back went the Master home again to have another look into his Book of Knowledge. There he saw as clear as day what sort of trick had been played upon him. Off he started again after the lad at such a rate that the ground smoked under his feet.

But the lad had lost no time either, so that when he looked over his shoulder and saw the Grey Master coming across the hills behind him, he had gone as far as the brook.

"One good turn deserves another," said the brook, and it made itself small and smaller, so that the lad stepped over without wetting so much as the sole of his foot. Then it spread itself out again three times as broad as before. Presently up came the Master, fuming like a pot on the fire.

"Brook," says he, "did you see the fisher-lad go by this way?"

"Yes," said the brook; "there he is just on the other side." And there he was sure enough.

The Grey Master never stopped to take off his shoes and stockings, but into the water he splashed as fast as he could go. Just as he reached the middle of the stream the brook began to swell, and grew large and larger until it carried away the Grey Master like a cork in the gutter, and there was an end of him.

After that the lad went on without hurrying any more than he chose, until he came to the side of the mountain. He took the eagle's feather from out his cap and threw it up in the air, and there was the eagle before he had time to grow tired of waiting.

He sat him upon the eagle's back, and away they flew, and on and on without stopping until they came to the house where the queen of the birds lived. There was Father Longlegs (the stork) waiting for them, He took his turn of carrying the lad, and when they stopped it was just over beyond the king's castle.

But the lad had been out into the world, and had learned a thing or two.

"See now," says he, "it was hasty cooking that burned the broth;" and so he would not go up to the castle with his key of wish-house without first trying what door he could unlock with it himself. He took it out of his pocket and struck it a rap or two upon the ground.

"I should like," says he, "to have golden clothes upon my back, and to have a golden horse and a golden greyhound that shall chase a golden hare." That was what he said, and he did not have to say it twice; for before he could wink there they were standing beside him just as he wanted. He leaped upon his horse and away he rode after the greyhound and the golden hare.

How the people in the castle did stare when they saw him riding past! The princess herself ran to the window to see the fine sight, and as for the

he Grey Master is caught in the stream and is swept away, but ye Fisher Lad crosses it dry=shod.

):(

king, he sent six of his knights posting after the fisher-lad, for he thought that it was some great lord who had come into those parts.

By and by the lad came to a thicket, and there he jumped off of his horse and rapped upon the ground with his key.

"I wish to be as I was before," says he, and then he was the poor fisher-lad and nothing else. As for the golden clothes, the golden horse, the golden greyhound, and the golden hare, they went back to Nomansland whither they had come; and when the king's people came riding up there was nobody but a lad in rags and tatters whistling into a key.

They hunted up and they hunted down, but they could find neither sign nor trace of the golden rider and the golden horse. So after a while they had to ride back to the castle without them.

"You should have brought the lad who blew upon the key," said the princess.

The next day the lad rapped upon the ground with his key again.

"I should like to have," says he, "a golden coach drawn by six milk-white horses, with coachman and footman and out-riders dressed in clothes of gold and silver."

That was what he said; and there they were just as he wanted. Into the coach he got, and off he rode down by the king's castle.

Dear, dear, how the folks did stare, to be sure! This time the king sent twelve knights after the golden coach, for he thought it must be a king or a prince for certain who rode by in such style.

Pretty soon the lad came to a woods, and there he jumped out of the coach and rapped upon the ground with his key.

"I want to be just as I was before," says he; and, sure enough, he was.

Up clattered the twelve knights on their horses, and there sat the lad in rags and tatters whistling upon his key.

The twelve knights hunted high and hunted low, and not another soul could they find, and so they had to ride back to the castle again.

"See now," said the princess, "did I not say that you should have brought the lad who blew upon the key?"

The next day the lad went out and rapped upon the ground for the third time.

"I should like," said he, "to have a splendid castle all built of silver and gold, such as nobody ever saw before."

That was what he said, and before the words had left his tongue just such a great castle grew up out of nothing like a soap-bubble.

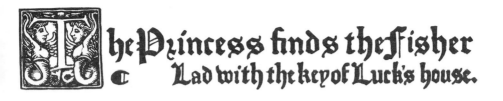

The Princess finds the Fisher Lad with the key of Luck's house.

The king chanced to look out of the window just then, and there was the great splendid gold-and-silver castle. He took off his spectacles and rubbed them and rubbed them, but there was the castle just the same as ever.

He bade them saddle the horses, and he and the princess, and all of the court besides, rode away to find out who it was that had built such a fine castle all in one night.

But the lad saw them coming, and rapped upon the ground with his key. "I should like," said he, "for things to be just as they were before;" and puff! away went the castle like the light of a candle when one blows it out.

Up came the king and the princess and all the court, and not a speck of the grand castle could they find, but only a lad in rags and tatters who sat upon a great round stone and whistled upon a key.

But the princess was a lass who could see through a millstone with a hole in it. So soon as she set eyes upon him she knew the whole business from beginning to end. Up she marched to him, before them all, and took him by the hand. "Now I will marry you," said she, "for I see that you have brought the key of wish-house with you;" and there she was as wise as ever. For there be many kings and princes in the world, but I have never yet heard of any one except the fisher-lad who had the key of wish-house. Have you?

Nine O'clock.

The *School-bell* rings;
The *Children* all
Must answer to
The *Master's* call.

The *Master* has
A crooked *Nose*;
He whips the *Boys*,
And puffs, and blows;

He makes them stand
And walk by *Rule*,
And bow before
They leave the *School*.

K.P.

Cloudy and warm.

The White Bird.

IX.

NCE there was a king, who, as time went on, found himself waxing old in years and feeble in body, so he began to think of giving up the cares of government and of taking his ease for as much of life as was left him. But here was the trouble: there were three princes, and each one of them was just as clever as the other two, so that the old king could not tell which to choose as the right one to sit in his place. He thought and thought and thought, until at last he plucked an apple off of his thinking-tree, as folks say. All three of the princes should go out into the world, and whichever of them should fetch back an apple from the Tree of Happiness should rule over all of the kingdom. And I speak the truth when I say that the apple was cheap enough even at that price.

So off went the three to seek for what they wanted. They travelled along without let or stay until towards evening they came to a place where two houses stood, the one on the one side of the road and the other on the other.

One of them was as fine a house as a body ever saw. Every window was lit up by the warm fires and the bright lights within, and even out on the high-road one could hear the merry times the folks were having; laughing and singing and clinking their glasses together. As for the good things cooking in the kitchen, why it was enough to make one hungry just to smell the steam of them. Over the door was a sign, and on the sign was written,

" WHO ENTERS HERE SHALL HAVE WHAT
HE LIKES AND PAY NOTHING FOR IT."

The other house was a poor, mean, little, tumble-down hut, as silent as death, and with never a spark of light or fire shining at the windows. There was also a sign over the door, and on the sign was written,

" WHO ENTERS HERE SHALL HAVE WHAT HE
NEEDS AND PAY WHAT HE CAN."

" Yonder is the place for us," said the older brothers, and they pointed with their thumbs to the grand house, where there was good company with plenty to eat and drink and nothing to pay.

" Yes," says the youngest of the three, " that is all very well, but I would rather pay for what I need than get what I like for nothing."

Dear, dear, how the two did laugh at the one to be sure! but all the same, the one held to what he had said, and so at last the two flew into a huff. " Go your way," said they, " and we will go ours." And into the grand house they went. There they gave themselves up to ease and comfort, and it was a merry time they had of it, I can tell you.

But the youngest brother went over to the little dark house and knocked upon the door, and it was opened by a poor old man whose head and beard were as white as the snow, and whose clothes hung about him all in tags and tatters.

" Come in and welcome," said he, " for you are the first who has been here for twenty-seven ages;" and that is a long time, as anybody knows without the telling.

But in the little house there was no wood to make a fire, and there was no water to boil in the pot. So the prince took the axe and went out and chopped an armful of wood, and then he took the pot and filled it at the well.

Out in the stable stood a white cow with silver horns; but there was never a straw for it to lie upon, and never a bit of hay for it to eat. So the prince shook down a bed for it, and then he filled the rack with hay and left it munching away for dear life.

Out in the yard was a red cock and a white hen, but though they scratched and scratched it was never a grain that they found. So the prince threw them a handful of barley and left them pecking away at it, as though they had not seen the like for a week of Sundays.

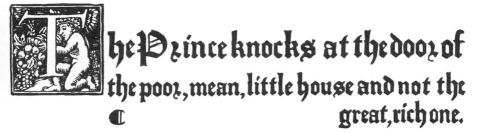

The Prince knocks at the door of
the poor, mean, little house and not the
great, rich one.

After he had done all these things, he and the old man sat down to supper together, and, if it was not of the finest, why the prince had a good
appetite, and one can have no better sauce to a crust than that.

The prince stayed all night, and the next morning he was for jogging on
his way. But before he went he offered the old man what money he had,
because anybody could read the sign over the door.

But the old man shook his head. "No, no," said he, "you have paid
your score. You have given what you can, and you shall have what you
need. Here is a little book, and in it you may read whatever you wish
to know. Go out into the stable and you will find a barley straw back of
the white cow's ear. Take that with you, for you will need it. Look in the
manger and you will find an egg that the white hen has laid; take it with
you also, for it is worth the having."

Then he said good-bye and shut the door, and that was the last the
prince saw of him.

The prince went to the stable, and there he found the barley straw and
the egg, just as the old man had said, and off he marched with them.

He went to the grand house over the way and called his brothers, but
they only came to the windows and laughed and jeered at him. "No, no,"
said they, "we are going no farther along the road, for we know very well
when the world is smooth with us. The Fruit of Happiness can bring us
nothing better than what we have at hand."

And so the young prince had to trudge away by himself. But what to
do with the straw and the egg he knew no more than my grandmother's
cat. So he opened his little book, and this was what it said between the
leaves:

"*Mount the straw and ride it whither it takes you.*"

"So," said the prince; "that would be a strange thing to do for sure and
certain. All the same, an easy task is worth the trying;" so he just flung
his leg over the straw and—whisk! pop!—there he was, astride of a great
splendid horse with smooth hair as yellow as gold.

That straw was a straw worth having!

And the best part of the matter was that the prince had no need to
draw the bridle-rein either to the right or to the left; for the yellow horse
took the bit in his teeth and away he pounded so that the ground smoked
under his hoofs, and the wind whistled back of the prince's ears. By and
by they came to a great sandy desert-place where not a twig or a leaf was
to be seen, but only white bones scattered here and there, for the prince was

he Prince finds ẏ three giants
sleeping under the tree of life & snozing
away like everything.

not the first by many who had tried to cross that desert to the Tree of Happiness.

But he had better luck than the others, for the yellow horse carried him along like the wind, and on and on until at last he came within sight of the Tree of Happiness. There sat three terrible giants, an old giant and his two sons, and alongside of each lay a great iron club with sharp spikes in the end of it. But all three sat with their eyes shut, sleeping away as though they would never awaken. And that was a good thing for the prince, for he had never seen such terrible, wicked-looking creatures as the old giant and his two sons. He leaped from off the back of the yellow horse, and there it was, nothing but a barley straw. He put it in his pocket and took out his Book of Knowledge and opened it. This was what it said:

"*Fear not the giants, for they will not awake; but touch neither the golden fruit nor the silver fruit, for they are not for you.*"

When the prince read what the Book of Knowledge said, he knew that it was so. Up he marched to the Tree of Happiness as bold as bold could be, and the giants snored away so that the leaves shook.

There hung three apples; the first was of gleaming gold, the second was of shining silver, and the third was just a poor, weazened, shrivelled thing, that looked as though there were not three drops of juice in it.

"Prut!" says the prince, "it can never be that I have travelled all this way for nothing in the world but a dead apple. After all, it must be the golden fruit that I am to take, in spite of what the Book of Knowledge said; for if happiness is to be found in anything, it is to be found in such as it."

So he reached up his hand and plucked the golden apple, and then—hi! what a hubbub, for the Tree of Happiness began to clamor and call as though every leaf on it had become a tongue to speak with.

"Help! help!" it cried. "Here is one coming to rob us of our golden fruit!"

Up jumped the three giants, and each one snatched up his iron club and came at the prince as though to put an end to him without any more talk over the business. But the prince begged and prayed and prayed and begged that they would spare his life.

"Listen," said the old giant; "if you will promise to bring us the Sword of Brightness that shines in the darkness and cuts whatsoever the edge is turned against, we will not only spare your life, but give you the Fruit of Happiness into the bargain." That was what the old giant said, and the others agreed to it; for if they could once lay hand upon such a sword as that they would be masters of all the world.

Well, the prince promised that he would get them the Sword of Brightness, for one will promise much before one will be knocked on the head with an iron club; and then the giant let him go, and glad enough he was to get away.

Off he went back of the hill. He drew out his barley straw and threw his leg over it, and there he sat astride of his yellow horse again.

"I should like," said he, "to be carried to where I can find the Sword of Brightness that shines in the darkness and cuts whatever its edge is turned against." That was all that he had to say, and away clattered the yellow horse over stock and stone so that the ground smoked beneath his hoofs. On they went and on they went for a great long while, until at last they came to a tall castle as black as your hat, and there was where the Sword of Brightness was to be found. In front of the castle gate lay two great fiery dragons, with smoke coming up out of their nostrils instead of the breath of life, and all over their bodies were brazen scales that shone like gold in the sunlight. But both dragons were sound asleep.

Inside of the court-yard were many and one fierce soldiers armed in shining armor and each with a battle-axe or a sword or an iron club lying beside him; but they too were as sound asleep as the dragon.

Down jumped the prince from the great yellow horse, and there was the barley straw again. He took out the Book of Knowledge from his pocket, and this was what it said:

"*Fear not the dragons nor the fierce soldiers, for they will not awaken; but take only the old leathern scabbard with the sword.*"

So up walked the prince as bold as brass, and the soldiers and the dragons said never a word, but just snored away so that the windows rattled. Into the castle he walked, and nobody said "No" to him. There sat an old man, as wicked as sin and as grey as the ashes in the hearth. He never moved a hair, only his little red eyes turned here and there, and were never still for a wink. A great keen sword lay on the table in front of him, and the light on the blade was like the bright flash of lightning. The prince took the sword up from the table, and the little old man looked at him, but said never a word, good or bad.

On the wall hung three scabbards; one was of gold studded all over with precious stones; another of silver that gleamed like the light of the moon in frosty weather; and the third was of nothing but old, shabby,

8

worm-eaten leather that looked as though they had just fetched it down from the dusty garret.

"It would be a pity," said the prince, "to put such a fine sword into such a poor scabbard. I'll not choose the gold because of what happened to me over at the Tree of Happiness yonder, but surely silver is none too good for the Sword of Brightness."

So he took down the silver scabbard and thrust the sword into it, and therewith dipped his spoon into the wrong pot again; for, no sooner had he sheathed the sword in the silver scabbard than the old gray man began to thump on the table in front of him and to bawl at the top of his voice, "Help! help! here is one come to steal our Sword of Brightness."

At this the soldiers outside woke up and began to clash and rattle with their battle-axes and swords and iron clubs, and the dragons began to roar and send up clouds of smoke like a chimney afire.

In ran the soldiers, and were for putting an end to the prince without another word being said, but he begged and prayed and prayed and begged that his life might be spared, just as he had done with the giants over yonder at the Tree of Happiness.

"Listen," says the old grey man at last; "if you will promise to bring me the White Bird from the black mountain, I will not only spare your life, but will give you the Sword of Brightness into the bargain."

Yes, the prince would get the White Bird if anybody in the world could get it. And thereupon they let him go, and glad enough he was to get away.

Back of the hedge he threw his leg over the barley straw.

"I would like," said he, "to be taken to where I can find the White Bird that lives on the black mountain;" and away thundered the yellow horse, like a storm in June.

If it was far that they travelled before, it was farther that they travelled this time. But at last they came to the black mountain, and the prince jumped off the nag and thrust the straw into his pocket.

There was not a blade of grass nor a bit of green to be seen on the hill, but only a great lot of round, black stones scattered from top to bottom. That was all that was left of the lads who had come that way before to find the White Bird.

On the top of the mountain sat an old witch with golden hair, and in her hand was the White Bird. The prince opened his Book of Knowledge, and there he read that if one would gain the White Bird one would have

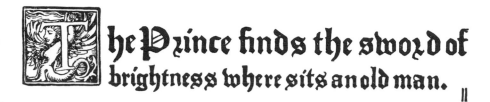

The Prince finds the sword of brightness where sits an old man.

II

to catch the witch by her golden hair, for then she would be compelled
to grant whatever was asked of her; only he would have to be very
careful in his doings, for if the witch caught sight of him upon the black
hill she would change him into a stone just as she had all the rest who
had come that way.

But how was he to climb the hill without the witch seeing him? That
was what the prince would like to know. So he turned over another leaf
of the Book of Knowledge, and there it was all in plain black and white.
This was what it said:

"*Crack the egg of the white hen and put on the cap.*"

The prince cracked the egg, and, sure enough, inside of it was a little
cap of feathers. He put on the feather cap and—whisk!—as quick as a
wink he was changed into a titmouse, which is the least of all the birds
in that land.

He spread his wings and flew and flew and flew, until he was close
behind the witch where she sat on the black mountain. He took off his
cap and there he was in his own shape again. He caught the old witch
by her golden hair and held her fast. And you should have heard how
she screamed and scolded, and you should have seen how she twisted and
turned!

But the prince just held fast, and she could make nothing of it for all
her trying.

"And what do you want, that you come here to torment me?" said she
at last.

"I want the White Bird," said the prince; "and I will be satisfied with
nothing else." It was all to no purpose that the old witch stormed and
scolded, for what he had said he had said, and he would be satisfied with
nothing else. So at last, willy-nilly, she had to give him what he asked
for.

The prince took it in his hands, and it was a white bird no longer, but
the prettiest lass that ever a body's eyes looked upon, with cheeks as red
as roses and a skin as white as snow.

But still the prince held tight to the old witch's hair, and now what else
was it he was wanting.

Why, before he would let her go, she must change all the round stones
back again into the lads of flesh and blood they had been before.

So the old witch had to do that also, and there stood so many good
stout lads in the place of the hard, round stones.

But still the prince held fast to her golden hair. And what else was it he was wanting?

Why, this! The old witch must promise to do no harm to him or to anybody else who should come that way. The old witch had to promise. And then he let go of her hair, and you can guess what a rage she was in.

But the prince cared nothing for that, for he had found what he came for.

He took the barley straw out of his pocket and threw his leg over it. Then he took the princess up behind him on the great yellow horse, and away he clattered, leaving the witch scolding behind him.

After a while he came to the black castle; there he took out his Book of Knowledge, for now that he had the White Bird he could not bear to think of giving her up; and this was what the book said:

"*Take the White Bird to the old grey man and he will give you the Sword of Brightness, turn the edge against him and against the fierce soldiers and against the two dragons, and then ride away with your White Bird.*"

So up he rode to the black castle, and the fiery dragons let him pass when they saw that the White Bird rode behind him. The old grey man gave the lad the Sword of Brightness quickly enough, for the White Bird was worth that and a great deal more, I can tell you.

As soon as the prince had hold of the Sword of Brightness, he turned the keen edge of the blade against the wicked old man and the soldiers and the dragons; off flew their heads, and there they lay as dead as red herrings in a box.

Then he thrust the Sword of Brightness into the leathern scabbard, for he had learned a grain or two of wisdom by this time, and away he rode with the White Bird sitting behind him.

On they rode and on they rode until they came to the desert place and the Tree of Happiness. And then the prince took out his Book of Wisdom and turned over the leaves, for he was of no mind to give up the Sword of Brightness if he could help doing so.

"*Turn the edge of the blade against the three giants.*"

Thus said the book, and the lad did so, and there they lay all three of them as dead as stocks.

I know that this is true which I tell, because since then there have been no cruel giants to keep a body from getting a taste of the Fruit of Happiness now and then, if a body chooses to travel that far to find it. But that is neither here nor there, and what I have to tell is this:

The young prince rode away towards home with the White Bird sitting behind him, the Sword of Brightness hanging by his side, and the Fruit of Happiness in his pocket.

By and by he came to the place where the two houses stood, the one on the one side of the road, and the one on the other, and there he took out his Book of Knowledge to have a peep at it, and this was what it said :

"*Buy no black sheep.*"

"Prut !" says the prince, "what should I want with black sheep I should like to know ?"

By and by he met a great crowd, and in the midst of all the rest were his two brothers with their hands tied behind them with stout ropes.

And what were they going to do with the two ?   That was what the prince would like to know.

"Why," said those who held them, "they have spent all their money at the great house over yonder, and have run up a score for good things besides, and now they are packing off to prison because they cannot pay what they owe."

"Come, come," says the prince, "let them go and I will pay their reckoning ;" and so he did, and that was what the Book of Wisdom meant by buying black sheep.

After that they all stepped away homeward, right foot foremost ; for since the young prince had brought the Fruit of Happiness along with him, there was no need of the other brothers going to look for it.

By and by they felt weary and sat down by the roadside to rest, and as they sat there the youngest prince fell asleep.   While he slept the elder brothers stole away the Sword of Brightness and the Fruit of Happiness. Then they wakened him and made him strip off his fine clothes, and gave him a parcel of rags and tatters fit for no one but a beggar, and he had to put them on or go without.

As for the White Bird, they made her vow and swear that she would say nothing of all this.   Then off they marched with her and with the Sword of Brightness, and left the prince with never a stitch or a thread that was worth the having.

"See," said they, as soon as they came home, "not only have we brought the Fruit of Happiness, but the Sword of Brightness and the White Bird into the bargain."

As for the youngest brother, they told the king that he had stopped over at the tavern yonder, and had spent all his money in eating and drinking, just as they themselves had really done.

The Prince sits down beside y͏ garden gate and only one knoweth him.

But the White Bird did nothing but weep and weep, and neither this brother nor that could draw the Sword of Brightness from its leathern scabbard. And when the king came to taste the Fruit of Happiness, it was as bitter as gall. So, after all, the two gained nothing by what they had done.

But the young prince was not for giving up all that he had lost, without trying to get what he could back again. Off he marched in his rags and tatters until he came to the castle where the king, his father, lived. Up he stepped to the door and knocked, but nobody would let him in because he looked like nothing but a beggar. So down he sat beside the gate of the castle garden, since he could not come into the house.

After a while the folks came out, one by one and two by two, to walk in the garden and take the air, and all the time the prince sat there and nobody knew him.

Last of all came the old king, and with him walked the White Bird. The king was for passing the lad by as all the rest had done. But as soon as the White Bird saw him, she knew who he was and ran to him and threw her arms around his neck and kissed him.

"Here is my own sweetheart," said she, "and he has come back to me again."

The prince told the king all that had happened from beginning to end, and how it really was he who had found the White Bird, the Sword of Brightness, and the Fruit of Happiness.

"Yes, yes," says the king, "that is all very well, but it is just the tale that your brothers tell; now can you draw the Sword of Brightness from the leathern scabbard?"

"Oh, yes," said the prince, "I can do that easily enough." So the sword was brought and—whisk!—he whipped the blade out of the scabbard so that the light of it dazzled the eyes of everybody that looked upon it.

Then the king saw what had happened as plain as the nose on his face, and was for punishing the elder brothers as they deserved, but nobody could find them, for as soon as they heard that the youngest prince had come home again they packed off without waiting to learn more news.

And why do I call this the story of the White Bird? Listen: any Tom or Jake or Harry might have found the Sword of Brightness or the Fruit of Happiness; but you may depend upon it that nobody but a real prince could ever have found the White Bird.

Ten O'clock.

The *Children* drone
In sing-song tone,
The *Master's* shoes creak on the *Floor*.
They're baking *Pies*
At *Home*, and *Flies*
Buzz in and out the open *Door*.

The *Beds* are made;
The *Pans* are laid
Out in the pleasant *Sun* to dry.
Good *Gretchen* takes
Some *Dough*, and makes,
For litte *John*, a *Saucer Pie*.

Good weather for farming.

KP

How the Good Gifts were used by Two.

X.

HIS is the way that this story begins:

Once upon a time there was a rich brother and a poor brother, and the one lived across the street from the other.

The rich brother had all of the world's gear that was good for him and more besides; as for the poor brother, why, he had hardly enough to keep soul and body together, yet he was contented with his lot, and contentment did not sit back of the stove in the rich brother's house; wherefore in this the rich brother had less than the poor brother.

Now these things happened in the good old times when the saints used to be going hither and thither in the world upon this business and upon that. So one day, who should come travelling to the town where the rich brother and the poor brother lived, but Saint Nicholas himself.

Just beside the town gate stood the great house of the rich brother; thither went the saint and knocked at the door, and it was the rich brother himself who came and opened it to him.

Now, Saint Nicholas had had a long walk of it that day, so that he was quite covered with dust, and looked no better than he should.   Therefore he seemed to be only a common beggar; and when the rich brother heard him ask for a night's lodging at his fine, great house, he gaped like a toad in a rain-storm.   What!   Did the traveller think that he kept a free lodging-house for beggars?   If he did he was bringing his grist to the wrong mill; there was no place for the likes of him in the house, and that was the truth. But yonder was a poor man's house across the street, if he went over there perhaps he could get a night's lodging and a crust of bread.   That was what the rich brother said, and after he had said it he banged to the door, and left Saint Nicholas standing on the outside under the blessed sky.

So now there was nothing for good Saint Nicholas to do but to go across the street to the poor brother's house, as the other had told him to do.   Rap! tap! tap! he knocked at the door, and it was the poor brother who came and opened it for him.

"Come in, come in!" says he, "come in and welcome!"

So in came Saint Nicholas, and sat himself down behind the stove where it was good and warm, while the poor man's wife spread before him all that they had in the house—a loaf of brown bread and a crock of cold water from the town fountain.

"And is that all that you have to eat?" said Saint Nicholas.

Yes; that was all that they had.

"Then, maybe, I can help you to better," said Saint Nicholas.   "So bring me hither a bowl and a crock."

You may guess that the poor man's wife was not long in fetching what he wanted.   When they were brought the saint blessed the one and passed his hand over the other.

Then he said, "Bowl be filled!" and straightway the bowl began to boil up with a good rich meat pottage until it was full to the brim.   Then the saint said, "Bowl be stilled!" and it stopped making the broth, and there stood as good a feast as man could wish for.

Then Saint Nicholas said, "Crock be filled!" and the crock began to bubble up with the best of beer.   Then he said, "Crock be stilled!" and there stood as good drink as man ever poured down his throat.

Down they all sat, the saint and the poor man and the poor man's wife, and ate and drank till they could eat and drink no more, and whenever the bowl and the crock grew empty, the one and the other became filled at the bidding.

The next morning the saint trudged off the way he was going, but he

aint Nicholas knocks at the
rich man's door but finds only a chill
welcome & cold faring.

left behind him the bowl and the crock, so that there was no danger of hunger and thirst coming to that house.

Well, the world jogged along for a while, maybe a month or two, and life was as easy for the poor man and his wife as an old shoe. One day the rich brother said to *his* wife. "See now, Luck seems to be stroking our brother over yonder the right way; I'll just go and see what it all means."

So over the street he went, and found the poor man at home. Down he sat back of the stove and began to chatter and talk and talk and chatter, and the upshot of the matter was that, bit by bit, he dragged out the whole story from the poor man. Then nothing would do but he must see the bowl and the crock at work. So the bowl and the crock were brought and set to work and—Hui!—how the rich brother opened his eyes when he saw them making good broth and beer of themselves.

And now he must and would have that bowl and crock. At first the poor brother said "No," but the other bargained and bargained until, at last, the poor man consented to let him have the two for a hundred dollars. So the rich brother paid down his hundred dollars, and off he marched with what he wanted.

When the next day had come, the rich brother said to his wife, "Never you mind about the dinner to-day. Go you into the harvest-field, and I will see to the dinner." So off went the wife with the harvesters, and the husband stayed at home and smoked his pipe all the morning, for he knew that dinner would be ready at the bidding. So when noontide had come he took out the bowl and the crock, and, placing them on the table, said, "Bowl be filled! crock be filled!" and straightway they began making broth and beer as fast as they could.

In a little while the bowl and the crock were filled, and then they could hold no more, so that the broth and beer ran down all over the table and the floor. Then the rich brother was in a pretty pickle, for he did not know how to bid the bowl and the crock to stop from making what they were making. Out he ran and across the street to the poor man's house, and meanwhile the broth and beer filled the whole room until it could hold no more, and then ran out into the gutters so that all the pigs and dogs in the town had a feast that day.

"Oh, dear brother!" cried the rich man to the poor man, "do tell me what to do or the whole town will soon be smothered in broth and beer."

But, no; the poor brother was not to be stirred in such haste; they would have to strike a bit of a bargain first. So the upshot of the matter

Saint Nicholas blesses the poor man's crock and bowl with food and drink.

was that the rich brother had to pay the poor brother another hundred dollars to take the crock and the bowl back again.

See, now, what comes of being covetous!

As for the poor man, he was well off in the world, for he had all that he could eat and drink, and a stockingful of money back of the stove besides.

Well, time went along as time does, and now it was Saint Christopher who was thinking about taking a little journey below. "See, brother," says Saint Nicholas to him, "if you chance to be jogging by yonder town, stop at the poor man's house, for there you will have a warm welcome and plenty to eat."

But when Saint Christopher came to the town, the rich man's house seemed so much larger and finer than the poor man's house, that he thought that he would ask for lodging there.

But it fared the same with him that it had with Saint Nicholas. Prut! Did he think that the rich man kept free lodgings for beggars? And— bang!—the door was slammed in his face, and off packed the saint with a flea in his ear.

Over he went to the poor man's house, and there was a warm welcome for him, and good broth and beer from the bowl and the crock that Saint Nicholas had blessed. After he had supped he went to bed, where he slept as snug and warm as a mouse in the nest.

Then the good wife said to the husband, "See, now, the poor fellow's shirt is none too good for him to be wearing. I'll just make him another while he is sleeping, so that he'll have a decent bit of linen to wear in the morning."

So she brought her best roll of linen out of the closet, and set to work stitching and sewing, and never stopped till she had made the new shirt to the last button. The next morning, when the saint awoke, there lay the nice, new, clean shirt, and he put it on and gave thanks for it.

Before he left the house the poor man took him aside, and emptied the stockingful of silver money on the table, and bade the saint take what he wanted, "for," says he, "a penny or two is never amiss in the great world."

After that it was time for the traveller to be jogging; but before he went he said, "See, now, because you have been so kind and so good to a poor wayfarer, I will give you a blessing; whatever you begin doing this morning, you shall continue doing till sunset." So saying, he took up his staff and went his way.

The Poor man welcomes Saint Christopher to his house.

After Saint Christopher had gone the poor man and his wife began talking together as to what would be best for them to be doing all of the day, and one said one thing and the other said the other, but every plug was too small for the hole, as we say in our town, for nothing seemed to fit the case.

"Come, come," said the good woman, "here we are losing time that can never be handled again. While we are talking the matter over I will be folding the linen that is left from making the shirt."

"And I," said the good man, "will be putting the money away that the holy man left behind him."

So the wife began folding the linen into a bundle again, and the man began putting away the money that he had offered in charity. Thus they began doing, and thus they kept on doing; so that by the time that the evening had come the whole house was full of fine linen, and every tub and bucket and mug and jug about the place was brimming with silver money. As for the good couple, their fortune was made, and that is the heart of the whole matter in four words.

That night who should come over from across the street but the rich brother, with his pipe in his mouth and his hands in his pockets. But when he saw how very rich the poor man had become all of a sudden, and what a store of fine linen and silver money he had, he was so wonder-struck that he did not know whither to look and what to think.

Dear heart's sake alive! Where did all these fine things come from? That was what he should like to know.

Oh! there was nothing to hide in the matter, and the poor man told all about what had happened.

As for the rich brother, when he found how he had shut his door in the face of good-fortune, he rapped his head with his knuckles because he was so angry at his own foolishness. However, crying never mended a torn jacket, so he made the poor brother promise that if either of the saints came that way again, they should be sent over to his house for a night's lodging, for it was only fair and just that he should have a share of the same cake his brother had eaten.

So the poor brother promised to do what the other wanted, and after that the rich brother went back home again.

Well, a year and a day passed, and then, sure enough, who should come along that way but both the saints together, arm in arm. Rap! tap! tap! they knocked at the poor man's door, for they thought that where they had

had good lodging before they could get it again. And so they could and welcome, only the poor brother told them that his rich brother across the street had asked that they should come and lodge at the fine house when they came that way again.

The saints were willing enough to go to the rich brother's house, though they would rather have stayed with the other. So over they went, and when the rich brother saw them coming he ran out to meet them, and shook each of them by the hand, and bade them to come in and sit down back of the stove where it was warm.

But you should have seen the feast that was set for the two saints at the rich brother's house! I can only say that I never saw the like, and I only wish that I had been there with my legs under the table. After supper they were shown to a grand room, where each saint had a bed all to his very own self, and before they were fairly asleep the rich man's wife came and took away their old shirts, and laid a shirt of fine cambric linen in the place of each. When the next morning came and the saints were about to take their leave, the rich brother brought out a great bag of golden money, and bade them to stuff what they would of it into their pockets.

Well, all this was as it should be, and before the two went on their way they said that they would give the same blessing to him and his wife that they had given to the other couple — that whatsoever they should begin doing that morning, that they should continue doing until sunset.

After that they put on their hats and took up their staffs, and off they plodded.

Now the rich brother was a very envious man, and was not contented to do only as well as his brother had done, no indeed! He would do something that would make him even richer than counting out money for himself all day. So down he sat back of the stove and began turning the matter over in his mind, and rubbing up his wits to make them the brighter.

In the meantime the wife said to herself, " See, now, I shall be folding fine cambric linen all day, and the pigs will have to go with nothing to eat. I have no time to waste in feeding them, but I'll just run out and fill their troughs with water at any rate."

So out she went with a bucketful of water which she began pouring into the troughs for the pigs. That was the first thing she did, and after that there was no leaving off, but pour water she must until sunset.

All this while the man sat back of the stove, warming his wits and saying to himself, " Shall I do this? shall I do that?" and answering " No " to himself every time. At last he began wondering what his wife was doing, so out he went to find her. Find her he did, for there she was pouring out water to the pigs. Then if anybody was angry it was the rich man. " What!" cried he, " and is this the way that you waste the gifts of the blessed saints?"

So saying, he looked around, and there lay a bit of a switch on the ground near by. He picked up the bit of a switch and struck the woman across the shoulders with it, and that was the first thing that he began doing. After that he had to keep on doing the same.

So the woman poured water and poured water, and the man stood by and beat her with the little switch until there was nothing left of it, and that was what they did all day.

And what is more, they made such a hubbub that the neighbors came to see what was going forward.   They looked and laughed and went away again, and others came, and there stood the two—the woman pouring water and the man beating her with the bit of a switch.

When the evening came, and they left off their work, they were so weary that they could hardly stand; and nothing was to show for it but a broken switch and a wet sty, for even the blessed saints cannot give wisdom to those who will have none of it, and that is the truth.

And such is the end of this story, with only this to tell: Tommy Pfouce tells me that there are folks, even in these wise times, who, if they did all day what they began in the morning, would find themselves at sunset doing no better work than pouring pure water to pigs.

That is the small kernel to this great nut.

Eleven O'clock.

The *Cook* undoes the *Oven Door*;
   The *Kobold* smells the baking *Pies*;
   Licking his *Lips*, with glistening *Eyes*,
He hops across the *Floor*.

Our fat, old *Betty* sweats and blows;
   She does not see how near he stands,
   And when she bangs the *Door, Good* *
It 'most cuts off his *Nose.*   *Lands!*

How Boots befool-
ed the King.

XI.

NCE upon a time there was a king who was the wisest in all of the world. So wise was he that no one had ever befooled him, which is a rare thing, I can tell you. Now, this king had a daughter who was as pretty as a ripe apple, so that there was no end to the number of the lads who came asking to marry her. Every day there were two or three of them dawdling around the house, so that at last the old king grew tired of having them always about.

So he sent word far and near that whoever should befool him might have the princess and half of the kingdom to boot, for he thought that it would be a wise man indeed who could trick him. But the king also said, that whoever should try to befool him and should fail, should have a good whipping. This was to keep all foolish fellows away.

The princess was so pretty that there was no lack of lads who came to have a try for her and half of the kingdom, but every one of these went away with a sore back and no luck.

Now, there was a man who was well off in the world, and who had three sons; the first was named Peter, and the second was named Paul. Peter and Paul thought themselves as wise as anybody in all of the world, and their father thought as they did.

As for the youngest son, he was named Boots. Nobody thought anything of him except that he was silly, for he did nothing but sit poking in
the warm ashes all of the day.

One morning Peter spoke up and said that he was going to the town
to have a try at befooling the king, for it would be a fine thing to have
a princess in the family. His father did not say no, for if anybody was
wise enough to befool the king, Peter was the lad.

So, after Peter had eaten a good breakfast, off he set for the town, right
foot foremost. After a while he came to the king's house and—rap! tap!
tap!—he knocked at the door.

Well; what did he want?

Oh! he would only like to have a try at befooling the king.

Very good; he should have his try. He was not the first one who had
been there that morning, early as it was.

So Peter was shown in to the king.

"Oh, look!" said he, "yonder are three black geese out in the court-
yard!"

But no, the king was not to be fooled so easily as all that. "One goose
is enough to look at at a time," said he; "take him away and give him a
whipping!"

And so they did, and Peter went home bleating like a sheep.

One day Paul spoke up. "I should like to go and have a try for the
princess, too," said he.

Well, his father did not say no, for, after all, Paul was the more clever
of the two.

So off Paul went as merrily as a duck in the rain. By and by he came
to the castle, and then he too was brought before the king just as Peter
had been.

"Oh, look!" said he, "yonder is a crow sitting in the tree with three
white stripes on his back!"

But the king was not so silly as to be fooled in that way. "Here is
a Jack," said he, "who will soon have more stripes on his back than he
will like. Take him away and give him his whipping!"

Then it was done as the king had said, and Paul went away home
bawling like a calf.

One day up spoke Boots. "I should like to go and have a try for the
pretty princess, too," said he.

At this they all stared and sniggered. What! he go where his clever

**P**eter goes to the castle to befool the King, dressed in his finest clothes.

brothers had failed, and had nothing to show for the trying but a good beating? What had come over the lout! Here was a pretty business, to be sure! That was what they all said.

But all of this rolled away from Boots like water from a duck's back. No matter, he would like to go and have a try like the others. So he begged and begged until his father was glad to let him go to be rid of his teasing, if nothing else.

Then Boots asked if he might have the old tattered hat that hung back of the chimney.

Oh, yes, he might have that if he wanted it, for nobody with good wits was likely to wear such a thing.

So Boots took the hat, and after he had brushed the ashes from his shoes set off for the town, whistling as he went.

The first body whom he met was an old woman with a great load of earthenware pots and crocks on her shoulders.

"Good-day, mother," said Boots.

"Good-day, son," said she.

"What will you take for all of your pots and crocks?" said Boots.

"Three shillings," said she.

"I will give you five shillings if you will come and stand in front of the king's house, and do thus and so when I say this and that," said Boots.

Oh, yes! she would do that willingly enough.

So Boots and the old woman went on together, and presently came to the king's house. When they had come there, Boots sat down in front of the door and began bawling as loud as he could—"No, I will not! I will not do it, I say! No, I will not do it!"

So he kept on, bawling louder and louder until he made such a noise that, at last, the king himself came out to see what all of the hubbub was about. But when Boots saw him he only bawled out louder than ever. "No, I will not! I will not do it, I say!"

"Stop! stop!" cried the king, "what is all this about?"

"Why," said Boots, "everybody wants to buy my cap, but I will not sell it! I will not do it, I say!"

"But, why should anybody want to buy such a cap as that?" said the king.

"Because," said Boots, "it is a fooling cap and the only one in all of the world."

"A fooling cap!" said the king. For he did not like to hear of such

aul comes home again from the king's castle with no luck. C

a cap as that coming into the town. "Hum-m-m-m! I should like to see you fool somebody with it. Could you fool that old body yonder with the pots and the crocks?"

"Oh, yes! that is easily enough done," said Boots, and without more ado he took off his tattered cap and blew into it. Then he put it on his head again and bawled out, "Break pots! break pots!"

No sooner had he spoken these words than the old woman jumped up and began breaking and smashing her pots and crocks as though she had gone crazy. That was what Boots had paid her five shillings for doing, but of it the king knew nothing. "Hui!" said he to himself, "I must buy that hat from the fellow or he will fool the princess away from me for sure and certain." Then he began talking to Boots as sweetly as though he had honey in his mouth. Perhaps Boots would sell the hat to him?

Oh, no! Boots could not think of such a thing as selling his fooling cap.

Come, come; the king wanted that hat, and sooner than miss buying it he would give a whole bag of gold money for it.

At this Boots looked up and looked down, scratching his head. Well, he supposed he would have to sell the hat some time, and the king might as well have it as anybody else. But for all that he did not like parting with it.

So the king gave Boots the bag of gold, and Boots gave the king the old tattered hat, and then he went his way.

After Boots had gone the king blew into the hat and blew into the hat, but though he blew enough breath into it to sail a big ship, he did not befool so much as a single titmouse. Then, at last, he began to see that the fooling cap was good on nobody else's head but Boots's; and he was none too pleased at that, you may be sure.

As for Boots, with his bag of gold he bought the finest clothes that were to be had in the town, and when the next morning had come he started away bright and early for the king's house. "I have come," said he, "to marry the princess, if you please."

At this the king hemmed and hawed and scratched his head. Yes; Boots had befooled him sure enough, but, after all, he could not give up the princess for such a thing as that. Still, he would give Boots another chance. Now, there was the high-councillor, who was the wisest man in all of the world. Did Boots think that he could fool him also?

Oh, yes! Boots thought that it might be done.

he old woman smashes pots and things at Boots' bidding.)(

Very well; if he could befool the high-councillor so as to bring him to the castle the next morning against his will, Boots should have the princess and the half of the kingdom; if he did not do so he should have his beating.

Then Boots went away, and the king thought that he was rid of him now for good and all.

As for the high-councillor, he was not pleased with the matter at all, for he did not like the thought of being fooled by a clever rogue, and taken here and there against his will. So when he had come home, he armed all of his servants with blunderbusses, and then waited to give Boots a welcome when he should come.

But Boots was not going to fall into any such trap as that! No indeed! not he! The next morning he went quietly and bought a fine large meal-sack. Then he put a black wig over his beautiful red hair, so that no one might know him. After that he went to the place where the high-councillor lived, and when he had come there he crawled inside of the sack, and lay just beside the door of the house.

By and by came one of the maid servants to the door, and there lay the great meal-sack with somebody in it.

"Ach!" cried she, "who is there?"

But Boots only said, "Sh-h-h-h-h!"

Then the serving maid went back into the house, and told the high-councillor that one lay outside in a great meal-sack, and that all that he said was, "Sh-h-h-h-h!"

So the councillor went himself to see what it was all about. "What do you want here?" said he.

"Sh-h-h-h-h!" said Boots, "I am not to be talked to now. This is a wisdom-sack, and I am learning wisdom as fast as a drake can eat peas."

"And what wisdom have you learned?" said the councillor.

Oh! Boots had learned wisdom about everything in the world. He had learned that the clever scamp who had fooled the king yesterday was coming with seventeen tall men to take the high-councillor, willy-nilly, to the castle that morning.

When the high-councillor heard this he fell to trembling till his teeth rattled in his head. "And have you learned how I can get the better of this clever scamp?" said he.

Oh, yes! Boots had learned that easily enough.

The Councilor finds one in the Sack who teaches him wisdom.

So, good! then if the wise man in the sack would tell the high-councillor how to escape the clever rogue, the high-councillor would give the wise man twenty dollars.

But no, that was not to be done; wisdom was not bought so cheaply as the high-councillor seemed to think.

Well, the councillor would give him a hundred dollars then.

That was good! A hundred dollars were a hundred dollars. If the councillor would give him that much he might get into the sack himself, and then he could learn all the wisdom that he wanted, and more besides.

So Boots crawled out of the sack, and the councillor paid his hundred dollars and crawled in.

As soon as he was in all snug and safe, Boots drew the mouth of the sack together and tied it tightly. Then he flung sack, councillor, and all over his shoulder, and started away to the king's house, and anybody who met them could see with half an eye that the councillor was going against his will.

When Boots came to the king's castle he laid the councillor down in the goose-house, and then he went to the king.

When the king saw Boots again, he bit his lips with vexation. "Well," said he, "have you fooled the councillor?"

"Oh, yes!" says Boots, "I have done that."

And where was the councillor now?

Oh, Boots had just left him down in the goose-house. He was tied up safe and sound in a sack, waiting till the king should send for him.

So the councillor was sent for, and when he came the king saw at once that he had been brought against his will.

"And now may I marry the princess?" said Boots.

But the king was not willing for him to marry the princess yet; no! no! Boots must not go so fast. There was more to be done yet. If he would come to-morrow morning he might have the princess and welcome, but he would have to pick her out from among fourscore other maids just like her; did he think that he could do that?

Oh, yes! Boots thought that that might be easy enough to do.

So, good! then come to-morrow; but he must understand that if he failed he should have a good whipping, and be sent packing from the town.

So off went Boots, and the king thought that he was rid of him now, for he had never seen the princess, and how could he pick her out from among eighty others?

But Boots was not going to give up so easily as all that! No, not he! He made a little box, and then he hunted up and down until he had caught a live mouse to put into it.

When the next morning came he started away to the king's house, taking his mouse along with him in the box.

There was the king, standing in the doorway, looking out into the street. When he saw Boots coming towards him he made a wry face. "What!" said he, "are you back again?"

Oh, yes! Boots was back again. And now if the princess was ready he would like to go and find her, for lost time was not to be gathered again like fallen apples.

So off they marched to a great room, and there stood eighty-and-one maidens, all as much alike as peas in the same dish.

Boots looked here and there, but, even if he had known the princess, he could not have told her from the others. But he was ready for all that. Before any one knew what he was about, he opened the box, and out ran the little mouse among them all. Then what a screaming and a hubbub there was! Many looked as though they would have liked to swoon, but only one of them did so. As soon as the others saw what had happened, they forgot all about the mouse, and ran to her and fell to fanning her and slapping her hands and chafing her temples.

"This is the princess," said Boots.

And so it was.

After that the king could think of nothing more to set Boots to do, so he let him marry the princess as he had promised, and have half of the kingdom to boot.

That is all of this story.

Only this: It is not always the silliest one that sits kicking his feet in the ashes at home.

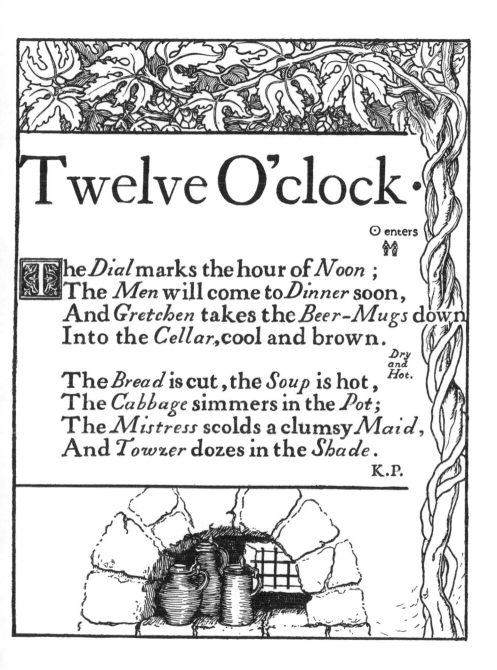

Twelve O'clock·

⊙ enters
♊

The *Dial* marks the hour of *Noon*;
The *Men* will come to *Dinner* soon,
And *Gretchen* takes the *Beer-Mugs* down
Into the *Cellar*, cool and brown.

*Dry
and
Hot.*

The *Bread* is cut, the *Soup* is hot,
The *Cabbage* simmers in the *Pot*;
The *Mistress* scolds a clumsy *Maid*,
And *Towzer* dozes in the *Shade*.

K.P.

The Step-mother.

XII.

NCE upon a time there was a man who was well off in the world so far as good things were concerned; but all the flesh and blood that belonged to him was a daughter, for his wife was dead, and he lived alone.

One day he went away from home and was gone for a long, long time, and when he came back again he brought a new wife with him, for that was the business that he had been about. As for the woman, she was as wicked as she was handsome, and as handsome as she was wicked, and whichever of the two one said of her one spoke the truth; for, though she was the most beautiful woman in all of the land, she was as great a witch as ever turned over the leaves of the black book with the red letters in it.

At first things went as smoothly in the rich man's house as butter and eggs, for the Step-mother was forever petting and caressing the man's daughter, and could not make enough of her. But that was only for a while, for as the maid grew in years she grew prettier and prettier, until there was none like her in all of that land.

One day the Step-mother and the step-daughter walked together in the fields, for it was in the spring-time, the weather was pleasant, and the grass was fresh and green. Two crows sat on a flowering thorn.

"Look," says one crow, "yonder go two beauties."

"Yes," says the other, "but when you talk of good looks, the old one is to the young one as a cabbage is to a rose."

Then, "Caw! caw!" they both cried, and flapped their wings and flew away.

That was what the two crows said; and though the maiden knew nothing, the Step-mother could tell what passed between them as well as could be, for she had eaten a bite of the white snake, and knew all that the birds and the beasts said to one another. So her heart grew bitter with hatred and envy, and she began to cudgel her brains for some means to put the girl out of the way. That night she made a ball of hollow gold and wrote this and that upon it, which nobody but herself could read. The next day she and the girl walked in the fields again, and when nobody was near the wicked Step-mother took the golden ball out of her pocket.

"See," said she, "here is a new plaything for you." She threw it upon the ground, and it rolled and rolled and rolled, and, whether she liked it or not, the maiden had to follow wherever it went. On and on rolled the ball, for no matter how fast the girl ran she could not catch it. By and by she came to a dark, lonesome place, where was a great, deep pit. Into the pit rolled the golden ball, and the poor girl had to follow. So into the pit she fell, and there she lay, for the sides were as smooth as glass, and one would have to have feet like a fly to climb from the bottom to the top.

As for the witch Step-mother, she was well content with what she had done, for the two crows sat on the thorn-tree. And—

"Look," said the first, "yonder goes the beauty."

"It is the truth that you speak," said the second. "For the other followed the golden ball and fell into the deep pit!" And then they clapped their wings and away they flew.

But the poor girl lay in the deep pit all alone, and cried and cried.

Suddenly a little door opened—click! clack!—and there was a little grey man no higher than a body's knee, but with a long white beard that touched the ground.

"Hi!" says he to the step-daughter, "and how came you here in the pit?"

The girl told him all from beginning to end, and the little man listened to every word.

"See, now," said he, when she had ended her story. "Since you are here in the deep pit and cannot get out, you shall be the queen of all the

The Step=daughter follows ye golden ball in spite of herself.   )(

little men like myself, and we shall serve you, for you are the most beautiful maiden that ever my eyes looked upon."

So there the maiden lived for many a long day, and the little man and others like him brought her rich food and wine, and covered all the inside of the pit with jewels and with gold, so that it was most splendid to see. And every day the maiden grew more and more beautiful.

One day the young king of that country went a-hunting, and all of his court with him, and four-and-twenty hounds besides. They came riding by the pit where the maiden sat, and there the hounds stopped and began to whimper and to howl, for they knew very well that human flesh and blood was down below.

"Listen to the hounds," says the king; "there is somebody fallen into the pit; now who will go down and bring the unfortunate up again?"

At this everybody looked at his neighbor, but nobody said, "I will go."

"Very well," said the king, "then I myself will go down into the pit, if no one else dares to venture."

So the others lowered the king into the pit, and when he reached the bottom you can guess how he stared and how he wondered; but he had no eyes for the jewels and gold that covered the walls; he had often seen the like of them, but never in all of his days had he beheld such a beauty as the maiden he found there.

Then the people above hauled them up together, and the king set her upon a milk-white horse, and then they all rode away to the palace, for that was where he was to take her. There they dressed her in splendid clothes and put a golden crown upon her head, and then she and the king were married. Around her neck he hung a golden chain and a locket, and in the locket was a picture of himself; on her finger he slipped a ring, and within were secret words which nobody but he and she knew.

One day the wicked Step-mother was walking in the fields, and the two crows sat on the thorn-tree.

"Look," says the first crow, "yonder goes the beauty."

"Yes," says the second, "but she is only as a cabbage to a rose when compared to the lass who followed the golden ball down into the pit, and who has married the handsome young king over at the castle yonder."

Then, "Caw! caw!" they cried, and flapped their wings and flew away.

As for the Step-mother, her heart was ready to burst with anger and with spite. Home she went and began to think of what she should do to put her step-daughter out of the way again.

The Young King goeth down
into the pit and bringeth up ye maiden.

She took some dough and some feathers, and of them she made an old hen and six chicks. She put them in the oven and baked them, and when she drew them out again they were all of pure gold. But the strangest of all was, that when she set them upon the table the little golden hen strutted and clucked, and the chicks cried, "Peep! peep!" and followed at her heels.

Then the woman clad herself in a strange dress, so that no one might know who she was. She hid a long, keen silver pin in her bosom, and off she set for the castle with the golden hen and the golden chickens in a basket wrapped up in a white napkin.

She set her basket on the ground under the palace window, and when the folks within saw the little clucking hen and her chicks, all made of pure gold that shone in the sunlight, they could not look enough.

Off ran one and told the queen, who came and looked and looked, and wondered and wondered, until by and by she longed for the golden hen and the golden chickens as she had never longed for anything in all of her life before. So she called one of her maids, and sent her down to ask the strange woman the price of her golden chickens.

"Prut!" says the wicked witch of a Step-mother, "who are you that you should come to talk with me? If the young queen would buy my wares she must come and bargain with me herself."

So down went the young queen to the wicked Step-mother; "And what is the price of your hen and chicks, my good woman," said she, for she did not know the other, because of the strange dress in which she was clad.

"Oh! it is little or nothing I ask for my hen and chickens," said the wicked Step-mother to the beautiful queen. "If you will give me a kiss down in the garden back of the rose-tree yonder, you may have the chickens and welcome."

Oh, yes; the queen was willing enough to pay the price, if that was all the woman wanted. So off they went back of the rose-tree, she and the Step-mother. There the witch drew out the silver pin from her bosom, and as she kissed the queen she thrust the pin deep into her head. Then quick as a wink the queen was changed into a white dove and flew away over the tree-tops.

Off went the Step-mother, and was as pleased with what she had done this time as with what she had done that time; for the two crows sat on the thorn-tree, and the first crow said to the second crow, "Yonder goes

The Step=mother bringeth mischief upon the Young Queen by sundry magic spells.

the beauty." And the second crow said to the first, " Yes, there is none to compare with her now that the young queen has been changed to a white dove.

At the king's castle they hunted for the queen high, and they hunted for the queen low, but could find neither thread nor hair of her. As for the white dove, it had flown in at a window, and there the little cook-boy found it, and caught it and sold it to the cook for a penny. So the beautiful white dove sat over the kitchen window, and did nothing but mourn from the dawn to the gloaming.

One day the folk in the kitchen were talking together. The king was lying sick abed and dying of a broken heart because his beautiful young queen was nowhere to be found. That was what they said, and the white bird heard every word of it.

The next morning when they came to the kitchen there was a beautiful sweet cake lying upon a white napkin, and on the cake were written these words :

" Break this, my king, and ease thy sorrow."

They took the sweet cake to the king where he lay, and he broke it as the words told him to. Within it he found the ring which he had given to the queen, inside of which were written words which no one but he and she knew.

" Where did this come from?" said he ; but nobody could tell him.

" Where the ring came from," said he, " there will the queen be found." And up he got from his bed and dressed himself, and ate his breakfast with a cheerful face.

They talked about what had happened down in the kitchen, and the white dove heard it all.

Next morning there, on a fine linen napkin, lay another cake like the first, and on it was written:

" Break this, my king, and be comforted."

They took it up to the king as they had done the first. And the king snatched it like a hungry man. He broke the cake, and there was the necklace and the locket that he had given the queen.

" Where did this come from?" said he.

But they could tell him no more about that than about the other.

All the same, they talked about it down in the kitchen, and the white dove heard what was said.

But that night the little cook-boy hid in the closet to watch, for he

The Young King caresses ỹ white dove.

wanted to see who it was that brought the cakes that they took up-stairs to the king. So he watched and watched, and by and by the clock struck twelve. And when the last stroke sounded the dove flew down from over the window, and as soon as it lit upon the floor it was the white dove no longer, but the queen herself. She made a sweet cake of sugar and of flour, and in it she put a feather as white as silver. Then she became the white dove again, and flew back over the window where she had sat before.

The next morning they found the third cake lying upon a white napkin, and on the cake was written:

"Break this, my king, for the time has come."

They took it up to the king and he broke it, and there was the white feather.

Then the king called everybody that was in the castle, and asked each one in turn if he or she could tell where the sweet cake had come from. But no; nobody knew, until last of all they questioned the kitchen-boy.

"Oh, yes," said he, "I know who it was that brought the cake. Last night the white dove in the kitchen flew down from over the window and became the queen herself; she made the sweet cake and laid it upon the white napkin, for I saw her do it with my own eyes."

Up they brought the white dove from the kitchen, and the king took it in his own hands and held it up to his bosom, and stroked it and caressed it.

"If thou art my queen," said he, "why dost thou not speak to me?"

But the dove answered never a word, and the king stroked it and stroked it.

By and by he felt something, and when he came to look it was the head of the silver pin. He drew it forth, and there stood the young queen again in her own true shape.

She told everything that had happened to her from the first to the last, and how her Step-mother had treated her. Then, hui! but the king was angry! He sent a great lot of soldiers off to the father's house to bring the Step-mother to the castle so that she might be punished for her wickedness. But she was not to be caught as easily as a sparrow in a rain-storm; she jumped upon a broom straw, and — puff! — away she flew up the chimney, and that was the last that anybody saw of her so far as ever I heard.

But they brought the father over to the king's castle, where he sat in the warmest corner and had the best that was to be had.

That is all of this story, and if you see a blind mouse run across the floor throw your cap over it and catch it, for it is yours.

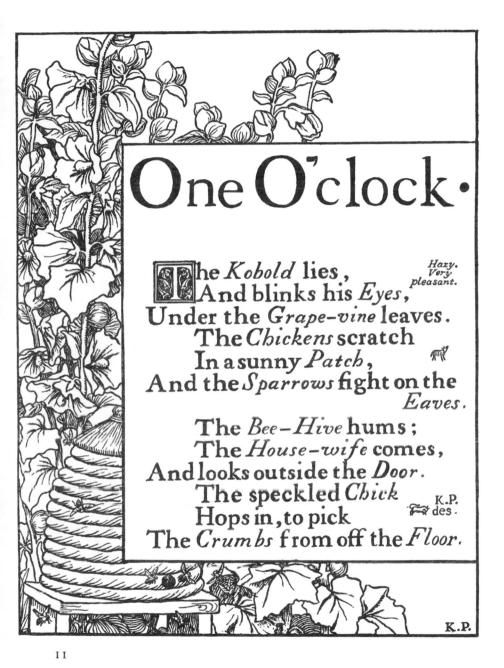

One O'clock·

Hazy.
Very
pleasant.

The *Kobold* lies,
And blinks his *Eyes*,
Under the *Grape-vine* leaves.
The *Chickens* scratch
In a sunny *Patch*,
And the *Sparrows* fight on the
Eaves.

The *Bee-Hive* hums;
The *House-wife* comes,
And looks outside the *Door*.
The speckled *Chick*
Hops in, to pick
The *Crumbs* from off the *Floor*.

K.P.
des.

K.P.

II

XIII.

NCE upon a time there was a man whose name was
just Master Jacob and nothing more.

All that Master Jacob had in the world was a
good fat pig, two black goats, a wife, and a merry
temper—which was more than many a better man
than he had, for the matter of that.

"See, now," says Master Jacob, "I will drive the
fat pig to the market to-morrow; who knows but
that I might strike a bit of a sale."

"Do," says Master Jacob's wife, for she was of the good sort, and always
nodded when he said "yes," as the saying goes.

Now there were three rogues in the town over the hill, who lived in
plenty; one was the priest, one was the provost, and one was the master
mayor; and which was the greatest rogue of the three it would be a hard
matter to tell, but perhaps it was the priest.

"See, now," says the priest to the other two, "Master Jacob, who lives
over yonder way, is going to bring his fat pig to market to-morrow. If you
have a mind for a trick, we will go snacks in what we win, and each of us
will have a rib or two of bacon hanging in the pantry, and a string or so of
sausages back in the chimney without paying so much as a brass button for
them."

Well, of course that was a tune to which the others were willing to dance. So the rogue of a priest told them to do thus and so, and to say this and that, and they would cheat Master Jacob out of his good fat pig as easily as a beggar eats buttered parsnips.

So the next morning off starts Master Jacob to the market, driving his fat pig before him with a bit of string around the leg of it. Down he comes into the town, and the first one whom he meets is the master priest.

"How do you find yourself, Master Jacob?" says the priest, "and where are you going with that fine, fat dog?"

"Dog!" says Master Jacob, opening his eyes till they were as big and as round as saucers. "Dog! Prut! It is as fine a pig as ever came into this town, I would have you know."

"What!" says the priest. "Do you try to tell me that that is a pig, when I can see with both of my ears and all of my eyes that it is a great, fat dog?"

"I say it is a pig!" says Master Jacob.

"I say it is a dog!" says the priest.

"I say it is a pig!" says Master Jacob.

"I say it is a dog!" says the priest.

"I say it is a pig!" says Master Jacob.

Just then who should come along but the provost, with his hands in his pockets and his pipe in his mouth, looking as high and mighty as though he owned all of that town and the sun and the moon into the bargain.

"Look, friend," says the priest. "We have been saying so and so and so and so, just now. Will you tell me, *is* that a pig, or *is* it a dog?"

"Prut!" says the provost, "how you talk, neighbor! Do you take me for a fool I should like to know? Why, it is as plain as the nose on your face that it is a great, fat dog."

"I say it is a pig!" bawled Master Jacob.

"I say it is a dog!" says the provost.

"I say it is a pig!" says Master Jacob.

"I say it is a dog!" says the provost.

"I say it is a pig!" says Master Jacob.

"Come, come," says the priest, "let us have no high words over the matter. No, no; we will take it to the mayor. If he says that it is a pig we two will give you ten shillings; and if he says it is a dog, you will give the animal to us as a penance."

Well, Master Jacob was satisfied with that, for he was almost certain that it was a pig. So off they marched to the mayor's house. There the

aster Jacob comes to ẙ town with his fine, fat pig and there falls in with the Priest and the Probost.

priest told all about the matter, for he was used to talking. "And now,"
says he, "*is* it a pig, or *is* it a dog?"

"Why," says the mayor, "I wish I may be choked to death with a
string of sausages if it is not a dog, and a big dog and a fat dog into the
bargain."

So there was an end of the matter, and Master Jacob had to march off
home without his pig and with no more in his pockets than he had before.
All the same, he saw what kind of trick had been played on him, and,
says he to himself, "What is sauce for the goose is sauce for the gander.
If one can pipe another can whistle; I'll just try a bit of a trick myself."
So he went to his wife and told her that he had a mind to do thus and so,
and that she must do this and that; for he thought of trying his hand at a
little trickery as well as other folks.

Now, as I told you before, Master Jacob had two goats, both of them as
black as the inside of your hat at midnight; moreover, they were as like as
two spoons in the same dish; for no one could have told them apart unless
he had lived with them year in and year out, rainy weather and clear, as
Master Jacob had done.

Well, the next day Master Jacob tied a rope around the neck of one of
the goats, took down a basket from the wall, and started off to the town
over the hill, leading his goat behind him. By and by he came to the market place and began buying many and one things, until his basket was as
full as it could hold. After a while whom should he see coming along but
the priest and the provost and the mayor, walking arm-in-arm as bold as
you please.

"Halloa, Master Jacob," said they, "and what have you there?"

"The blessed saints only know that," said Master Jacob. "It may be a
black cat for all that I know; it *was* a black goat when I left home this
morning."

And what was Master Jacob going to do with his little black goat?
That was what they should like to know.

"Oh," said Master Jacob, "I am about to send my little black goat on
an errand; if you will wait you shall see for yourselves."

Then what did he do but hang the basket around the goat's neck.
"Go home to your mistress," said he, "and tell her to boil the beef and
cabbage for dinner to-day; and, stop! tell her to go to Neighbor Nicholas's house and borrow a good big jug of beer, for I have a masterful thirst
this morning." Then he gave the goat a slap on the back, and off it went

Master Jacob takes his black goat to town.

as though the ground were hot under it. But whether it ever really went home or not, I never heard.

As for the priest, the provost, and the mayor, you may guess how they grinned at all of this. Good land sake's alive! And did Master Jacob really mean to say that the little black goat would tell the mistress all that?

Oh, yes; that it would. It was a keen blade, that little black goat, and if they would only come home with him, Master Jacob would show them.

So off they all went, Master Jacob and the priest and the provost and the mayor, and after a while they came to Master Jacob's house. Yes, sure enough, there was a black goat feeding in the front yard, and how should the priest and the provost and the mayor know that it was not the same

one that they had seen at the market-place! And just then out came
Master Jacob's wife. "Come in, Jacob," says she, "the cabbage and the
meat are all ready. As for the beer, Neighbor Nicholas had none to spare,
so I just borrowed a jugful of Neighbor Frederick, and it is as good as the
other for certain and sure."

Dear, dear! how the three cronies did open their eyes when they heard
all of this! They would like to have such a goat as that, indeed they would.
Now, if Master Jacob had a mind to sell his goat, they would give as much
as twenty dollars for it.

Oh, no; Master Jacob could not think of selling his nice little, dear little
black goat for twenty dollars.

For thirty, then.

No; Master Jacob would not sell his goat for thirty dollars, either.

Well, they would give as much as forty.

No; forty dollars was not enough for such a goat as that.

So they bargained and bargained till the upshot of the matter was that
they paid Master Jacob fifty dollars, and marched off with the goat as
pleased as pleased could be.

Well, the three rogues were not long in finding out what a trick had
been played upon them, I can tell you. So, in a day or two, whom should
Master Jacob see coming down the road but the priest, the provost, and the
master mayor, and anybody could see with half an eye that they were in an
awful fume.

"Hi!" says Master Jacob, "there will be hot water boiling presently."
In he went to his good wife. "Here," says he, "take this bladder of blood
that we were going to make into pudding, and hide it under your apron,
and then when I do this and that, you do thus and so."

Presently in came the priest, the provost, and the mayor, bubbling and
sizzling like water on slake lime. "What kind of a goat was that that you
sold us?" bawled they, as soon as they could catch their breaths.

"My black goat," says Master Jacob.

Then look! He would run on no errands, and would do nothing that
it was told. It was of no more use about the house than five wheels
to a wagon. Now Master Jacob might just go and put his hat on
and come along with them, for they were about to take him away to
prison.

"But stop a bit," says Master Jacob. "Did you say 'by the great horn
spoon,' when you told the goat to do this or that?"

No; the cronies had done nothing of the kind, for Master Jacob had said nothing about a great horn spoon when he sold them the goat.

"Why didn't you remind me?" says Master Jacob to his good wife.

"I didn't think of it," says she.

"You didn't?" says he.

"No," says she.

"Then take that!" says he, and he out with a great sharp knife and jabbed it into the bladder under her apron, so that the blood ran out like everything.

"Ugh!" says the good wife, and then fell down and lay quite still, just for all the world as though she were dead.

When the three cronies saw this, they gaped like fish out of water. Just look now! Master Jacob had gone and killed his good wife, and all for nothing at all. Dear, dear! what a hasty temper the man had. Now he had gotten himself into a pretty scrape, and would have to go before the judge and settle the business with him.

"Tut! tut!" says Master Jacob, "the broth is not all in the ashes yet. Perhaps I am a bit hasty, but we will soon mend this stocking."

So he went to the closet in the corner of the room, and brought out a little tin horn. He blew a turn or two over his wife, whereat she sneezed, and then sat up as good and as sound as ever.

As for the priest and the provost and the mayor, they thought that they had never seen anything so wonderful in all of their lives before. They must and would have that tin horn if it was to be had; now, how much would Master Jacob take for it, money down?

Oh, Master Jacob did not want to part with his horn; all the same, if he had to sell it, he would just as lief that they should buy it as anybody. So they bargained and bargained, and the end of the matter was that they paid down another fifty dollars and marched off with the little tin horn, blowing away at it for dear life.

By and by they came home, and there stood the goat, nibbling at the grass in front of the house and thinking of no harm at all. "So!" says the provost, "was it you that would do nothing for us without our saying, 'By the great horn spoon?' Take that then!" And he fetched the goat a thwack with his heavy walking-staff so that it fell down, and lay with no more motion than a stone. "There," says he, "that business is done; and now lend me the horn a minute, brother, till I fetch him back again."

Well, he blew and he blew, and he blew and he blew, till he was as red in the face as a cherry, but the goat moved never so much as a single hair. Then the priest took a turn at the horn, but he had no better luck than the provost. Last of all the mayor had a try at it; but he might as well have blown the horn over a lump of dough for all the answer he had for his blowing.

Then it began to work into their heads that they had been befooled again. Phew! what a passion they were in. I can only say that I am glad that I was not in Master Jacob's shoes. "We'll put him in prison right away," said they, and off they went to do as they said.

But Master Jacob saw them coming down the road, and was ready for them this time too. He took two pots and filled them with pitch, and over the top of the pitch he spread gold and silver money, so that if you had looked into the pots you would have thought that there was nothing in them but what you saw on the top. Then he took the pots off into the little woods back of the house. Now in the woods was a great deep pit, and all around the pit grew a row of bushes, so thick that nothing was to be seen of the mouth of the hole.

By and by came the priest and the mayor and the provost to Master Jacob's house, puffing and blowing and fuming.

Rap! rap! tap! they knocked at the door, but nobody was there but Master Jacob's wife.

Was Master Jacob at home? That was what they wanted to know, for they had a score to settle with him.

Oh, Master Jacob's wife did not know just where he was, but she thought that he was in the little woods back of the house yonder, gathering money.

Phew! and did money grow so near to the house as all that? This was a matter to be looked into, for if money was to be gathered they must have their share. So off they went to the woods, hot-foot.

Yes; there was Master Jacob, sure enough, and what was more, he was carrying two pots, one on each arm.

"Hi! Master Jacob, and what have you there?" said they.

"Oh, nothing much," says Master Jacob.

Yes; that was all very good, but they would like to look into those pots that he was carrying; that was what the three cronies said.

"Well," says Master Jacob, "you may look into the pots if you choose;

he Priest, the Provost and the Master Mayor blow and blow the little tin trumpet over ỹ black goat.

all the same, I will tell you that they are both full of pitch, and that
there is only just a little money scattered over the top.

Yes, yes; that was all very well, but the three cronies knew the
smell of money from the smell of pitch. See now, they had been
fooled twice already, and were not to be caught again. Now, where
did Master Jacob get that money, that was what they wanted to
know.

"Oh," says Master Jacob, "I cannot tell you that; if you want to
gather money you will have to look for it yourselves. But you must not
go too near to those thick bushes yonder, for there is a deep pit hidden
there, and you will be sure to fall into it."

When the priest and the provost and the mayor heard this, they nudged
one another with their elbows and winked with one eye. They knew how
much of that cheese to swallow. They would just take a look at this wonderful pit, for they thought that the money was hidden in the bushes for
sure and certain. So off they went as fast as they could lay foot to the
ground.

"Just you stay here," said the priest to the others, "while I go and
see whether there really is a pit as he said." For he thought to himself
that he would go and gather a pocketful of the money before it would be
share and share with his comrades. So, into the thicket he jumped, and—
plump!—he fell into the great, deep pit; and there was an end of number
one.

By and by the others grew tired of tarrying. "I'll go and see what he
is waiting for," says the provost. For he thought to himself, "He is filling
his pockets, and I might as well have my share." So, into the thicket he
jumped, and—plump!—he fell into the great, deep pit; and there was an
end of number two.

As for the mayor, he waited and waited. "What a fool am I," said he
at last, "to sit here twiddling my thumbs while the two rogues yonder are
filling their pockets without me. It is little or nothing but the scraps and
the bones that I will come in for."

So the upshot of the matter was that he too ran and jumped into the
thicket, and heels over head into the great, deep pit, and there was an end
of number three. And if Master Jacob ever helped them out, you may
depend upon it that he made them promise to behave themselves in time
to come.

And this is true that I tell you: it would have been cheaper for them to

aster Jacob with his two pots meets the three cronies in the woods. ⊂

have bought their pork in the first place, for, as it was, they paid a pretty penny for it.

As for Master Jacob and his good wife, they had a hundred dollars in good hard money, and if they did not get along in the world with that, why I, for one, want nothing more to do with them.

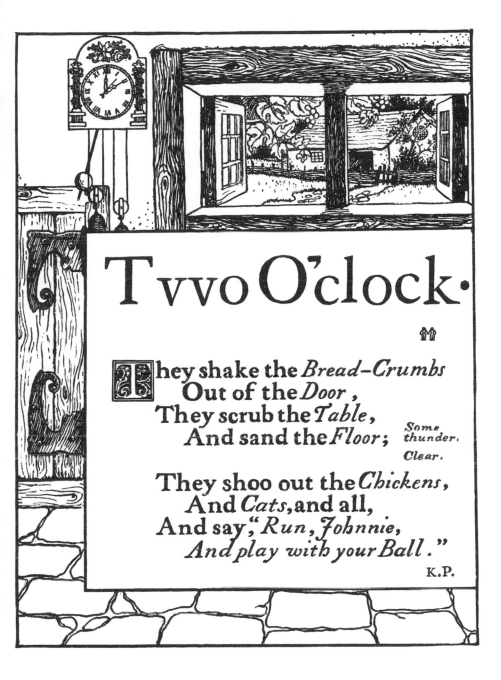

Tvvo O'clock·

They shake the *Bread–Crumbs*
Out of the *Door*,
They scrub the *Table*,
And sand the *Floor*; *Some thunder.*
Clear.

They shoo out the *Chickens*,
And *Cats*, and all,
And say, "*Run, Johnnie,*
And play with your Ball."

K.P.

Peterkin and the Little Grey Hare.

XIV.

HERE was a man who died and left behind him three sons, and nothing but two pennies to each. So, as there was little to be gained by scraping the dish at home, off they packed to the king's house, where they might find better faring. The two elder lads were smart fellows enough; as for Peterkin, he was the youngest—why, nobody thought much of him.

So off they went—tramp! tramp! tramp!—all three together. By and by they came to a great black forest where little was to be seen either before or behind them.

There old Father Hunger met them, and that was the worse for them, for there was nothing at all to eat. They looked here and there, and, after a while, what should they come across but a little grey hare caught in a snare.

Then, if anybody was glad, it was the two elder brothers. " Here is something to stay our stomachs," said they.

But Peterkin had a soft heart in his breast. " See, brothers," said he, " look how the poor thing turns up its eyes. Sure it would be a pity to take its life, even though our stomachs do grumble a bit."

But the two elder brothers were deaf in that ear. They had gone without their dinners long enough, and they were no such foolish fellows as to throw it away, now that it had come to them.

But Peterkin begged and begged, until, at last, the two said that they would let the Little Grey Hare go free if he would give them the two pennies that he had in his pocket.

Well, Peterkin let them have the pennies, and they let the hare go, and glad enough it was to get away, I can tell you.

"See, Peterkin," it said, speaking as plainly as a Christian, "you shall lose nothing by this. When you are in a tight place, whistle on your fingers—thus—and perhaps help will come to you."

Then it thumped its feet on the ground and away it scampered.

As for Peter's brothers, they laughed and laughed. A fool and his money were soon parted, said they. How could a little grey hare help him, they should like to know?

After a while they came to the town, where Peterkin's brothers took up their lodgings at a good inn. As for Peterkin, he had to go and sleep in the straw, for one cannot spend money and have it both. So while the brothers were eating broth with meat in it, Peterkin went with nothing.

"I wonder," said he, "if the Little Grey Hare can help me now." So he whistled on his fingers, just as it had told him.

Then who should come hopping and skipping along but the Little Grey Hare itself. "What do you want, Peterkin?" it said.

"I should like," said Peterkin, "to have something to eat."

"Nothing easier than that," said the Little Grey Hare; and before one could wink twice a fine feast, fit for a king, was spread out before him, and he fell to as though he had not eaten a bite for seven years.

After that he slept like a flat stone, for one can sleep well even in the straw, if one only has a good supper within one.

When the next morning had come, the two elder brothers bought them each a good new coat with brass buttons. Peterkin they said would have to go as he was, for patches and tatters were good enough for such a spend-thrift.

But Peterkin knew a way out of that hole. Back of the house he went, and there he blew on his fingers.

"What will you have?" said the Little Grey Hare.

"I should like," said Peterkin, "to have a fine new suit of clothes, so that I can go to the king's house with my brothers and not be ashamed."

"If that is all that you want," said the Hare, "it is little enough;" and there lay the finest suit of clothes that Peterkin had ever seen, for it was all of blue silk sewed with golden threads. So Peterkin dressed himself in his fine clothes, and you may guess how his brothers stared when they saw him.

Peterkin's brothers marvel at the fine clothes that the hare gave him.

Off they all went to the king's house, and there was the king feeding his chickens; for that was all the work he had upon his hands, and an easy life he led of it. The king looked at Peterkin, and thought that he had never seen such fine clothes. Did they want service? Well, the king thought that he might give it to them. The oldest brother might tend the pigs, the second might look after the cows. But as for Peterkin, he was so spruce and neat that he might stay in the house and open the door when folks knocked. That was what his fine clothes did for him.

So Peterkin had the soft feathers in that nest, for he sat in the warm chimney all day, and had the scraping of the pipkins when good things had been cooked.

Well, things went quietly enough for a while, but the elder brothers kept up a great buzzing in their heads, I can tell you; for one does not like to see another step in front of one, and that is the truth.

So, one day, who should come to the king but the two elder brothers. Perhaps, said they, the king did not know it, but there was a giant over yonder who had a grey goose that laid a golden egg every day of her life. Now Peterkin had said more than once, and over and over again, that he was man enough to get the grey goose for the king whenever the king wanted it. You can guess how this tickled the king's ears. Off he sent for Peterkin, and Peterkin came.

Hui! how Peterkin opened his eyes when he heard what the king wanted. He had never said that he could get the giant's goose; he vowed and swore that he had not. But it was to no purpose that he talked, the king wanted the grey goose, and Peterkin would have to get it for him. He might have three days for the business, and that was all. Then, if he brought the grey goose, he should have two bags of gold money; if he did not bring it he should pack off to the prison.

So Peterkin left the king, and if anybody was down in the mouth in all of the world it was Peterkin.

"Perhaps," said he, "the Little Grey Hare can help me." So he blew a turn or two on his fingers, and the Little Grey Hare came hopping and skipping up to him.

What was Peterkin in the dumps about now? That was what it wanted to know.

Why, the king wanted him to get such and such a grey goose from over at the giant's house, and Peterkin knew no more about it than a red herring in a box; that was the trouble.

"Oh, well," says the Little Grey Hare, "maybe that can be cured; just go to the king and ask for this and that and the other thing, and we will see what can be done about the business."

So off went Peterkin to the king; perhaps he could get the grey goose after all, but he must have three barrels of soft pitch, and a bag of barley-corn, and a pot of good tallow.

The king let him have all that he wanted, and then the Little Grey Hare took Peterkin and the three barrels of soft pitch and the bag of barley-corn and the pot of good tallow on its back, and off it went till the wind whistled behind Peterkin's ears.

(Now that was a great load for a little grey hare; but I tell the story to you just as Time's Clock told it to me.)

After a while they came to a river, and then the Little Grey Hare said:

"Brother Pike! Brother Pike! Here are folks would like to cross the wide river."

Then up came a great river pike, and on his back he took Peterkin and the Little Grey Hare and the three barrels of pitch and the sack of barley-corn and the pot of good tallow, and away he swam till he had brought them from this side to that.

(Now that was a great load for a river pike to carry; but as Time's Clock told the story to me I tell it to you.)

Then the Little Grey Hare went on and on again until it came to a high hill, and on the top of the high hill was a great house; that was where the giant lived.

Then Peterkin took the soft pitch and made a wide pathway of it. After that he smeared his feet all over with the tallow, so that he stuck to the soft pitch no more than water sticks to a cabbage leaf. Then he shouldered his bag of barley-corn and went up to the giant's castle, and hunted around and hunted around until he had found where the grey goose was; and it was in the kitchen and would not come out. But Peterkin had a way to bring it; he scattered the barley-corn all about, and when the grey goose saw that, it came out quickly enough and began to eat the grains as fast as it could gobble. But Peterkin did not give it much time for this, for up he caught it, and off he went as fast as he could scamper.

Then the grey goose flapped its wings and began squalling. "Master! master! Here I am! here I am! It is Peterkin who has me!"

Out ran the giant with his great iron club, and after Peterkin he came

as fast as he could lay foot to the ground.   But Peterkin had the buttered
side of the cake this time, for he ran over the pitch road as easily as though
it were made of good stones; that was because his boots were smeared with
tallow.   As for the giant, he stuck to it as a fly sticks to the butter, so that
it was very slow travelling that he made of it.

Then the hare took Peterkin up on its back, and away it scampered till
the wind whistled behind his ears.   When it had come to the river it said:

" Brother Pike! Brother Pike!   Here are folks would like to cross the
wide river."

Then the pike took them on its back and away they went.   But it was
a tight squeeze through that crack, I can tell you, for they had hardly left
the shore when up came the giant, fuming and boiling like water in the pot.

" Is that you, Peterkin?" said he.

" Yes; it is I," said Peterkin.

" And did you steal my grey goose?" said the giant.

" Yes; I stole your grey goose," said Peterkin.

" And what would you do if you were me and I were you?" said the
giant.

" I would do what I could," said Peterkin.

After that the giant went back home, shaking his head and talking to
himself.

So the king got the grey goose, and was as glad as glad could be.   And
Peterkin got the bags of gold, and was glad also.   Thus there were two in
the world pleased at the same time.

And now the king could not make too much of Peterkin.   It was
Peterkin here and Peterkin there, till Peterkin's brothers were as sour as
bad beer over the matter.

So, one day, they came buzzing in the king's ear again; perhaps the king
did not know it, but that same giant had a silver bell, and every time that
the bell was rung a good dinner was spread ready for the eating.   Now,
Peterkin had been saying to everybody that he could get that bell for the
king just as easily as he had gotten the grey goose.   At this the king
pricked up his ears, for it tickled them to hear such talk.   He sent for
Peterkin to come to him, and Peterkin came.   He vowed and swore that
he had said nothing about getting the giant's bell.   But it was of no use;
he only wasted his breath.   The king wanted the silver bell, and the king
must have it.   Peterkin should have three days in which to get it.   If he
brought it at the end of that time, he should have half of the kingdom to

Peterkin, with y̎ help of the hare, carries off the Giant's goose. ‑(

rule over. If he did not bring it he should have his ears clipped; so there was an end of that talk.

It was a bad piece of business, but off Peterkin went and blew on his fingers, and up came the Little Grey Hare.

"Well," said the Little Grey Hare, "and what is the trouble with us now?"

Why, the king wanted a little silver bell that was over at the giant's house, and he had to go and get it for him; that was the trouble with Peterkin.

"Well," says the Little Grey Hare, "there is no telling what one can do till one tries; just get a little wad of tow and come along, and we will see what we can make of it."

So Peterkin got the wad of tow, and then he sat him on the Little Grey Hare's back, and away they went till the wind whistled behind his ears. When they came to the river the Little Grey Hare called on the pike, and up it came and carried them over as it had done before. By and by they came to the giant's house, and this time the giant was away from home, which was a lucky thing for Peterkin.

Peterkin climbed into the window, and hunted here and there till he had found the little silver bell. Then he wrapped the tow around the clapper, but, in spite of all that he could do, it made a jingle or two. Then away he scampered to the Little Grey Hare. He mounted on its back, and off they went.

But the giant heard the jingle of the little silver bell, and home he came as fast as his legs could carry him.

He hunted here and there till he found the track of Peterkin, then after him he went, three miles at a step.

When he came to the river, there was Peterkin, just out of harm's way.

"Is that you, Peterkin?" bawled the giant.

"Yes; it is I," said Peterkin.

"And have you stolen my silver bell?" said the giant.

"Yes; I have stolen your silver bell," said Peterkin.

"And have you stolen my grey goose too?" said the giant.

Yes; Peterkin had stolen that too.

"And what would you do if you were me and I were you?" said the giant.

"I would do what I could," said Peterkin.

At this the giant went back home, grumbling and muttering to himself, and if Peterkin had been by it would have been bad for Peterkin.

P eterkin bringeth ẏ little sil=ver bell of the Giant to the King.

Dear, dear! but the king was glad to get the silver bell; as for Peterkin, he was a great man now, for he ruled over half of the kingdom.

But now the two elder brothers were less pleased than ever before; they grumbled and talked together until the upshot of the matter was that they went to the king for the third time.   Peterkin had been bragging and talking again.   This time he had said that the giant over yonder had a sword of such a kind that it gave more light in the dark than fourteen candles, and that he could get the sword as easily as he had gotten the grey goose and the little silver bell.

After that nothing would satisfy the king but for Peterkin to go and get the sword.   Peterkin argued and talked, and talked and argued, but it was for no good; he might have talked till the end of all things.   The king wanted the sword, and the king must have it.   If Peterkin could bring it to him in three days' time he might have the princess for his wife; if he came back empty-handed he should have a good thong of skin cut off of his back from top to bottom; that was what the king said.

So there was nothing for it but for Peterkin to whistle on his fingers for the Little Grey Hare once more.

"And what is it this time?" said the Little Grey Hare.

Why, the king wanted such and such a kind of sword, and Peterkin must go and get it for him; that was the trouble.

Well, well; there might be a hole in this hedge as well as another. But this time Peterkin must borrow one of the princess's dresses and her golden comb; then one might see what could be done.

So Peterkin went to the king and said that he must have the dress and the comb, and the king let him have them.   Then he mounted on the Little Grey Hare and—whisk!—away they went as fast as before.

Well, they crossed the river and came to the giant's house once more. There Peterkin dressed himself in the princess's dress, and combed his hair with her golden comb; and as he combed his hair it grew longer and longer, and the end of the matter was that he looked for all the world like as fine and strapping a lass as ever a body saw.   Then he went up to the giant's house, and—rap! tap! tap!—he knocked at the door as bold as brass.   The giant was in this time, and he came and opened the door himself.   But when he saw what he thought was a fine lass, he smiled as though he had never eaten anything in all his life but soft butter.

Perhaps the pretty lass would come in and sit down for a bit; that was what he said to Peterkin.

Peterkin as a girl combs the Giant's hair

Oh, yes! that suited Peterkin; of course he would come in. So in he came, and then he and the giant sat down to supper together. After they had eaten as much as they could the giant laid his head in Peterkin's lap, and Peterkin combed his hair and combed his hair, until he fell fast asleep and began to snore so that he made the cinders fly up the chimney.

Then Peterkin rose up softly and took down the Sword of Light from the wall. After that he went out on tiptoes and mounted the Little Grey Hare, and away they went till the chips flew behind them.

By and by the giant opened his eyes and saw that Peterkin was gone, and, what was more, his Sword of Light was gone also. Then what a rage he was in! Off he went after Peterkin and the Little Grey Hare, seven

miles at a step.   But he was just a little too late, though there was no
room to spare between Peterkin and him, and that is the truth.

"Is that you, Peterkin?" said he.

"Yes; it is I," said Peterkin.

"And have you stolen my grey goose?" said the giant.

Oh, yes; Peterkin had done that.

"And what would you do if you were me and I were you?" said the giant.

"I would drink the river dry and follow after," said Peterkin.

"That is good," said the giant.   So he laid himself down and drank and
drank and drank, until he drank so much that he burst with a great noise,
and there was an end of him!

The king was so pleased with the Sword of Light that it seemed as
though he could not look at it and talk about it enough.   As for Peterkin,
he got the princess for his wife, and that pleased him also, you may be sure.
The princess was pleased too, for Peterkin was a good, smart, tight bit of a
lad, and that is what the girls like.   So it was that everybody was pleased
except the two elder brothers, who looked as sour as green gooseberries.
But now Peterkin was an apple that hung too high for them to reach, and
so they had to let him alone.

The next day after the wedding, whom should Peterkin come across but
the Little Grey Hare.

"See, Peterkin," it said, "I have done much for you; will you do a little
for me?"

"Yes, indeed, that I will," said Peterkin.

"Then take the Sword of Light and cut off my head and feet," said the
Little Grey Hare.

No, no; Peterkin could never do such a thing as that; that would be a
pretty way to treat a good friend.

But the Little Grey Hare begged and begged and begged, until at last
Peterkin did as he asked; he cut off his head and his feet.   Then who
should stand before him but a handsome young prince, with yellow hair and
blue eyes.   That was what the Little Grey Hare had been all the time, only
the giant had bewitched him.

As for Peterkin—well, this is the way of it; the youngest will step ahead
of the others sometimes.

Three O'clock·

Make
hay.

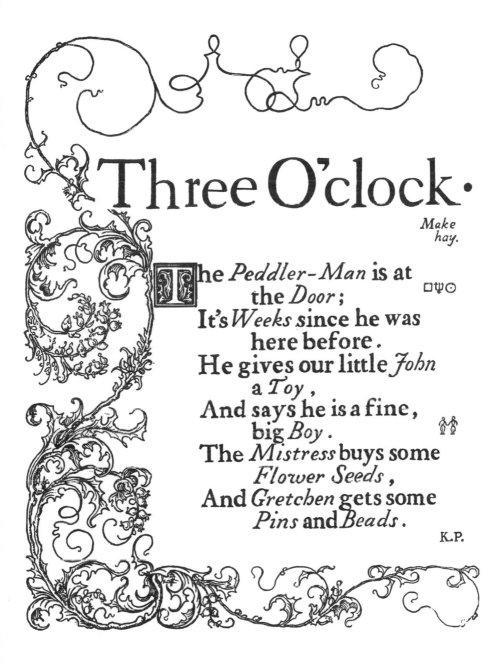

The *Peddler-Man* is at
the *Door*;
It's *Weeks* since he was
here before.
He gives our little *John*
a *Toy*,
And says he is a fine,
big *Boy*.
The *Mistress* buys some
Flower Seeds,
And *Gretchen* gets some
Pins and *Beads*.

K.P.

Mother Hildegarde.

XV.

ONCE upon a time there lived a king who had an only daughter, and the princess was more handsome than I can tell you. But the queen had been dead for so long that the king began to think about marrying a second time. So the upshot of the matter was that by and by there came a step-mother into the house, and a step-sister besides, for the new queen had a daughter of her own. And that was a sorrowful thing for the princess.

At first the new queen was kind enough to the poor girl; but before long there were other cakes baking in that oven, for the step-mother began saying to herself: "See, now, if this hussy were out of the way my own dear girl would be the first in the land, and might, in time, have the kingdom for her very own." So, in the end, the poor princess found but little peace in the same house with the woman and her daughter.

One day the step-mother, the step-sister, and the pretty princess sat together in the castle garden beside a deep cistern of water. By the cistern hung a silver cup for the use of those who wished to drink. And as they sat there the princess grew thirsty, and would have taken the cup to quench her thirst, but the step-mother stopped her.

"See, now," said she, "if you must drink you will have to stoop to the water, for the silver cup is too good for such as you."

"Alas!" said the poor princess, "the time was when a cup of gold was not too good for me!" And thereupon she began to weep as though her heart would break. But there was no help for it; if she would drink she must stoop for it; so down she knelt and began to drink from the deep water without any thought or fear of harm.

But as the princess thus stooped and drank, the wicked step-mother came behind her without her knowing it, and gave her a push so that she fell headlong into the cistern and sank to the bottom. After that the step-mother and the step-sister went back to the castle again, rejoicing and thinking that now they were rid of the princess for good and all, and that the step-sister would be the first in all of the land.

But in this they counted black chicks before they were hatched; for when the princess sank down to the bottom of the cistern, she found herself in a great wide meadow, all covered over with bright flowers, as many as there are stars in the sky at night.

Across this meadow she went on and on and on; but never a single soul did she see until at last she came to a great, fine house that stood all alone by itself, without another to be seen, near or afar. In the doorway of the house stood an old woman, whom the princess saw very plainly was not like common folk.

And she was right, for the old woman was none other than Mother Hildegarde, who is so wise that she knows almost as much as Father Time himself. Thus it was that she knew all about the princess, and who she was and whence she came, without the asking. "Listen," said she, "I will give you food and lodging, and will pay you well if you will serve me faithfully for the space of a year and a day."

That the princess was willing enough to do, for she was both tired and hungry; so into the house she went to serve Mother Hildegarde for a year and a day.

But it was no common work that the princess did, I can tell you; for listen: When she blew the bellows that the fire might blaze the brighter, the wind swept over the great brown world so that every windmill turned around and around from Jacob Pfennigdrummel's to the shores of the great black sea at the north end of the earth; and when she sprinkled the clothes, the blessed rain came tumbling down till all the gutters ran with water so

The Princess cometh into a
wonderful country and to the house
of a strange old woman.

that little folk had either to stay home from school or to go thither under great, wide umbrellas.

But of all this the pretty princess knew nothing whatever, but only thought that she blew the fire and sprinkled the clothes. And that is often the way of the world—at least, so Tommy Pfouce tells me.

Well, one day Mother Hildegarde said to the princess: "See, now; I am going off on a journey, and it may be a while before I am back again. Here are the keys of all of the house, and you are free to go wherever you choose. Only here is a black key that unlocks a little room into which you must not go; for if you do I will be sure to know it, and ill-luck will be certain to happen to you." Then off she went, and the princess was left all alone.

The first day the lass went here, and the second day she went there, and the third day she had gone everywhere except into the little room where Mother Hildegarde had told her not to go; and she never wanted anything in all of her life as much as she wanted just to peep into that little room.

"I wonder," said she to herself—"I wonder what harm there could be in it if I were only to take one little peep?" So the upshot of the matter was that she went there just to look at the outside of the door.

"I wonder," said she, "if the key will fit the lock?"

Yes; it did fit it.

"I wonder," said she, "if the key will turn the bolt?"

Yes; it did turn it.

"I wonder," said she, "whether it would do any harm just to peep into the room?"

And she did peep into it.

Believe me or not, all the same I tell you the truth when I say that there was not one thing in the room but a covered jar, that stood in the middle of the floor. Of course the princess must have just one peep into the jar, for as she had gone as far as she had, there could be no more harm in this than in the other. So she went to the jar and took off the lid and peeped into it.

And what do you think was in it? Nothing but water!

But as the princess looked into the water she saw Mother Hildegarde as though she were a great way off, and the Mother Hildegarde whom she saw in the water was looking at nobody in all of the world but her. As soon as the princess saw what she saw, she clapped down the lid of the jar

 **he Princess looks into that which she should not have done.** 1

again; but she clapped it down just a moment too late, for a lock of hair fell down over her face, and one single hair touched the water in the jar.

Yes; only one single hair. But when the princess looked she saw that every lock upon her head was turned to pure gold. Then if anybody in all of the world was frightened it was the poor princess. She twisted up the hair upon the top of her head and bound her kerchief about it so that it was all hidden; but all the same the hair was there, and could never be changed from the gold again.

Just then who should come walking into the house but Mother Hildegarde herself. "Have you obeyed all that I have told you?" said she.

"Yes," said the princess, but all the same she was so frightened that her knees knocked together.

"Did you go into the little room?" said Mother Hildegarde.

"No," said the princess; but her heart beat so that she could hardly speak.

Then Mother Hildegarde snatched the kerchief off of the princess's head, and her golden hair came tumbling down all about her shoulders, glittering, so that it was the finest sight that you could see between here and Nomansland.

"Then how came your hair to be like that?" said Mother Hildegarde.

"I do not know," said the princess; and then she began crying and sobbing as though her heart would break.

"See now," said Mother Hildegarde; "you have served me well for all of the time that you have been with me, therefore I will have pity upon you, only you must tell me the truth. Did you go into the little room while I was away?"

But for all that Mother Hildegarde spoke ever so kindly the princess could not bring herself to speak the truth.

"No," said she.

"Then how came your hair to be like that?" said Mother Hildegarde.

"I do not know," said the princess.

At this Mother Hildegarde frowned till her eyes burned like sparks of fire. She caught the princess by the arm and struck her staff upon the ground, and away they flew through the air till the wind whistled behind them. So by and by they came to a great forest, out of which there was no path to be found either to the east or the west or the north or the south.

"See now," said Mother Hildegarde, "because you have been faithful in your labor with me I will give you still another chance. But if you do not

he Princess dwells in the oak tree where ỹ wild pigeons come to feed her.

answer me truthfully this time, I will leave you alone here in the forest, and will take away your speech so that you will be as dumb as the beasts of the field.   Did you go into the little room?"

But still the princess hardened her heart and answered " No."

" Then how came your hair to be like that?" said Mother Hildegarde.

" I do not know," said the princess.

Then Mother Hildegarde went away, and left the princess alone in the forest as she had promised to do; and not only that, but she took away the princess's speech, so that she was quite dumb.   So in the forest the princess dwelt for a long, long time, and there she would have died of hunger, only that Mother Hildegarde still cared for her and sent the wood-pigeons to feed her, which they did from day to day and from week to week and from month to month.   As for the princess, she lived in the branches of the trees, for she was afraid of the wild beasts that roamed through the wood.

By and by her clothes became nothing but rags and tatters, and then she had to weave her beautiful hair about her, so that she was clad all from head to foot in her golden tresses, and in them alone.

Well, one time it happened that a young king came riding into the forest to hunt the wild boars, and many of his people came along with him. Some of those who rode on before came suddenly to where a great flock of wood-pigeons flew about in the tree-tops above them.   But when they looked up, you may guess how wonder-struck they were when they saw that the pigeons were feeding a beautiful maiden who sat in the branches above, clad all in her golden hair.   Back they rode to the young king and told him all that they had seen, and up he came as fast as he could ride.   There he saw the maiden and how beautiful she was, and he called to her to come down.   But she only shook her head, for she could not speak, and she was ashamed of being found where she was.   Then the young king, seeing that she would not come down from the branches to him, climbed up himself and brought her.

He wrapped his cloak about her and set her on his horse in front of him, and then he and all that were with him rode away out of the dark forest and under the blue sky, until they had come to the king's castle. But all the time the princess did nothing but weep and weep, for she could not speak a single word.   The young king gave her to his mother to care for, who was none too glad to have such a dumb maiden brought into the house, even though the lass was as pretty as milk and rose-leaves.

But the young king cared nothing whatever for what his mother thought

**M**other Hildegarde carries ye baby away from the castle of the king.

about the matter, for the more he looked at the princess, the more beautiful she appeared in his eyes. So the end of the matter was that he married her, even though she had not a word to say for herself.

Well, time went on and on, till one day the storks that lived on the castle roof brought a baby boy to the poor dumb princess, whereat everybody was as glad as glad could be.

But their gladness was soon changed to sadness, for that night, when every one in the king's house was fast and sound asleep, Mother Hildegarde came softly into the princess's room. She gave her back her speech for the time being, and then she said. " I will still have pity upon you. If you will only tell me the truth you shall have your speech again, and all will go well with you. But if you tell me a falsehood once more, still greater troubles will come upon you. Now tell me, did you go into the little room ?"

" No," said the princess, for still she could not bring herself to confess to Mother Hildegarde.

" Then how came your hair to be like that ?"

" I do not know," said the princess.

So Mother Hildegarde took away her speech once more.

After that she smeared the mouth of the princess with blood, and then, wrapping the baby in her mantle, she carried it away with her, leaving the mother weeping alone.

You can guess what a hubbub there was the next morning in the castle, when they came and found that the baby was gone, and that the princess's mouth was smeared with blood. " See," said the king's mother, " what did I tell you from the very first. Do you not see that you have brought a wicked witch into the house, and that she has killed her own child ?"

But the king would listen to no such words as these, for it seemed to him that the princess was too beautiful and too good to do such a wicked thing.

After a time there came another baby to the princess, and once more Mother Hildegarde came to her and said, " Did you go into the little room ?"

" No," said the princess.

" Then how came your hair to be like that ?"

" I do not know," said the princess.

So Mother Hildegarde took this baby away as she had done the other, and left the princess with her lips smeared with blood.

And now every one of the king's household began to mutter and to whisper to his neighbor, and the king had nothing to say, but only left the room silently, for his heart was like heavy lead within his breast. Still he would not hear of harm coming to the princess, no matter what had happened.

In time there came a third baby, but still the princess could not soften her heart, and Mother Hildegarde took it away as she had done the others. This time the king could do nothing to save the princess, for every one cried out upon her that she was a wicked witch who killed her children, and that she should be burned at the stake, as was fitting for such a one. So a great pile of fagots was built out in the castle courtyard, and the princess was brought out and tied to a stake that stood in the midst. Then they lit the pile of fagots, and it began to crackle and burn around her where she stood.

Then suddenly Mother Hildegarde stood beside her in the midst of the fire. In her arms she held the princess's youngest baby, and the others stood, one upon one side and the other upon the other, and held on to her skirts.

She gave the princess her speech again, and then she said, " Now, tell me, did you go into the little room ?"

Even yet the princess would have answered " No;" but when she saw her children standing in the midst of the fire with her, her heart melted away within her.

" Yes !" she cried, " I went in and I saw."

" And how came your hair to be like that ?" said Mother Hildegarde.

" Alas !" said the princess, " I gazed upon that which I should not have gazed upon, and looked into that which I should not have looked into, and one hair touched the water and all was turned to gold."

Then Mother Hildegarde smiled till her face shone as white as the moon. " The truth is better late than not at all," said she : " and if you had but spoken in the first place, I would have freely forgiven you." As she spoke a shower of rain fell down from the sky, and the fire of the fagots was quenched.

And now you can guess what joy there was in the king's castle when every one knew all that had happened, and it was seen how the right thing had come about at last, though it was the toss of a farthing betwixt this and that. Even the king's mother was glad enough when she came to know that it was a real princess whom her son had married after all.

And now listen to what happened in the end.

They gave a great feast, and everybody was asked to come from far and near. Then who should come travelling along with the others, as grand as you please, but the wicked step-mother and step-sister of the princess.

Dear, dear, how they stared and goggled when they saw who the young queen really was, and that the poor princess had married the richest and greatest king in all of the land!

Their hearts were so filled with envy that they swelled and swelled until they burst within them, and they fell down dead, and there was an end of them.

Thus it is that everything turns out right in the long run—that is in fairy tales.

But, after all, if the princess had only told the truth in the first place, she would never have gotten in all this peck of trouble.

And then who knows what Mother Hildegarde would have done for her, for she is a strange woman, is Mother Hildegarde.

Four O'clock .

⊙ K.P.U
*Warm
and
Dusty .*

Bare-necked *Gretchen* combs her hair
At the *Looking-Glass* .
This is *Grease*, and these are *Beads*
She takes to early *Mass* .

Her *Water-Pitcher*, blue and white,
Has got a broken *Nose* ,
And both the *Stockings* that she wears
Are ravelled at the *Toes* .

Which is Best ?

XVI.

THERE was a rich man who lived on a hill, and a poor man who lived down in the valley, and they were brothers, the one was older and the other younger. The one lived in a grand house and the other in a little, rickety, tumbledown hut, and the one was covetous and greedy and the other was kind and merciful. All the same, it was a merry life that the poor brother led of it, for each morning when he took a drink he said, " Thank Heaven for clear water ;" and when the day was bright he said, " Thank Heaven for the warm sun that shines on us all ;" and when it was wet it was, " Thank Heaven for the gentle rain that makes the green grass grow."

One day the poor brother was riding in the forest, and there he met the rich brother, and they jogged along the way together. The one rode upon a poor, old, spavined, white horse, and the other rode upon a fine, prancing steed.

By and by they met an old woman, and it was all that she could do to hobble along the way she was going.

" Dear, good, kind gentlemen," said she, " do help a poor old body with a penny or two, for it is nothing I have in the world, and life sits heavy on old shoulders."

The rich brother was for passing along as though he heard never a word of what she said, but the poor brother had a soft heart, and reined in his horse.

"It is only three farthings that I have in the world," said he; "but such as they are you are welcome to them," and he emptied his purse into her hand.

"You shall not have the worst of the bargain," said the old woman; "here is something that is worth the having," and she gave him a little black stone about as big as a bean. Then off she went with what he had given her.

"See, now," said the rich brother, "that is why you are so poor as hardly to be able to make both ends meet in the world."

"That may be so, or may not be so," said the poor brother; "all the same, mercy is better than greed."

How the elder did laugh at this, to be sure! "Why, look," says he, "here I am riding upon a grand horse with my pockets full of gold and silver money, and there you are astride of a beast that can hardly hobble along the road, and with never a copper bit in your pocket to jingle against another."

Yes; that was all true enough; nevertheless, the younger brother stuck to it that mercy was better than greed, until, at last, the other flew into a mighty huff.

"Very well," says he, "I will wager my horse against yours that I am right, and we will leave it to the first body we meet to settle the point."

Well, that suited the poor brother, and he was agreed to do as the other said.

So by and by they met a grand lord riding along the road with six servants behind him; and would he tell whether mercy or greed were the best for a body in this world?

The rich lord laughed and laughed. "Why," said he, "greed is the best, for if it were otherwise, and I had only what belonged to me, I should never be jogging along through the world with six servants behind me."

So off he rode, and the poor brother had to give up his horse to the other, who had no more use for it than I have for five more fingers. "All the same," says the poor brother, "mercy is better than greed." Goodness! what a rage the rich brother fell into, to be sure! "There is no teaching a simpleton," said he; "nevertheless, I will wager all the money in my purse against your left eye that greed is better than mercy, and we will leave it to the next body we meet, since you are not content with the other."

 aving been thrice adjudged in the wrong, the poor man is left by the rich man blind upon the highway.

That suited the younger brother well enough, and on they jogged until they met a rich merchant driving a donkey loaded with things to sell. And would he judge between them whether mercy or greed were the best for a body?

"Poof!" says the merchant, "what a question to ask! All the world knows that greed is the best. If it were not for taking the cool end of the bargain myself, and leaving the hot end for my neighbor to hold, it is little or nothing that I should have in the world to call my own." And off he went whither he was going.

"There," says the rich brother, "now perhaps you will be satisfied;" and he put out the poor man's left eye.

But no, the other still held that mercy was better than greed; and so they made another wager of all the rich man had in the world against the poor man's right eye.

This time it was a poor ploughman whom they met, and would he tell whether mercy or greed were the best?

"Prut!" said he, "any simpleton can tell that greed is the best, for all the world rides on the poor man's shoulders, and he is able to bear the burden the least of all."

Then the rich man put out the poor man's right eye; "for," says he, "a body deserves to be blind who cannot see the truth when it is as plain as a pikestaff."

But still the poor man stuck to it that mercy was the best. So the rich man rode away and left him in his blindness.

As all was darkness to his eyes, he sat down beside the road at the first place he could find, and that was underneath the gallows where three wicked robbers had been hung. While he sat there two ravens came flying, and lit on the gallows above him. They began talking to one another, and the younger brother heard what they said, for he could understand the speech of the birds of the air and of the beasts of the field, just as little children can, because he was innocent.

And the first raven said to the second raven, "Yonder, below, sits a fellow in blindness, because he held that mercy was better than greed."

And the second raven said to the first, "Yes, that is so, but he might have his sight again if he only knew enough to spread his handkerchief upon the grass, and bathe his eyes in the dew which falls upon it from the gallows above."

And the first raven said to the second, "That is as true as that one and

one make two; but there is more to tell yet, for in his pocket he carries a little black stone with which he may open every door that he touches. Back of the oak-tree yonder is a little door; if he would but enter thereat he would find something below well worth the having."

That was what the two ravens said, and then they flapped their wings and flew away.

As for the younger brother, you can guess how his heart danced at what he heard. He spread his handkerchief on the grass, and by and by,

14

when night came, the dew fell upon it until it was as wet as clothes on the line. He wiped his eyes with it, and when the dew touched the lids they were cured, and he could see as well and better than ever.

By and by the day broke, and he lost no time in finding the door back of the oak-tree. He touched the lock with the little black stone, and the door opened as smoothly as though the hinges were greased. There he found a flight of steps that led down into a pit as dark as a beer vault. Down the steps he went, and on and on until, at last, he came to a great room, the like of which his eyes had never seen before. In the centre of the room was a statue as black as ink; in one hand it held a crystal globe which shone with a clear white light, so that it dazzled one's eyes to look upon it; in the other hand it held a great diamond as big as a hen's egg. Upon the breast of the statue were written these words in letters of gold:

"WHAT THOU DESERVEST
THAT THOU SHALT HAVE."

On three sides of the room sat three statues, and at the feet of each statue stood a heavy chest:

The first statue was of gold, and over its head were written these words:

"WHO CHOOSES HERE TAKES THE BEST THAT THE EARTH HAS TO GIVE."

The second statue was of silver, and over its head was written these words:

"WHO CHOOSES HERE TAKES WHAT THE RICH MAN LOVES."

The third statue was of dull lead, and over its head was written:

"WHO CHOOSES HERE TAKES WHAT HE SHOULD HAVE."

The man touched the chest at the feet of the golden statue with the little black stone. And—click! clack!—up flew the lid, and the chest was full of all kinds of precious stones.

"Pugh!" says the younger brother; "and if this is the best that the world has to give, it is poor enough." And he shut down the lid again.

He touched the chest at the feet of the silver statue with his little black stone, and it was full of gold and silver money.

"Pish!" says he; "and if this is what the rich man loves, why, so do not I." And he shut down the lid again.

Last of all he touched the chest at the feet of the leaden statue.

 he poor man finds that which is the best.

In it was a book, and the letters on it said that whoever read within would know all that was worth the knowing. Beside the book was a pair of spectacles, and whoever set them astride of his nose might see the truth without having to rub the glasses with his pocket-handkerchief. But the best of all in the chest was an apple, and whoever ate of it would be cured of sorrow and sickness.

"Hi!" said the younger brother, "but these are worth the having, for sure and certain." And he put the spectacles upon his nose and the apple and the book in his pocket. Then off he went, and the spectacles showed him the way, although it was as crooked as sin and as black as night.

So by and by he came out into the blessed sunlight again, and at the same place where he had gone in.

Off he went to his own home as fast as his legs could carry him, and you can guess how the rich brother stared when he saw the poor brother back in that town again, with his eyesight as good as ever.

As for the poor brother, he just turned his hand to being a doctor; and there has never been one like him since that day, for not only could he cure all sickness with his apple, but he could cure all sorrow as well. Money and fame poured in on him; and whenever trouble lit on his shoulders he just put on his spectacles and looked into the business, and then opened the book of wisdom and found how to cure it. So his life was as happy as the day was long; and a body can ask for no more than that in this world here below.

One day the rich brother came and knocked at the other's door. "Well, brother," says he, "I am glad to see you getting along so well in the world. Let us let bygones be bygones and live together as we should, for I am sorry for what I did to you."

Well, that suited the younger brother well enough; he bore no malice against the other, for all that had been done had turned out for the best. All the same, he was more sure than ever now that mercy was better than greed.

The elder brother twisted up his face at this, as though the words were sour; all the same, he did not argue the question, for what he had come for was to find why the world had grown so easy with the other all of a sudden. So in he came, and they lit their pipes and sat down by the stove together.

He was a keen blade, was the elder brother, and it was not long before he had screwed the whole story out of the other.

The rich man findeth that which he deserveth.

" Dear, dear, dear !" said he, " I only wish I could find a black pebble like
that one of yours."

" It would do you no good if you had it," said the younger brother, " for
I have brought away all that is worth the having.   All the same, if you want
my black pebble now you are welcome to it."

Did the elder brother want it !   Why, of course he wanted it, and he
could not find words enough to thank the younger.

Off he went, hot-foot, to find the door back of the oak-tree ; " For," said
he to himself, " I will bring something back better worth the having than
a musty book, an old pair of spectacles, and a red apple."

He touched the door with the black stone, and it opened for him just
as it had for the younger brother.

Down the steps he went, and on and on and on, until by and by he came
to the room where the statues were.   There was the black statue holding
out the crystal ball and the diamond as big as a hen's egg, and there sat the
golden statue and the silver statue and the leaden statue, just as they had
sat when the younger brother had been there, only there was nothing in the
chest at the feet of the leaden statue.

The rich brother touched the lock of the chest in front of the
silver statue.   Up flew the lid, and there lay all the gold and silver
money.

" Yes," says he, " that is what the rich man loves, sure enough.   Nevertheless, there may be something else that is better worth the having."   So
he let the money lay where it was.

He touched the chest in front of the golden statue.   Up flew the lid,
and he had to blink and wink his eyes because the precious stones dazzled
them so.

" Yes," says he, " this is the best the world has to give, and there is
no gainsaying that ; all the same, there may be something better worth
the having than these."

So he looked all about the room, until he saw the golden letters on
the breast of the black statue that stood in the middle.   First he read
the words :

" WHAT THOU DESERVEST

THAT THOU SHALT HAVE."

And then he saw the great diamond that the statue held in its left
hand.

" Why," said he, " it is as plain as daylight that I deserve this precious stone, for not being so simple as my brother, and taking what I could find without looking for anything better."

So up he stepped and took the diamond out of the statue's hand.

Crash!—and all was darkness, darker than the darkest midnight; for, as quick as a wink, the black statue let the crystal globe of light fall from its right hand upon the stone floor, where it broke into ten thousand pieces.

And now the rich brother might wander up and wander down, but wander as he chose he could never find his way out of that place again, for the darkness shut him in like a blanket.

So, after all, mercy and temperance were better in the long run than greed and covetousness, in spite of what the great lord and the rich merchant and the poor ploughman had said.

Maybe I have got this story twisted awry in the telling; all the same, Tommy Pfouce says that it is a true-enough story, if you put on your spectacles and look at it from the right side.

Five O'clock.

Pussy-Cat, *Pussy-Cat* what do you dream,
Sleeping out there in the *Sun* ?
The *Red Cow* and *White Cow* are out
in the *Lane* ;
I guess that the *Milking* is done .

Pussy-Cat, *Pussy-Cat* open your *Eyes*,
And see what your *Kitten*'s about ;
She's found a great *Rat-Hole* that's close
to the *Step* ,
And is watching for him to come out.

The Simpleton
and his Little Black Hen.

XVII.

HERE were three brothers left behind when the father died. The two elder, whose names were John and James, were as clever lads as ever ate pease with a fork.

As for the youngest, his name was Caspar, he had no more than enough sense to blow his potatoes when they were hot. Well, when they came to divide things up between themselves, John and James contrived to share all of the good things between them. As for Caspar, "why, the little black hen is enough for him," says John and James, and that was all the butter he got from that churn.

"I'll take the little black hen to the fair," says Caspar, "and there I'll sell her and buy me some eggs. I'll set the eggs under the minister's speckled hen, and then I'll have more chicks. Then I'll buy me more eggs and have more chicks, and then I'll buy me more eggs and have more chicks, and after that I'll be richer than Uncle Henry, who has two cows and a horse, and will marry my sweetheart into the bargain." So off he went to the fair with the black hen under his arm, as he had promised himself to do.

"There goes a goose to the plucking," says John and James, and then they turned no hairs grey by thinking any more about the case.

As for him, why, he went on and on until he came to the inn over the hill not far from the town, the host of which was no better than he should be, and that was the long and the short of it.

" Where do you go with the little black hen, Caspar?" says he.

" Oh," says Caspar, " I take it to the fair to sell it and buy me some eggs.   I'll set the eggs under the minister's speckled hen, and then I'll have more chicks.   Then I'll buy me more eggs and have more chicks, and then I'll buy me more eggs and have more chicks, and after that I'll be richer than Uncle Henry, who has two cows and a horse, and will marry my sweetheart into the bargain."

Prut! And why should Caspar take his hen to the fair?   That was what the landlord said.   It was a silly thing to tramp to the river for water before the well was dry at home.   Why, the landlord had a friend over yonder who would give ten pennies to one that he could get at the fair for his black hen.   Now, had Caspar ever heard tell of the little old gentleman who lived in the old willow-tree over yonder?

No, Caspar had never heard tell of him in all of his life.   And there was no wonder in that, for no more had anybody else, and the landlord was only up to a bit of a trick to get the little black hen for himself.

But the landlord sucked in his lips—" tsch "—so! Well, that was a pity, for the little old gentleman had said, time and time again, that he would give a whole bagful of gold and silver money for just such a little black hen as the one that Caspar carried under his arm.

Dear, dear! How Caspar's eyes did open at this, to be sure.   Off he started for the willow-tree.   " Here's the little black hen," said he, " and I'll sell her for a bagful of gold and silver money."   But nobody answered him ; and you may be sure of that, for there was nobody there.

" Well," says Caspar, " I'll just tie the hen to the tree here, and you may pay me to-morrow."   So he did as he had said, and off he marched. Then came the landlord and took the hen off home and had it for his supper ; and there was an end of that business.

An end of that business?   No, no ; stop a bit, for we will not drive too fast down the hill.   Listen: there was a wicked robber who had hidden a bag of gold and silver money in that very tree ; but of that neither Caspar nor the landlord knew any more than the chick in the shell.

" Hi!" says Caspar, " it is the wise man who gets along in the world." But there he was wrong for once in his life, Tommy Pfouce tells me.

" And did you sell your hen?" says John and James.

" Oh, yes ; Caspar had done that.

And what had he got for it?

Oh, just a bag of gold and silver money, that was all.   He would show

 he cunning landlord telleth
Caspar where to take his hen to sell it
for a good price.

it to them to-morrow, for he was to go and get it then from the old gentleman who lived in the willow-tree over yonder by the inn over the hill.

When John and James heard that they saw as plain as the nose on your face that Caspar had been bitten by the *fool dog*.

But Caspar never bothered his head about that; off he went the next day as grand as you please. Up he marched to the willow-tree, but never a soul did he find there; for why, there was nobody.

Rap! tap! tap! He knocked upon the tree as civil as a beggar at the kitchen door, but nobody said, " Come in !"

" Look," says he, " we will have no dilly-dallying; I want my money and I will have it," and he fetched a kick at the tree that made the bark fly. But he might as well have kicked my grandfather's bedpost for all the good he had of it. " Oh, very well !" says he, and off he marched and brought the axe that stood back of the stable door.

Hui! how the chips flew! for Caspar was bound to get to the bottom of the business. So by and by the tree lay on the ground, and there was the bag of gold and silver money that the wicked robber had hidden. " So !" says Caspar, " better late than never !" and off he marched with it.

By and by whom should he meet but John and James. Bless me, how they stared ! And did Caspar get all of that money for one little black hen ?

Oh, yes; that he had.

And where did he get it ?

Oh ! the little old man in the willow-tree had paid it to him.

So, good ! that was a fine thing, and it should be share and share alike among brothers; that was what John and James said, and Caspar did not say " No ;" so down they all sat on the grass and began counting it out.

" This is mine," said John.

" And this is mine," said James.

" And this is mine," said John.

" And this is mine," said James.

" And where is mine ?" says Caspar. But neither of the others thought of him because he was so simple.

Just then who should come along but the rogue of a landlord. " Hi ! and where did you get all that ?" says he.

Caspar findeth money in the willow-tree.

"Oh," says Caspar, "the little old man in the willow-tree paid it to me for my little black hen."

Yes, yes, the landlord knew how much of that cake to eat. He was not to have the wool pulled over his eyes so easily. See, now, he knew very well that thieving had been done, and he would have them all up before the master mayor for it. So the upshot of the matter was that they had to take him in to share with them.

"This is mine," says the landlord.

"And this is mine," says John.

"And this is mine," says James.

"And where do I come in?" says poor Caspar. But nobody thought of him because he was so simple.

Just then came along a company of soldiers—tramp! tramp! tramp!—and there they found them all sharing the money between them, except Caspar.

"Hi!" says the captain, "here are a lot of thieves, and no mistake!" and off he marched them to the king's house, which was finer than any in our town, and as big as a church into the bargain.

And how had they come by all that money? that was what the king would like to know.

As for the three rogues, they sang a different tune now than they had whistled before.

"It's none of mine, it's his," said the landlord, and he pointed to John.

"It's none of mine, it's his," said John, and he pointed to James.

"It's none of mine, it's his," said James, and he pointed to Caspar.

"And how did you get it?" says the king.

"Oh!" says Caspar, "the little old man in the willow-tree gave it to me for my little black hen;" and then he told the whole story without missing a single grain.

Beside the king sat the princess, who was so serious and solemn that she had never laughed once in all her life. So the king had said, time and time again, that whoever should make her laugh should have her for his wife. Now, when she heard Caspar's story, and how he came in behind all the rest, so that he always had the pinching, like the tail of our cat in the crack of the door, she laughed like everything, for she could not help it. So there was the fat in the fire, for Caspar was not much to look at, and that was the truth. Dear, dear, what a stew the king was in, for he had no notion for Caspar as a son-in-law. So he began to think about striking a bargain. "Come," says he to Caspar, "how much will you take to give up the princess instead of marrying her?"

Well, Caspar did not know how much a princess was worth. So he scratched his head and scratched his head, and by and by he said that he would be willing to take ten dollars and let the princess go.

At this the king boiled over into a mighty fume, like water into the fire. What! did Caspar think that ten dollars was a fit price for a princess!

Oh, Caspar had never done any business of this kind before. He had a sweetheart of his own at home, and if ten dollars was too much for the princess he would be willing to take five.

Sakes alive! what a rage the king was in! Why, I would not have

The three share the money amongst them.

stood in Caspar's shoes just then—no, not for a hundred dollars. The king would have had him whipped right away, only just then he had some other business on hand. So he paid Caspar his five dollars, and told him that if he would come back the next day he should have all that his back could carry—meaning a whipping.

As for Caspar and his brothers and the rogue of a landlord, they thought that the king was talking about dollars. So when they had left the king's house and had come out into the road again, the three rogues began to talk as smooth and as soft as though their words were buttered.

See, now, what did Caspar want with all that the king had promised him; that was what they said. If he would let them have it, they would give him all of their share of the money he had found in the willow-tree.

"Ah, yes," says Caspar, "I am willing to do that. For," says he to

15

himself, "an apple in the pocket is worth three on the tree." And there he was right for once in his life.

Well, the next day back they all tramped to the king's house again to get what had been promised to Caspar.

So! Caspar had come back for the rest, had he?

Oh, yes, he had come back again; but the lord king must know that he had sold all that had been promised to him to these three lads for their share of the money he had found in the willow-tree over yonder.

"Yes," says the landlord, "one part of what has been promised is mine."

"And one part of it is mine," says John.

"Stop a bit, brother," says James; "remember, one part of it is mine too."

At this the king could not help laughing, and that broke the back of his anger.

First of all he sent the landlord for his share, and if his back did not smart after he had it, why, it was not the fault of those who gave it to him. By and by he came back again, but he said nothing to the others of what had been given to him; but all the same he grinned as though he had been eating sour gooseberries. Then John went, and last of all James, and what they got satisfied them, I can tell you.

After that the king told Caspar that he might go into the other room and fill his pockets with money for what he had given up to the others; so he had the cool end of that bargain, and did not burn his fingers after all.

But the three rogues were not satisfied with this. No, indeed! Caspar should have his share of the smarting, see if he shouldn't! So back they went to the king's house one fine day, and said that Caspar had been talking about the lord king, and had said that he was no better than an old hunks. At this the king was awfully angry. And so off he sent the others to fetch Caspar along so that he might settle the score with him.

When the three came home, there was Caspar lying on a bench in the sun, for he could take the world easy now, because he was so rich.

"Come along, Caspar," said they, "the king wants to see you over at his house yonder."

Yes, yes, but there was too much hurrying in this business, for it was over-quick cooking that burned the broth. If Caspar was to go to the king's house he would go in fitting style, so they would just have to wait till he found a horse, for he was not going to jog it afoot; that was what Caspar said.

 he three rogues lend Caspar sundry things so that he may go to the king's castle.

"Yes," says the landlord, "but sooner than you should lose time in the waiting, I will lend you my fine dapple-grey."

But where was the bridle to come from? Caspar would have them know that he was not going to ride a horse to the king's house without a good bridle over the nag's ears.

Oh, John would lend him the new bridle that he bought in the town last week; so that was soon settled.

But how about the saddle?—that was what Caspar wanted to know— yes, how about the saddle? Did they think that he was going to ride up to the king's house with his heels thumping against the horse's ribs as though he were no better than a ploughman?

Oh, James would lend him a saddle if that was all he wanted.

So off they went, all four of them, to the king's house.

There was the king, walking up and down, and fussing and fuming with anger till he was all of a heat.

"See, now," says he, as soon as he saw Caspar, "what did you call me an old hunks for?"

"I didn't call you an old hunks," said Caspar.

"Yes, you did," said the king.

"No, I didn't," said Caspar.

"Yes, you did," said the king, "for these three lads told me so."

"Prut!" said Caspar, "who would believe what they say? Why, they would just as lief tell you that this horse and saddle and bridle belong to them."

"And so they do!" bawled the three rogues.

"See there, now," said Caspar.

The king scratched his head, for here was a tangled knot, for certain. "Yes, yes," said he, "these fellows are fooling either Caspar or me, and we are both in the same tub, for the matter of that. Take them away and whip them!" So it was done as he said, and that was all that they got for their trouble.

Wit and Luck are not always hatched in the same nest, says Tommy Pfouce, and maybe he is right about it, for Caspar married his sweetheart, and if she did not keep his money for him, and himself out of trouble, she would not have been worth speaking of, and I, for one, would never have told this story.

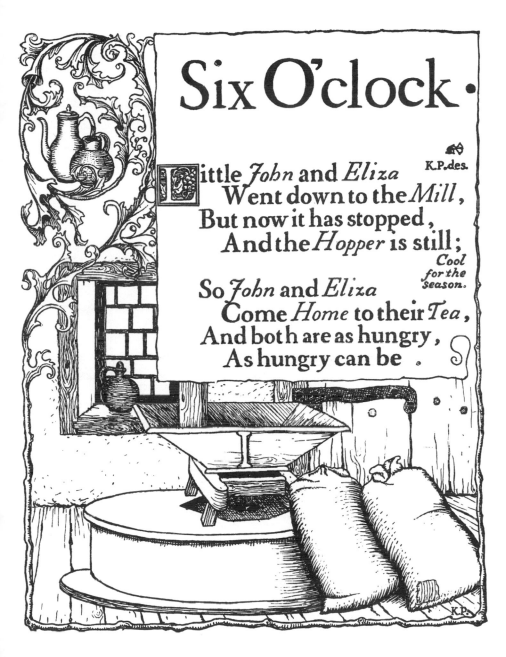

Six O'clock .

K.P.des.

Little *John* and *Eliza*
   Went down to the *Mill*,
But now it has stopped,
   And the *Hopper* is still;

Cool
for the
season.

So *John* and *Eliza*
   Come *Home* to their *Tea*,
And both are as hungry,
   As hungry can be .

K.P.

The Swan Maiden.

XVIII.

ONCE there was a king who had a pear-tree which bore four-and-twenty golden pears. Every day he went into the garden and counted them to see that none were missing.

But, one morning, he found that a pear had been taken during the night, and thereat he was troubled and vexed to the heart, for the pear-tree was as dear to him as the apple of his eye. Now, the king had three sons, and so he called the eldest prince to him.

"See," said he, "if you will watch my pear-tree to-night, and will find me the thief who stole the pear, you shall have half of my kingdom now, and the whole of it when I am gone."

You can guess how the prince was tickled at this: oh, yes, he would watch the tree, and if the thief should come he should not get away again as easily.

Well, that night he sat down beside the tree, with his gun across his knees, to wait for the coming of the thief.

He waited and waited, and still he saw not so much as a thread or a hair. But about the middle of the night there came the very prettiest music that his ears had ever heard, and before he knew what he was about he was asleep and snoring until the little leaves shook upon the tree.

When the morning came and he awoke, another pear was gone, and he could tell no more about it than the man in the moon.

The next night the second son set out to watch the pear-tree. But he fared no better than the first. About midnight came the music, and in a little while he was snoring till the stones rattled. When the morning came another pear was gone, and he had no more to tell about it than his brother.

The third night it was the turn of the youngest son, and he was more clever than the others, for, when the evening came, he stuffed his ears full of wax, so that he was as deaf as a post. About midnight, when the music came, he heard nothing of it, and so he stayed wide awake. After the music had ended he took the wax out of his ears, so that he might listen for the coming of the thief. Presently there was a loud clapping and rattling, and a white swan flew overhead and lit in the pear-tree above him. It began picking at one of the pears, and then the prince raised his gun to shoot at it. But when he looked along the barrel it was not a swan that he saw up in the pear-tree, but the prettiest girl that he had ever looked upon.

"Don't shoot me, king's son! Don't shoot me!" cried she.

But the prince had no thought of shooting her, for he had never seen such a beautiful maiden in all of his days. "Very well," said he, "I will not shoot, but, if I spare your life, will you promise to be my sweetheart and to marry me?"

"That may be as may be," said the Swan Maiden. "For listen! I serve the witch with three eyes. She lives on the glass hill that lies beyond the seven high mountains, the seven deep valleys, and the seven wide rivers; are you man enough to go that far?"

"Oh, yes," said the prince, "I am man enough for that and more too."

"That is good," said the Swan Maiden, and thereupon she jumped down from the pear-tree to the earth. Then she became a swan again, and bade the king's son to mount upon her back at the roots of her wings. When he had done as she had told him, she sprang into the air and flew away, bearing him with her.

On flew the swan, and on and on, until, by and by, she said, "What do you see, king's son?"

"I see the grey sky above me and the dark earth below me, but nothing else," said he.

After that they flew on and on again, until, at last, the Swan Maiden said, "What do you see now, king's son?"

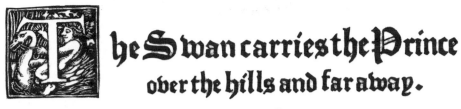

The Swan carries the Prince over the hills and far away.

HP.

"I see the grey sky above me and the dark earth below me, but nothing else," said he.

So once more they flew on until the Swan Maiden said, for the third time, "And what do you see by now, king's son?"

But this time the prince said, "I see the grey sky above me and the dark earth below me, and over yonder is a glass hill, and on the hill is a house that shines like fire."

"That is where the witch with three eyes lives," said the Swan Maiden; "and now listen: when she asks you what it is that you came for, ask her to give you the one who draws the water and builds the fire; for that is myself."

So, when they had come to the top of the hill of glass, the king's son stepped down to the ground, and the swan flew over the roof.

Rap! tap! tap! he knocked at the door, and the old witch herself came and opened it.

"And what do you want here?" said she.

"I want the one who draws the water and builds the fire," said the prince.

At this the old witch scowled until her eyebrows met.

"Very well," said she, "you shall have what you want if you can clean my stables to-morrow between the rise and the set of the sun. But I tell you plainly, if you fail in the doing, you shall be torn to pieces body and bones."

But the prince was not to be scared away with empty words. So the next morning the old witch came and took him to the stables where he was to do his task. There stood more than a hundred cattle, and the stable had not been cleaned for at least ten long years.

"There is your work," said the old witch, and then she left him.

Well, the king's son set to work with fork and broom and might and main, but—prut!—he might as well have tried to bale out the great ocean with a bucket.

At noontide who should come to the stable but the pretty Swan Maiden herself.

"When one is tired, one should rest for a while," said she; "come and lay your head in my lap."

The prince was glad enough to do as she said, for nothing was to be gained by working at that task. So he laid his head in her lap, and she combed his hair with a golden comb till he fell fast asleep. When he awoke the Swan Maiden was gone, the sun was setting, and the stable was as clean as a plate. Presently he heard the old witch coming, so up he

jumped and began clearing away a straw here and a speck there, just as though he were finishing the work.

"You never did this by yourself!" said the old witch, and her brows grew as black as a thunder-storm.

"That may be so, and that may not be so," said the king's son, "but you lent no hand to help; so now may I have the one who builds the fire and draws the water?"

At this the old witch shook her head. "No," said she, "there is more to be done yet before you can have what you ask for. If you can thatch the roof of the stable with bird feathers, no two of which shall be of the same color, and can do it between the rise and the set of sun to-morrow, then you shall have your sweetheart and welcome. But if you fail your bones shall be ground as fine as malt in the mill."

Very well; that suited the king's son well enough. So at sunrise he arose and went into the fields with his gun; but if there were birds to be shot, it was few of them that he saw; for at noontide he had but two, and they were both of a color. At that time who should come to him but the Swan Maiden.

"One should not tramp and tramp all day with never a bit of rest," said she; "come hither and lay your head in my lap for a while."

The prince did as she bade him, and the maiden again combed his hair with a golden comb until he fell asleep. When he awoke the sun was setting, and his work was done. He heard the old witch coming, so up he jumped to the roof of the stable and began laying a feather here and a feather there, for all the world as though he were just finishing his task.

"You never did that work alone," said the old witch.

"That may be so, and that may not be so," said the prince; "all the same, it was none of your doing. So now may I have the one who draws the water and builds the fire?"

But the witch shook her head. "No," said she, "there is still another task to do before that. Over yonder is a fir-tree; on the tree is a crow's nest, and in the nest are three eggs. If you can harry that nest to-morrow between the rising and the setting of the sun, neither breaking nor leaving a single egg, you shall have that for which you ask."

Very well; that suited the prince. The next morning at the rising of the sun he started off to find the fir-tree, and there was no trouble in the finding I can tell you, for it was more than a hundred feet high, and as smooth as glass from root to tip. As for climbing it, he might as well have

The Swan-Maiden helps ỹ young Prince.

tried to climb a moonbeam, for in spite of all his trying he did nothing but slip and slip. By and by came the Swan Maiden as she had come before.

"Do you climb the fir-tree?" said she.

"None too well," said the king's son.

"Then I may help you in a hard task," said she.

She let down the braids of her golden hair, so that it hung down all about her and upon the ground, and then she began singing to the wind. She sang and sang, and by and by the wind began to blow, and, catching up the maiden's hair, carried it to the top of the fir-tree, and there tied it to the branches. Then the prince climbed the hair and so reached the nest. There were the three eggs; he gathered them, and then he came down as he had gone up. After that the wind came again and loosed the maiden's hair from the branches, and she bound it up as it was before.

"Now, listen," said she to the prince: "when the old witch asks you for the three crow's eggs which you have gathered, tell her that they belong to the one who found them. She will not be able to take them from you, and they are worth something, I can tell you."

At sunset the old witch came hobbling along, and there sat the prince at the foot of the fir-tree. "Have you gathered the crow's eggs?" said she.

"Yes," said the prince, "here they are in my handkerchief. And now may I have the one who draws the water and builds the fire?"

"Yes," said the old witch, "you may have her; only give me my crow's eggs."

"No," said the prince, "the crow's eggs are none of yours, for they belong to him who gathered them."

When the old witch found that she was not to get her crow's eggs in that way, she tried another, and began using words as sweet as honey. Come, come, there should be no hard feeling between them. The prince had served her faithfully, and before he went home with what he had come for he should have a good supper, for it is ill to travel on an empty stomach.

So she brought the prince into the house, and then she left him while she went to put the pot on the fire, and to sharpen the bread knife on the stone door-step.

While the prince sat waiting for the witch, there came a tap at the door, and whom should it be but the pretty Swan Maiden.

"Come," said she, "and bring the three eggs with you, for the knife

Ⓣ he witch and ẏ woman of honey & meal ·

that the old witch is sharpening is for you, and so is the great pot on the
fire, for she means to pick your bones in the morning."

She led the prince down into the kitchen; there they made a figure
out of honey and barley-meal, so that it was all soft and sticky; then the
maiden dressed the figure in her own clothes and set it in the chimney-
corner by the fire.

After that was done, she became a swan again, and, taking the prince
upon her back, she flew away, over hill and over dale.

As for the old witch, she sat on the stone door-step, sharpening her
knife. By and by she came in, and, look as she might, there was no prince
to be found.

Then if anybody was ever in a rage it was the old witch; off she went,
storming and fuming, until she came to the kitchen. There sat the woman
of honey and barley-meal beside the fire, dressed in the maiden's clothes,
and the old woman thought that it was the girl herself. "Where is your
sweetheart?" said she; but to this the woman of honey and barley-meal
answered never a word.

"How now! are you dumb?" cried the old witch; "I will see whether I cannot bring speech to your lips." She raised her hand—*slap!*—she struck, and so hard was the blow that her hand stuck fast to the honey and barley-meal. "What!" cried she, "will you hold me?"—*slap!*—she struck with the other hand, and it too stuck fast. So there she was, and, for all that I know, she is sticking to the woman of honey and barley-meal to this day.

As for the Swan Maiden and the prince, they flew over the seven high mountains, the seven deep valleys, and the seven wide rivers, until they came near to the prince's home again. The Swan Maiden lit in a great wide field, and there she told the prince to break open one of the crow's eggs. The prince did as she bade him, and what should he find but the most beautiful little palace, all of pure gold and silver. He set the palace on the ground, and it grew and grew and grew until it covered as much ground as seven large barns. Then the Swan Maiden told him to break another egg, and he did as she said, and what should come out of it but such great herds of cows and sheep that they covered the meadow far and near. The Swan Maiden told him to break the third egg, and out of it came scores and scores of servants all dressed in gold-and-silver livery.

That morning, when the king looked out of his bedroom window, there stood the splendid castle of silver and gold. Then he called all of his people together, and they rode over to see what it meant. On the way they met such herds of fat sheep and cattle that the king had never seen the like in all of his life before; and when he came to the fine castle, there were two rows of servants dressed in clothes of silver and gold, ready to meet him. But when he came to the door of the castle, there stood the prince himself. Then there was joy and rejoicing, you may be sure! only the two elder brothers looked down in the mouth, for since the young prince had found the thief who stole the golden pears, their father's kingdom was not for them. But the prince soon set their minds at rest on that score, for he had enough and more than enough of his own.

After that the prince and the Swan Maiden were married, and a grand wedding they had of it, with music of fiddles and kettle-drums, and plenty to eat and to drink. I, too, was there; but all of the good red wine ran down over my tucker, so that not a drop of it passed my lips, and I had to come away empty.

And that is all.

Seven O'clock .

The *Work* is over for the *Day*;
The *Sky* is pale, and far away
The *Village Children* shout at *Play* .

K. P. del .
Grows
cool.

Now from his *Hole* the *Toad* comes out,
And blinks his *Eyes*, and hops about,
And likes the pleasant *Air*, no doubt.

The Three Little Pigs *and the* OGRE.

XIX.

HERE were three nice, fat little pigs. The first was small, the second was smaller, and the third was the smallest of all. And these three little pigs thought of going out into the woods to gather acorns, for there were better acorns there than here.

"There's a great ogre who lives over yonder in the woods," says the barn-yard cock.

"And he will eat you up, body and bones," says the speckled hen.

"And there will be an end of you," says the black drake.

"If folks only knew what was good for them, they would stay at home and make the best of what they had there," said the old grey goose who laid eggs under the barn, and who had never gone out into the world or had had a peep of it beyond the garden gate.

But no; the little pigs would go out into the world, whether or no; "for," said they, "if we stay at home because folks shake their heads, we will never get the best acorns that are to be had;" and there was more than one barleycorn of truth in that chaff, I can tell you.

So out into the woods they went.

They hunted for acorns here and they hunted for acorns there, and by and by whom should the smallest of all the little pigs meet but the great, wicked ogre himself.

" Aha!" says the great, wicked ogre, " it is a nice, plump little pig that I have been wanting for my supper this many a day past. So you may just come along with me now."

" Oh, Master Ogre," squeaked the smallest of the little pigs in the smallest of voices—" oh, Master Ogre, don't eat me! There's a bigger pig back of me, and he will be along presently."

So the ogre let the smallest of the little pigs go, for he would rather have a larger pig if he could get it.

By and by came the second little pig. " Aha!" says the great, wicked ogre, " I have been wanting just such a little pig as you for my supper for this many a day past. So you may just come along with me now."

" Oh, Master Ogre," said the middle-sized pig, in his middle-sized voice, " don't take me for your supper; there's a bigger pig than I am coming along presently. Just wait for him."

Well, the ogre was satisfied to do that; so he waited, and by and by, sure enough, came the largest of the little pigs.

" And now," says the great, wicked ogre, " I will wait no longer, for you are just the pig I want for my supper, and so you may march along with me."

But the largest of the little pigs had his wits about him, I can tell you. " Oh, very well," says he; " if I am the shoe that fits there is no use in hunting for another; only, have you a roasted apple to put in my mouth when I am cooked? for no one ever heard of a little pig brought on the table without a roast apple in its mouth."

No; the ogre had no roasted apple.

Dear, dear! that was a great pity. If he would wait for a little while, the largest of the little pigs would run home and fetch one, and then things would be as they should.

Yes, the ogre was satisfied with that. So off ran the little pig, and the ogre sat down on a stone and waited for him.

Well, he waited and he waited and he waited and he waited, but not a tip of a hair of the little pig did he see that day, as you can guess without my telling you.

And Tommy Pfouce tells me that the great, wicked ogre is not the only one who has gone without either pig or roast apple, because when he could get the one he would not take it without the other.

" And now," says the cock and the speckled hen and the black drake and the old grey goose who laid her eggs under the barn, and had never

he Ogre meets the three little pigs in the forest, whither they went to gather acorns.

been out into the world beyond the garden-gate—"and now perhaps you will run out into the world and among ogres no more. Are there not good enough acorns at home?

Perhaps there were; but that was not what the three little pigs thought. "See, now," said the smallest of the three little pigs, "if one is afraid of the water, one will never catch any fish. I, for one, am going out into the woods to get a few acorns."

So out into the woods he went, and there he found all of the acorns that he wanted. But, on his way home, whom should he meet but the great, wicked ogre.

"Aha!" says the ogre, "and is that you?"

Oh, yes, it was nobody else; but had the ogre come across three fellows tramping about in the woods down yonder?

No, the ogre had met nobody in the woods that day.

"Dear, dear," says the smallest little pig, "but that is a pity, for those three fellows were three wicked robbers, and they have just hidden a meal-bag full of money in that hole up in the tree yonder."

You can guess how the ogre pricked up his ears at this, and how he stared till his eyes were as big as saucers.

"Just wait," said he to the smallest little pig, "and I will be down again in a minute." So he laid his jacket to one side and up the tree he climbed, for he wanted to find that bag of money, and he meant to have it.

"Do you find the hole?" says the smallest of the little pigs.

Yes; the ogre had found the hole.

"And do you find the money?" says the smallest of the little pigs.

No; the ogre could find no money.

"Then good-bye," says the smallest of the little pigs, and off he trotted home, leaving the ogre to climb down the tree again as he chose.

"And now, at least, you will go out into the woods no more," says the cock, the speckled hen, the black drake, and the grey goose.

Oh, well, there was no telling what the three little pigs would do yet, they would have to wait and see.

One day it was the middle-sized little pig who would go out into the woods, for he also had a mind to taste the acorns there.

So out into the woods the middle-sized little pig went, and there he had all the acorns that he wanted.

But by and by the ogre came along. "Aha!" says he. "Now I have you for sure and certain."

he Ogre climbs the tree for the money that he believes to ❖ be there.

But the middle-sized little pig just stood and looked at a great rock just in front of him, with all of his might and main. "Sh-h-h-h-h-h!" says he, "I am not to be talked to or bothered now!"

Hoity-toity! Here was a pretty song, to be sure! And why was the middle-sized pig not to be talked to? That was what the ogre should like to know.

Oh, the middle-sized little pig was looking at what was going on under the great rock yonder, for he could see the little folk brewing more beer than thirty-seven men could drink.

So! Why, the ogre would like to see that for himself.

"Very well," says the middle-sized little pig, "there is nothing easier than to learn that trick! just take a handful of leaves from yonder bush and rub them over your eyes, and then shut them tight and count fifty."

Well, the ogre would have a try at that. So he gathered a handful of the leaves and rubbed them over his eyes, just as the middle-sized pig had said.

"And now are you ready?" said the middle-sized little pig.

Yes; the ogre was ready.

"Then shut your eyes and count," said the middle-sized little pig.

So the ogre shut them as tightly as he could and began to count, "One, two, three, four, five," and so on; and while he was counting, why, the little pig was running away home again.

By and by the ogre bawled out "*Fifty ! ! !*" and opened his eyes, for he was done. Then he saw not more, but less, than he had seen before, for the little pig was not there.

And now it was the largest of the three little pigs who began to talk about going out into the woods to look for acorns.

"You had better stay at home and take things as they come. The crock that goes often to the well gets broken at last;" that was what the cock, the speckled hen, the black drake, and the grey goose said; and they thought themselves very wise to talk as they did.

But no; the little pig wanted to go out into the woods, and into the woods the little pig would go, ogre or no ogre.

After he had eaten all of the acorns that he wanted he began to think of going home again, but just then the ogre came stumping along. "A'ha!" says he, "we have met again, have we?"

"Yes," said the largest of the three little pigs, "we have. And I want

The Ogre shuts his eyes and counts fifty

to say that I could find no roast apple at home, and so I did not come back again."

Yes, yes, that was all very fine; but they should have a settling of old scores now. The largest of the three little pigs might just come along home with the ogre, and to-morrow he should be made into sausages; for there was to be no trickery this time, so there was an end of the matter.

Come, come! the ogre must not be too testy. There was such a thing as having too much pepper in the pudding—that was what the largest of the little pigs said. If it were sausages that the ogre was after, maybe the pig could help him. Over home at the farm yonder was a storehouse filled with more sausages and good things than two men could count. There was a window where the ogre could just squeeze through. Only he must promise to eat what he wanted and to carry nothing away with him.

Well, the ogre promised to eat all he wanted in the storehouse, and then off they went together.

By and by they came to the storehouse at the farm, and there, sure enough, was a window, and it was *just* large enough for the ogre to squeeze through without a button to spare in the size.

Dear, dear! how the ogre did stuff himself with the sausages and puddings and other good things in the storehouse.

By and by the little pig bawled out as loud as he could, "*Have you had enough yet?*"

"Hush-sh-sh-sh-sh-sh-sh!" says the ogre, "don't talk so loud, or you'll be rousing the folks and having them about our ears like a hive of bees."

"No," bawled the little pig, louder than before, "but tell me, *have* you had enough yet?"

"Yes, yes," says the ogre, "I have had almost enough, only be still about it!"

"Very well!" bawled the little pig, as loud as he could, "if you have had enough, and if you have eaten all of the sausages and all of the puddings you can stuff, it is about time that you were going, for here comes the farmer and two of his men to see what all the stir is about."

And, sure enough, the farmer and his men were coming as fast as they could lay foot to the ground.

But when the ogre heard them coming, he felt sure that it was time that he was getting away home again, and so he tried to get out of the same window that he had gotten in a little while before. But he had stuffed himself with so much of the good things that he had swelled like everything, and there he stuck in the storehouse window like a cork in a bottle, and could budge neither one way nor the other; and that was a pretty pickle to be in.

"Oho!" says the farmer, "you were after my sausages and my puddings, were you? Then you will come no more."

And that was so; for when the farmer and his men were done with the ogre he never went into the woods again, for he could not.

As for the three little pigs, they trotted away into the woods every day of their lives, for there was nobody nowadays to stop them from gathering all the acorns that they wanted.

The Ogre sticks fast in the window. 2

Now, don't you believe folks when they say that this is *all* stuff and nonsense that I have been telling you; for if you turn it upside down and look in the bottom of it you will find that there is more than one grain of truth there; that is if you care to scratch among the chaff for it. And that is the end of this story.

Eight O'clock·

The little *Bats* fly
About in the *Sky*,
And the *Kobold*'s wide awake.
The great black *Trees*
Are stirred in the *Breeze*,
And a curious *Sound* they make.

The *Plays* are done,
And the *Prayers* are said,
And the *Children* are snugly
Tucked in *Bed*.

Cooler winds.

K.P.

XX.

THE wind of heaven blows the chips and the straws to-gether.

There was a fiddler, a tinker, and a shoemaker jogging along the road, but whatever brought them in company is more than I am able to tell you. All the same, there they were, and, after all, that is the kernel of the nut.

The fiddler was as merry a little toad as ever a body could wish to see; as for the tinker and the shoemaker, why, they were as sour as bad beer.

Well, they plodded along, all three of them, until by and by they came to a cross-road, and there sat an old body begging; "Dear, good, kind gentlemen, give a poor old woman a penny or two. Do now."

"Pooh!" says the tinker and the shoemaker, and off they walked with their noses in the air as though they were hunting for flies up yonder.

As for the fiddler, he had another kind of a heart under his jacket; "Come," says he, "we are all chicks in the same puddle." So he gave the old woman all that he had, which was only two pennies.

"A cake for a pie," said the old woman; "and what would you like to have in the way of a wish? for all that you have to do is to ask, and it shall be granted."

This old woman was a famous wise one, I can tell you, though the fiddler knew nothing of that.

The fiddler thought and thought, but there was little that he had to wish for; nevertheless, since they were in the way of asking and giving, and seeing that his body was none of the largest, he would like to have it for a wish that whenever he should say, " Rub-a-dub-dub," the staff in his hand would up and fight for him.

So! and was that all that he wanted? Then it was granted and welcome, for it was little enough.

After that they said, " Good-morning," and the fiddler went one way and the old woman the other.

So the three companions plodded along together until, by and by, night came, and there they were, in a deep forest, with branches over their heads and not a peep out from under the trees, no matter where they might look; and that was not the pleasantest thing for them, I can tell you. But by and by they saw a light, and then the world looked up with them again. So they hurried along more rapidly, and presently came to the house where the light was shining; and, after all, it was not much to look at.

Rap, tap, tap! they knocked at the door, but nobody came; so they opened it for themselves and walked in.

No; there was no one at home, but there was a table spread with a smoking hot supper, and places for three. Down they sat without waiting for the bidding, for their hunger was as sharp as vinegar.

Well, they ate and they ate and they ate until they could eat no more, and then they turned around and roasted their toes at the warm fire.

That was all very well and good, but by and by all the wood was burned, and then who was to go out into the dark forest and fetch another armful?

" Not I," says the tinker.

" Not I," says the shoemaker.

And so it fell to the lot of the fiddler, and off he went.

But many a one spills the milk-mug to save the water-jug, and so it was with the tinker and the shoemaker; for, while they sat warming their shins at the fire and rubbing their hands over their knees, in walked an ugly little troll no taller than a yard-stick, but with a head as big as a

 he Fiddler gives the old wo = man all that he has in his purse .
❰ ❱ ⦂ ❲ ❳

17

cabbage, and a good stout cudgel twice as long as himself in his hand; as for his eyes, why, they were as big as your mother's teacups.

" I want something to eat," says he.

" You'll get nothing here," says the tinker and the shoemaker.

" Yes, but I will," says the little manikin.

" No, but you will not," says the tinker and the shoemaker.

" That we'll see," says the manikin; whereupon he spat upon his hands, snatched up his club, and, without more ado, fell upon the tinker and the shoemaker, and began beating them with all his might and main. My goodness, you should have seen how they hopped about like two peas on a drum-head, and you should have heard how they bellowed and bawled for mercy! But the little ugly troll never stopped until he was too tired to drub them any more; then he went away whither he had come, and all that the two fellows could do was to rub the places that smarted the most.

By and by in came the fiddler with his armful of wood, but never a word did the tinker and the shoemaker say, for they had no notion of telling how such a little manikin had dusted the coats of two great hulking fellows like themselves; only the next day they thought that it would be well to rest where they were, for their bones were too sore to be jogging. So they lolled around the house all day, and found everything that they wanted to eat in the cupboards.

After supper there was more wood to be brought in from the forest, and this time it was the tinker and the shoemaker who went to fetch it, for they had settled it between them that the fiddler was to have a taste of the same broth that they had supped.

Sure enough, by and by in came the ugly little troll with the great long cudgel.

" I want something to eat," says he.

" There it is, brother," says the fiddler, " help yourself."

" It is you who shall wait on me," says the ugly little troll.

" Tut!" says the fiddler, " how you talk, neighbor; have you no hands of your own?"

" You shall wait on me," says the manikin.

" I shall not," says the fiddler.

" That we will see," says the manikin, and he spat upon his hands and gripped his cudgel.

" Hi!" says the fiddler, " and is that the game you are playing? Then, rub-a-dub-dub!" says he.

The Fiddler gives the word & the staff falls to drubbing the Dwarf as he deserves.

Pop!—up jumps his staff from the corner where he had stood it, and then you should have seen the dust fly! This time it was the manikin who hopped over the chairs and begged and bawled for mercy. As for the fiddler, he stood by with his hands in his pockets and whistled. By and by the manikin found the door, and out he jumped with the fiddler at his heels. But the fiddler was not quick enough, for, before he could catch him, the little troll popped into a great hole in the ground like a frog into a well; and there was an end to that business.

After a while the tinker and the shoemaker came back from the forest with their load of wood, and then how the fiddler did laugh at them, for he saw very well how the wind had been blowing with them. As for him, he was all for following the little manikin into the hole in the ground; so they hunted here and they hunted there, until they found a great basket and a rope, and then the tinker and the shoemaker lowered the fiddler and his staff down into the pit.

Down he went ever so deep until he reached the bottom, and there he found a great room. The first body whom he saw was a princess as pretty as a ripe apple, but looking, oh, so sad! at being in such a place. The next he saw was the ugly little troll, who sat in the corner and growled like our cat when the dog comes into the kitchen.

"So!" says the fiddler, "there you are, are you? Then it is rub-a-dub-dub again." And this time before the drubbing was stopped it was all over with the troll.

And then who was glad but the pretty princess. She flung her arms around the merry little fiddler's neck, and gave him a right good smacking kiss or two, and that paid a part of the score, I can tell you. Then they sat down and the pretty princess told him all about how the troll had carried her off a year and more ago, and had kept her in this place ever since. After that she took a pure gold ring off of her finger and broke it in two; half of it was for the fiddler and half of it was for her; for they were sweethearts now, and the ring was to be a love-token.

Then the fiddler put the princess into the basket, and the two fellows above hauled her up. By and by down came the basket again, and now it was the fiddler's turn. "Suppose," says he, "that they are up to some of their tricks!" So he tumbled a great stone into the basket in the place of himself. Sure enough, when the basket was about half-way up, down it came tumbling, for the rogues above had cut the rope, and if the fiddler had been there in the place of the stone, it would have been all over with him.

he Fiddler finds ỹ Princess
in the cavern of the Dwarf.

Then if anybody was ever down in the dumps the fiddler was the fellow. For there he was down in the pit, and he could no more get out of his pickle than a toad out of the cellar window. After he had been there for ever so long a time, he saw a pretty little fiddle that hung back of the cupboard. "Aha!" says he, "there is some butter to the crust after all; and now we will just have a bit of a jig to cheer us up a little." So down he sat and began to play.

And then what do you think happened? Why, up popped a little fellow no higher than your knee and as black as your hat!

"What do you want, master?" said he.

"So," said the fiddler, "and is that the tune we play? Well, I should like to get out of this pit, that I should."

No sooner said than done, for he had hardly time to pick up his staff and tuck the fiddle under his arm, when—whisk!—he was up above as quick as a wink.

"Hi!" said he, "but this is a pretty fiddle to own and no mistake!" and off he went, right foot foremost.

After a while he came to the town where the king lived, and there was a great buzzing and gossip, and this was why: all the folks were talking about how the tinker and the shoemaker had brought back the princess from the ugly little troll, and of how the king had promised that whoever did that was to have her for his wife and half of the kingdom to boot; but here were two lads, and the question was who was to have her. For before they had left the pit over yonder, the tinker and the shoemaker had made the princess vow and promise that she would say nothing about how they had treated the fiddler, and now each fellow was saying that he had brought her up out of the troll's den.

And the princess did nothing but sit and cry and cry; but, as for marrying, she vowed and declared that she would not do that till she had a pair of slippers of pure gold, and a real diamond buckle on each slipper; and nobody in all of the town was able to make the kind that she wanted.

When the fiddler heard all this he went straight to a shoemaker's shop. "Will you take a journeyman shoemaker?" says he.

"What can you do?" says the master shoemaker.

"I can make a pair of slippers such as the princess wants, only I must have a room all to myself to make them in," says the fiddler.

When the master shoemaker heard this, he was not long in making up his mind, so the bargain was closed and that settled the business.

The Fiddler and the little, black mannikin.

As soon as the fiddler was alone he drew out his fiddle and began to play a bit of a jig, and there stood the little black fellow, just as he had done before.

"What do you want?" says he.

"I should like," said the fiddler, "to have a pair of slippers such as the princess asks for, but I only want one buckle to the pair, and that must be made of real diamonds."

Oh! that was an easy thing to have, and there were the slippers just as the fiddler had ordered.

"But there is only one buckle," says the master shoemaker.

"Tut!" says the fiddler, "turn no hairs grey for that, brother. Just tell the princess that the fiddler has the other, and matters will be as smooth as cream."

Well, the master shoemaker did as the fiddler said, and you may guess how the princess opened her pretty eyes when she heard that her sweetheart was thereabouts. Nothing would suit her but that she must see that journeyman shoemaker. But when they sent to fetch him, he was gone.

And now the shoemaker and the tinker began to talk again; the princess had been promised to the man who saved her from the troll, and so she must and should choose one of them. But no; the princess was not ready yet; she would never marry till she had a pair of gloves of the finest silk, all embroidered with silver and pearls and with a ruby clasp at the wrist of each.

And now came the same dance with a different tune, for nobody was to be found in all of the town who could make such a pair of gloves as she wanted. By and by the matter came to the fiddler's ears, and off he set to the glover's shop. And did the glover want an apprentice?

Yes, the glover wanted an apprentice, but he must know first what the other could do.

"Well," said the fiddler, "if I have a room all to myself, I can make a pair of gloves such as the princess asks for." And after that he was not left to kick his toes in the cold.

As soon as he was alone, he drew out his fiddle and struck up an air, and there stood the little black man again.

"I would like," said the fiddler, "to have a pair of gloves such as the princess asks for. But there must be only one clasp to the wrist, and that made all of pure rubies." That is what he said, and there were the gloves without his having to ask twice for them.

"But there is only one clasp," said the glover.

"Never mind that," said the wonderful apprentice; "just tell the princess that the fiddler had the other, and she will be satisfied."

As for the princess, she sent off post-haste for the lad who had made her gloves. But she was behindhand this time too, for, when those whom she sent came to the glover's house, they found nobody there but the cat and the kettle, and the master glover, for the fiddler was gone.

And now the tinker and the shoemaker began again; the princess had her gloves, and she must and should choose one or the other of them.

But no. First of all the princess must have a fine dress all of white silk with both sleeves looped up with pearls as big as marbles.

But there was nobody to make such a dress as that in all of the town, till the fiddler went to the master tailor and offered himself as a journeyman workman. Then the dress came quickly enough, and with only the tune of a fiddle. But the loop of pearls on one sleeve was missing.

"And that will never do in the wide world," says the tailor.

"Oh," says the fiddler, "that is nothing; just tell the princess that the fiddler has the other, and she will be satisfied."

Well, the tailor did as he said, and when the princess heard who had the pearl loop, she was satisfied, just as the fiddler had said she would be.

By and by the tinker and the shoemaker began again; the princess must choose one or the other of them. And now there was nothing left for her to do but to say "Yes." She felt sure that the fiddler would be on hand at the right time, and so a day was fixed for choosing whom she would marry.

It was not long before the fiddler heard of that, for news flies fast. Off he went by himself and played a turn or two on his fiddle.

"And what do you want now?" says the little manikin.

"This time," said the fiddler, "I want a splendid suit of clothes for myself, all of silver and gold; besides that, I want a hat with a great feather in it and a fine milk-white horse.

So; good! Well, he could have those things easily enough, and there they were.

So the fiddler dressed himself in his fine clothes, and then, when it was about time for the princess to make her choice, he mounted upon his great milk-white horse and set off for the king's house with his staff across the saddle in front of him.

But you should have seen how the people looked as he rode along the street, for they had never laid eyes upon such a fine sight in all of their lives before. Up he rode to the castle, and when he knocked at the door they did not keep him waiting long out in the cold, I can tell you.

There they all sat at dinner, the tinker on one side of the princess and the shoemaker on the other. But when they saw the fiddler in his grand clothes, they thought that he was some great nobleman for sure and certain, for neither the princess nor the two rogues knew who he was. The folks squeezed together along the bench and made room for him; so he leaned his staff in the corner and down he sat, just across the table from the princess.

By and by he asked the princess if she would drink a glass of red wine with him.

Yes, the princess would do that.

So the fiddler drank, and then what did he do but drop his half of the ring that the princess had given him into the cup, before he passed it across to her.

Then the princess drank, but something bobbed against her lips; and when she came to look—lo and behold!—there was the half of her ring.

And if anybody in all of the world was glad, it was the princess at that very moment. Up she stood before them all; "There is my sweetheart," says she, "and I will marry him and no one else."

As for the fiddler, he just said, "Rub-a-dub-dub," and up jumped the staff and began to thump and bang the tinker and the shoemaker until they scampered away for dear life, and there was an end of them so far as I know, for if you would like to know what happened to them afterwards, you will have to ask some one else.

The king was ever so glad to have the fiddler for a son-in-law in the place either of the tinker or the shoemaker, for he was a much better-looking lad. Besides, the others had done nothing but brew trouble and worriment ever since they had come into the house.

After that there was a grand wedding. I too was there at the feasting, but I got nothing but empty sausage and wind pudding, and so I came away again.

And that is the end of this story.

Nine O'clock·

When all are wrapped in *Slumbers* sweet,
  About the *House*, with stealthy *Tread*,
  With flowered *Gown*, and night-capped
                                    Head,
Dame *Margery* goes, in *Stocking Feet*.

She stops and listens at the *Doors*;
  She sees that every thing is right,
  And safe, and quiet for the *Night*,
Then goes to *Bed*, and sleeps, and snores.

K. P.

How the Princess's Pride was broken.

XXI.

HERE was a princess who was as pretty as a picture, and she was so proud of that that she would not so much as look at a body; all the same, there was no lack of lads who came a-wooing, and who would have liked nothing so much as to have had her for a sweetheart because she was so good-looking. But, no, she would have nothing to do with any of them; this one was too young and that one was too old; this one was too lean and that one was too fat; this one was too little and that one was too big; this one was too dark and that one was too fair. So there was never a white sheep in the whole flock, as one might say.

Now there was one came who was a king in his own country, and a fine one at that. The only blemish about him was a mole on his chin; apart from that he was as fresh as milk and rose leaves.

But when the princess saw him she burst out laughing; "Who would choose a specked apple from the basket?" said she; and that was all the cake the prince bought at that shop, for off he was packed.

But he was not for giving up, not he; he went and dressed himself up in rags and tatters; then back he came again, and not a soul knew him.

Rap! tap! rap!—he knocked at the door, and did they want a stout lad about the place?

Well, yes; they were wanting a gooseherd, and if he liked the place he might have it.

Oh, that fitted his wants like a silk stocking, and the next day he drove the geese up on the hill back of the king's house, so that they might eat grass where it was fresh and green. By and by he took a golden ball out of his pocket and began tossing it up and catching it, and as he played with it the sun shone on it so that it dazzled one's eyes to look at it.

The princess sat at her window, and it was not long before she saw it, I can tell you. Dear, dear, but it was a pretty one, the golden ball. The princess would like to have such a plaything, that she would; so she sent one of the maids out to ask whether the gooseherd had a mind to sell it.

Oh, yes, it was for sale, and cheap at that; the princess should have it for the kerchief which she wore about her neck.

Prut! but the lad was a saucy one; that was what the princess said. But, after all, a kerchief was only a kerchief; fetch the gooseherd over and she would give it to him, for she wanted the pretty golden ball for her own, and she would have it if it were to be had.

But, no; the gooseherd would not come at the princess's bidding. If she wanted to buy the golden ball she must come up on the hill and pay him, for he was not going to leave his flock of geese, and have them waddling into the garden perhaps; that is what the gooseherd said. So the upshot of the matter was that the princess went out with her women, and gave the lad the kerchief up on the hill behind the hedge, and brought back the golden ball with her for her own.

As for the gooseherd he just tied the kerchief around his arm so that everybody might see it; and all the folks said, "Hi! that is the princess's kerchief."

The next day, when he drove his flock of geese up on the hill, he took a silver looking-glass and a golden comb out of his pocket and began to comb his hair, and you should have seen how the one and the other glistened in the sun.

It took the princess no longer to see the comb and the looking-glass than it had the golden ball, and then she must and would have them. So she sent one to find whether the lad was of a mind to sell them, for she thought that she had never seen anything so pretty in all of her life before.

he **Royal gooseherd playeth
with the golden ball .**

"Yes," said he, "I will sell them, but the princess must come up on the hill back of the hedge and give me the necklace she wears about her neck."

The princess made a sour enough face at this, but, as the gooseherd would take nothing more nor less than what he had said, she and her maids had to tuck up their dresses and go up on the hill; there she paid him his price, and brought home the silver looking-glass and the golden comb.

The lad clasped the necklace about his throat, and, dear, dear, how all the folks did goggle and stare. "See," said they, "the princess has been giving the gooseherd the necklace from about her own throat."

The third day it was a new thing the gooseherd had, for he brought out a musical box with figures on it, dressed up, and looking for all the world like real little men and women. He turned the handle, and when the music played it was sweeter than drops of honey. And all the while the little men and women bowed to one another and went through with a dance, for all the world as though they knew what they were about, and were doing it with their own wits.

Good gracious! how the princess did wonder at the pretty musical box! She must and would have it at any price; but this time it was five-and-twenty kisses that the lad was wanting for his musical box, and he would take nothing more nor less than just that much for it. Moreover, she would have to come up on the hillside and give them to him, for he could not leave his geese even for five-and-twenty kisses.

But you should have seen what a stew the princess was in at this! Five-and-twenty kisses, indeed! And did the fellow think that it was for the likes of her to be kissing a poor gooseherd? He might keep his musical box if that was the price he asked for it; that was what she said.

As for the lad, he just played the music and played the music, and the more the princess heard and saw the more she wanted it. "After all," said she, at last, "a kiss is only a kiss, and I will be none the poorer for giving one or two of them; I'll just let him have them, since he will take nothing else." So off she marched, with all of her maidens, to pay the gooseherd his price, though it was a sour face she made of it, and that is the truth.

Now, somebody had been buzzing in the king's ear, and had told him that the gooseherd over yonder was wearing the princess's kerchief and her golden necklace, and folks said she had given them to him of her own free will.

"What!" says the king, "is that so? her kerchief! golden necklace!

 he King peeps over the hedge
and sees what is going on upon the
other side.

we will have to look into this business." So off he marched, with his little dog at his heels, to find out what he could about it. Up the hill he went to where the gooseherd watched his flock; and when he came near the hedge where the kissing was going on, he heard them counting—"Twenty-one, twenty-two, twenty-three—" and he wondered what in the world they were all about. So he just peeped over the bushes, and there he saw the whole business.

Mercy on us! what a rage he was in! So; the princess would turn up her nose at folks as good as herself, would she? And here she was kissing the gooseherd back of the hedge. If he was the kind she liked she should have him for good and all.

So the minister was called in, and the princess and the gooseherd were married then and there, and that was the end of the business. Then off they were packed to shift for themselves in the wide world, for they were not to live at the king's castle, and that was the long and the short of it.

But the lad did nothing but grumble and growl, and seemed as sore over his bargain as though he had been trying to trick a Jew. What did he want with a lass for a wife who could neither brew nor bake nor boil blue beans? That is what he said. All the same, they were hitched to the same plough, and there was nothing for it but to pull together the best they could. So off they packed, and the poor princess trudged after him and carried his bundle.

So they went on until they came to a poor, mean little hut. There she had to take off her fine clothes and put on rags and tatters; and that was the way she came home.

"Well," said the gooseherd one day, "it's not the good end of the bargain that I have had in marrying; all the same, one must make the best one can of a crooked stick when there is none other to be cut in the hedge. It is little or nothing you are fit for; but here is a basket of eggs, and you shall take them to the market and sell them."

So off the poor princess went to the great town, and stood in the corner of the market with her eggs. By and by there came along a tipsy countryman—tramp! tramp! tramp! As for the basket of eggs, he minded them no more than so many green apples. Smash! and there they lay on the ground, and were fit for nothing but to patch broken promises, as we say in our town.

Then how the poor princess did wring her hands and cry and cry, for she was afraid to go home to her husband, because of the hard words he

The Princess taketh her eggs to the market.

would be sure to fling at her. All the same, there was no other place for her to go; so back she went.

"There!" said he, "I always knew that you were good for nothing but to look at, and now I am more sure of it than ever. The china pitcher was never fit to send to the well, and it was a rainy day for me when I married such a left-handed wife;" that was what the gooseherd said. All the same, the princess should try again; this time she should take a basket of apples to the market to sell; for whatever happened she could not break them; so off she went again.

Well, by and by came a fellow driving swine, and there sat the princess in the way; that was bad luck for her, for over tumbled the basket, and the apples went rolling all about the street. When the drove had passed there was not a single apple to be seen, for the pigs had eaten every one of them. So there was nothing for the princess but to go home crying, with her apron to her eyes.

"Yes, yes," said the gooseherd, "it is as plain as reading and writing and the nose on your face that you are just fit for nothing at all! All the same, we'll make one more try to mend the crack in your luck. The king up in the castle yonder is married and is going to give a grand feast. They are wanting a body in the kitchen to draw the water and chop the wood; and you shall go and try your hand at that; and see, here is a basket; you shall take it along and bring home the kitchen scrapings for supper."

So off went the princess to the castle kitchen, and there she drew the water and chopped the wood for the cook. After her work was done she begged so prettily for the kitchen scrapings that the cook filled her basket full of the leavings from the pots and the pans, for they were about having a grand dinner up-stairs and the king was going to bring home his wife that day.

By and by it was time for her to be going home, so she picked up her basket and off she went. Just outside stood two tall soldiers. "Halt!" said they. And was she the lass who had been chopping the wood and drawing the water for the cook that day? Yes? Then she must go along with them, for she was wanted up-stairs. No; it did no good for her to beg and to pray and to cry and to wring her hands, and it mattered nothing if her good man was waiting for her at home. She had been sent for, and she must go, willy-nilly. So she had only just time to fling her apron over her basket of kitchen scrapings, and off they marched her.

There sat the king on his golden throne, dressed all in splendid golden robes, and with a golden crown glittering upon his head. But the poor princess was so frightened that she neither looked at anything nor saw anything, but only stood there trembling.

"What have you under your apron?" said the king. But to this the princess could not answer a single word. Then somebody who stood near snatched away her apron, and there was the basket full of kitchen scrapings, and all the time the princess stood so heart-struck with shame that she saw nothing but the cracks in the floor.

But the king stepped down from his golden throne, dressed all in his

golden robes, just as he was, and took the princess by the hand. "And
do you not know me?" said he; "look! I am the gooseherd."

And so he was! She could see it easily enough now, but that made her
more ashamed than ever.

And listen: the king had more to tell her yet. He was the tipsy countryman and had knocked over her basket of eggs himself, and more than
that he was the swineherd who had driven his pigs over her basket of
apples so that they were spilled on the ground. But the princess only
bowed her head lower and lower, for her pride was broken.

"Come," says the king, "you are my own sweetheart now;" and he
kissed her on the cheek and seated her beside himself, and if the princess

cried any more the king wiped away her tears with his own pocket-hand-kerchief.   As for the poor and rough clothes in which she was dressed, he thought nothing of them, for they were nothing to him.

That is the end of this story, for everything ends aright in a story worth the telling.

But if the princess was proud and haughty before, she never was again; and that is the plain truth, fresh from the churn and no hairs in it, and a lump of it is worth spreading your bread with, I can tell you.

Ten O'clock.

Out of the *Cupboard*
   The *Kobold* takes
Some bits of the *Morning*
   Griddle-Cakes .

Cold
and
windy .   The *Windows* rattle,
   The *North Wind* blows,
But the *Ashes* are warm
   Between his *Toes* .

K.P.

The little grey *Mouse*
   Looks out of the *Wall*,
And wishes he had
   The *Crumbs* that fall .

How Two went into Partnership.

XXII.

HIS was the way of it.

Uncle Bear had a pot of honey and a big cheese, but the Great Red Fox had nothing but his wits.

The fox was for going into partnership, for he says, says he, " a head full of wits is worth more than a pot of honey and a big cheese," which was as true as gospel, only that wits cannot be shared in partnership among folks, like red herring and blue beans, or a pot of honey and a big cheese.

All the same, Uncle Bear was well enough satisfied, and so they went into partnership together, just as the Great Red Fox had said. As for the pot of honey and the big cheese, why, they were put away for a rainy day, and the wits were all that were to be used just now.

"Very well," says the fox, "we'll rattle them up a bit ;" and so he did, and this was how.

He was hungry for the honey, was the Great Red Fox. "See, now," said he, "I am sick to-day, and I will just go and see the Master Doctor over yonder."

But it was not the doctor he went to ; no, off he marched to the store-house, and there he ate part of the honey. After that he laid out in the sun and toasted his skin, for that is pleasant after a great dinner.

By and by he went home again.

"Well," says Uncle Bear, "and how do you feel now?"

"Oh, well enough," says the Great Red Fox.

"And was the medicine bitter?" says Uncle Bear.

"Oh, no, it was good enough," says the Great Red Fox.

"And how much did the doctor give you?" says Uncle Bear.

"Oh, about one part of a pot full," says the Red Fox.

Dear, dear! thinks Uncle Bear, that is a great deal of medicine to take, for sure and certain.

Well, things went on as smoothly as though the wheels were greased, until by and by the fox grew hungry for a taste of honey again; and this time he had to go over yonder and see his aunt. Off he went to the storehouse, and there he ate all the honey he wanted, and then, after he had slept a bit in the sun, he went back home again.

"Well," says Uncle Bear, "and did you see your aunt?"

"Oh, yes," says the Great Red Fox, "I saw her."

"And did she give you anything?" says Uncle Bear.

"Oh, yes, she gave me a trifle," says the Great Red Fox.

"And what was it she gave you?" says Uncle Bear.

"Why, she gave me another part of a pot full, that was all," says the Great Red Fox.

"Dear, dear! but that is a queer thing to give," says Uncle Bear.

By and by the Great Red Fox was thinking of honey again, and now it was a christening he had to go to. Off he went to the pot of honey, and this time he finished it all and licked the pot into the bargain.

And had everything gone smoothly at the christening? That was what Uncle Bear wanted to know.

"Oh, smoothly enough," says the Great Red Fox.

"And did they have a christening feast?" says Uncle Bear.

"Oh, yes, they had that," says the Great Red Fox.

"And what did they have?" says Uncle Bear.

"Oh, everything that was in the pot," says the Great Red Fox.

"Dear, dear," says Uncle Bear, "but they must have been a hungry set at that christening."

Well, one day Uncle Bear says, "We'll have a feast and eat up the pot of honey and the big cheese, and we'll ask Father Goat over to help us."

That suited the Great Red Fox well enough, so off he went to the storehouse to fetch the pot of honey and the cheese; as for Uncle Bear

 he Great Red Fox goeth to the store=house and helps him= self to the good things. ℂ

he went to ask Father Goat to come and help them eat up the good things.

"See, now," says the Great Red Fox to himself, "the pot of honey and the big cheese belong together, and it is a pity to part them." So down he sat without more ado, and when he got up again the cheese was all inside of him.

When he came home again there was Father Goat toasting his toes at the fire and waiting for supper; and there was Uncle Bear on the back door-step sharpening the bread-knife.

"Hi!" says the Great Red Fox, "and what are you doing here, Father Goat?"

"I am just waiting for supper, and that is all," says Father Goat.

"And where is Uncle Bear?" says the Great Red Fox.

"He is sharpening the bread-knife," says Father Goat.

"Yes," says the Great Red Fox, "and when he is through with that he is going to cut your tail off."

Dear, dear! but Father Goat was in a great fright; that house was no place for him, and he could see that with one eye shut; off he marched, as though the ground was hot under him. As for the Great Red Fox, he went out to Uncle Bear; "That was a pretty body you asked to take supper with us," says he; "here he has marched off with the pot of honey and the big cheese, and we may sit down and whistle over an empty table between us."

When Uncle Bear heard this he did not tarry, I can tell you; up he got and off he went after Father Goat. "Stop! stop!" he bawled, "let me have a little at least."

But Father Goat thought that Uncle Bear was speaking of his tail, for he knew nothing of the pot of honey and the big cheese; so he just knuckled down to it, and away he scampered till the gravel flew behind him.

And this was what came of that partnership; nothing was left but the wits that the Great Red Fox had brought into the business; for nobody could blame Father Goat for carrying the wits off with him, and one might guess that without the telling.

Now, as the pot of honey and big cheese were gone, something else must be looked up, for one cannot live on thin air, and that is the truth.

"See, now," says the Great Red Fox, "Farmer John over yonder has a storehouse full of sausages and chitterlings and puddings, and all sort

The Fox tells Father Goat a strange story.

of good things. As nothing else is left of the partnership we'll just churn our wits a bit, and see if we can make butter with them, as the saying goes;" that was what the Great Red Fox said, and it suited Uncle Bear as well as anything he ever heard; so off they marched arm in arm.

By and by they came to Farmer John's house, and nobody was about, which was just what the two rogues wanted; and, yes, there was the storehouse as plain as the nose on your face, only the door was locked. Above was a little window just big enough for the Great Red Fox to creep into, though it was up ever so high. "Just give me a lift up through the window yonder," says he to Uncle Bear, "and I will drop the good things out for you to catch."

So Uncle Bear gave the Great Red Fox a leg up, and—pop!—and there he was in the storehouse like a mouse in the cheese-box.

As soon as he was safe among the good things he bawled out to Uncle Bear, "What shall it be first, sausages or puddings?"

"Hush! hush!" said Uncle Bear.

"Yes, yes," bawled the Red Fox louder than ever, "only tell me which I shall take first, sausages or puddings?"

"Sh-h-h-h!" said Uncle Bear, "if you are making such a noise as that you will have them about our ears; take the first that comes and be quick about it."

"Yes, yes," bawled the fox as loud as he was able; "but one is just as handy as another, and you must tell me which I shall take first."

But Uncle Bear got neither pudding nor sausage, for the Great Red Fox had made such a hubbub that Farmer John and his men came running, and three great dogs with them.

"Hi!" said they, "there is Uncle Bear after the sausages and puddings;" and there was nothing for him to do but to lay foot to the ground as fast as he could. All the same, they caught him over the hill, and gave him such a drubbing that his bones ached for many a long day.

But the Great Red Fox only waited until all the others were well away on their own business, and then he filled a bag with the best he could lay his hands on, opened the door from the inside, and walked out as though it were from his own barn; for there was nobody to say "No" to him. He hid the good things away in a place of his own, and it was little of them that Uncle Bear smelt. After he had gathered all this, Master Fox came home, groaning as though he had had an awful drubbing; it would have moved a heart of stone to hear him.

"Dear, oh dear! what a drubbing I have had," said he.

"And so have I," said Uncle Bear, grinning over his sore bones as though cold weather were blowing snow in his teeth.

"See, now," said the Great Red Fox, "this is what comes of going into partnership, and sharing one's wits with another. If you had made your choice when I asked you, your butter would never have been spoiled in the churning."

That was all the comfort Uncle Bear had, and cold enough it was too.

 ncle Bear and the Great Red Fox visit the farmer's store-house.

All the same, he is not the first in the world who has lost his dinner, and had both the drubbing and the blame into the bargain.

But things do not last forever, and so by and by the good things from Farmer John's storehouse gave out, and the Great Red Fox had nothing in the larder.

"Listen," says he to Uncle Bear, "I saw them shaking the apple-trees at Farmer John's to-day, and if you have a mind to try the wits that belong to us, we'll go and bring a bagful apiece from the storehouse over yonder at the farm."

Yes, that suited Uncle Bear well enough; so off they marched, each of them with an empty bag to fetch back the apples. By and by they came to the storehouse, and nobody was about. This time the door was not locked, so in the both of them went and began filling their bags with apples. The Great Red Fox tumbled them into his bag as fast as ever he could, taking them just as they came, good or bad; but Uncle Bear took his time about it and picked them all over, for since he had come there he was bound to get the best that were to be had.

So the upshot of the matter was that the Great Red Fox had his bag full before Uncle Bear had picked out half a score of good juicy apples.

"I'll just peep out of the window yonder," says the Great Red Fox, "and see if Farmer John is coming." But in his sleeve he said to himself, "I'll slip outside and turn the key of the door on Uncle Bear, for somebody will have to carry the blame of this, and his shoulders are broader and his skin tougher than mine; he will never be able to get out of that little window." So up he jumped with his bag of apples, to do as he said.

But listen! A hasty man drinks hot broth. And so it was with the Great Red Fox, for up in the window they had set a trap to catch rats. But he knew nothing of that; out he jumped from the window — click! went the trap and caught him by the tail, and there he hung.

"Is Farmer John coming?" bawled Uncle Bear, by and by.

"Hush! hush!" said the Great Red Fox, for he was trying to get his tail out of the trap.

But the boot was on the other leg now. "Yes, yes," bawled Uncle Bear, louder than before, "but tell me, is Farmer John coming?"

"Sh-h-h-h!" says the Great Red Fox.

"No, no," bawled Uncle Bear, as loud as he could, "what I want to know is, is Farmer John coming?"

The Bear & the Fox go to farmer John's again.

Yes, he was, for he had heard the hubbub, and here he was with a lot of his men and three great dogs.

"Oh, Farmer John," bawled the Great Red Fox, "don't touch me, I am not the thief. Yonder is Uncle Bear in the pantry, he is the one."

Yes, yes, Farmer John knew how much of that cake to eat; here was the rogue of a fox caught in the trap, and the beating was ready for him. That was the long and the short of it.

When the Great Red Fox heard this, he pulled with all his might and main. Snap! went his tail and broke off close to his body, and away he scampered with Farmer John the men and the dogs close to his heels. But Uncle Bear filled his bag full of apples, and when all hands had gone racing away after the Great Red Fox, he walked quietly out of the door and off home.

And that is how the Great Red Fox lost his tail in the trap.

What is the meaning of all this? Why, here it is: When a rogue and another cracks a nut together, it is not often the rogue who breaks his teeth by trying to eat the hulls. And this too: But when one sets a trap for another, it is a toss of a copper whether or no it flies up and pinches his own fingers.

If there is anything more left in the dish you may scrape it for yourself.

Eleven O'clock.

Who goes about the *House* when all
    Are sleeping but the *Clock*,
  And no one hears it, all alone,
    Still saying tick-a-tock?

K.P.

It is not *Gretchen* goes about,
    She's snoring in her *Bed*;
It's not the *Hound* that goes about
    He never lifts his *Head*;

It is the *Wind* that goes about,
    And sighs around the *House*,
And never wakes the toothless *Hound*,
    Or stops the gnawing *Mouse*.

King Stork.

XXIII.

HERE was a drummer marching along the high-road—forward march!—left, right!—tramp, tramp, tramp!—for the fighting was done, and he was coming home from the wars. By and by he came to a great wide stream of water, and there sat an old man as gnarled and as bent as the hoops in a cooper shop. "Are you going to cross the water?" said he.

"Yes," says the drummer, "I am going to do that if my legs hold out to carry me."

"And will you not help a poor body across?" says the old man.

Now, the drummer was as good-natured a lad as ever stood on two legs. "If the young never gave a lift to the old," says he to himself, "the wide world would not be worth while living in." So he took off his shoes and stockings, and then he bent his back and took the old man on it, and away he started through the water—splash!

But this was no common old man whom the drummer was carrying, and he was not long finding that out, for the farther he went in the water the heavier grew his load—like work put off until to-morrow—so that, when he was half-way across, his legs shook under him and the sweat stood on his forehead like a string of beads in the shop-window. But by and by he reached the other shore, and the old man jumped down from his back.

"Phew!" says the drummer, "I am glad to be here at last!"

And now for the wonder of all this: The old man was an old man no longer, but a splendid tall fellow with hair as yellow as gold. "And who do you think I am?" said he.

But of that the drummer knew no more than the mouse in the haystack, so he shook his head, and said nothing.

"I am king of the storks, and here I have sat for many days; for the wicked one-eyed witch who lives on the glass hill put it upon me for a spell that I should be an old man until somebody should carry me over the water. You are the first to do that, and you shall not lose by it. Here is a little bone whistle; whenever you are in trouble just blow a turn or two on it, and I will be by to help you."

Thereupon King Stork drew a feather cap out of his pocket and clapped it on his head, and away he flew, for he was turned into a great, long, red-legged stork as quick as a wink.

But the drummer trudged on the way he was going, as merry as a cricket, for it is not everybody who cracks his shins against such luck as he had stumbled over, I can tell you. By and by he came to the town over the hill, and there he found great bills stuck up over the walls. They were all of them proclamations. And this is what they said:

The princess of that town was as clever as she was pretty; that was saying a great deal, for she was the handsomest in the whole world. ("Phew! but that is a fine lass for sure and certain," said the drummer.) So it was proclaimed that any lad who could answer a question the princess would ask, and would ask a question the princess could not answer, and would catch the bird that she would be wanting, should have her for his wife and half of the kingdom to boot. ("Hi! but here is luck for a clever lad," says the drummer.) But whoever should fail in any one of the three tasks should have his head chopped off as sure as he lived. ("Ho! but she is a wicked one for all that," says the drummer.)

That was what the proclamation said, and the drummer would have a try for her; "for," said he, "it is a poor fellow who cannot manage a wife when he has her"—and he knew as much about that business as a goose about churning butter. As for chopping off heads, he never bothered his own about that; for, if one never goes out for fear of rain one never catches fish.

Off he went to the king's castle as fast as he could step, and there he knocked on the door, as bold as though his own grandmother lived there.

But when the king heard what the drummer had come for, he took out

The Drummer carries the Old Body across the River.

his pocket-handkerchief and began to wipe his eyes, for he had a soft heart under his jacket, and it made him cry like anything to see another coming to have his head chopped off, as so many had done before him. For there they were, all along the wall in front of the princess's window, like so many apples.

But the drummer was not to be scared away by the king's crying a bit, so in he came, and by and by they all sat down to supper—he and the king and the princess. As for the princess, she was so pretty that the drummer's heart melted inside of him, like a lump of butter on the stove—and that was what she was after. After a while she asked him if he had come to answer a question of hers, and to ask her a question of his, and to catch the bird that she should set him to catch.

"Yes," said the drummer, "I have come to do that very thing." And he spoke as boldly and as loudly as the clerk in church.

"Very well, then," says the princess, as sweet as sugar candy, "just come along to-morrow, and I will ask you your question."

Off went the drummer; he put his whistle to his lips and blew a turn or two, and there stood King Stork, and nobody knows where he stepped from.

"And what do you want?" says he.

The drummer told him everything, and how the princess was going to ask him a question to-morrow morning that he would have to answer, or have his head chopped off.

"Here you have walked into a pretty puddle, and with your eyes open," says King Stork, for he knew that the princess was a wicked enchantress, and loved nothing so much as to get a lad into just such a scrape as the drummer had tumbled into. "But see, here is a little cap and a long feather —the cap is a dark-cap, and when you put it on your head one can see you no more than so much thin air. At twelve o'clock at night the princess will come out into the castle garden and will fly away through the air. Then throw your leg over the feather, and it will carry you wherever you want to go; and if the princess flies fast it will carry you as fast and faster."

"Dong! Dong!" The clock struck twelve, and the princess came out of her house; but in the garden was the drummer waiting for her with the dark-cap on his head, and he saw her as plain as a pikestaff. She brought a pair of great wings which she fastened to her shoulders, and away she flew. But the drummer was as quick with his tricks as she was with hers; he flung his leg over the feather which King Stork had given him, and away he flew after her, and just as fast as she with her great wings.

Thus the Princess cometh forth
from the Castle at twelve o'clock at night.

By and by they came to a huge castle of shining steel that stood on a mountain of glass. And it was a good thing for the drummer that he had on his cap of darkness, for all around outside of the castle stood fiery dragons and savage lions to keep anybody from going in without leave.

But not a thread of the drummer did they see; in he walked with the princess, and there was a great one-eyed witch with a beard on her chin, and a nose that hooked over her mouth like the beak of a parrot.

" Uff !" said she, " here is a smell of Christian blood in the house."

" Tut, mother!" says the princess, " how you talk! do you not see that there is nobody with me?" For the drummer had taken care that the wind should not blow the cap of darkness off of his head, I can tell you. By and by they sat down to supper, the princess and the witch, but it was little the princess ate, for as fast as anything was put on her plate the drummer helped himself to it, so that it was all gone before she could get a bite.

" Look, mother !" she said, " I eat nothing, and yet it all goes from my plate; why is that so?" But that the old witch could not tell her, for she could see nothing of the drummer.

" There was a lad came to-day to answer the question I shall put to him," said the princess. " Now what shall I ask him by way of a question ?"

" I have a tooth in the back part of my head," said the witch, " and it has been grumbling a bit; ask him what it is you are thinking about, and let it be that."

Yes ; that was a good question for sure and certain, and the princess would give it to the drummer to-morrow, to see what he had to say for himself. As for the drummer, you can guess how he grinned, for he heard every word that they said.

After a while the princess flew away home again, for it was nearly the break of day, and she must be back before the sun rose. And the drummer flew close behind her, but she knew nothing of that.

The next morning up he marched to the king's castle and knocked at the door, and they let him in.

There sat the king and the princess, and lots of folks besides. Well, had he come to answer her question? That was what the princess wanted to know.

Yes ; that was the very business he had come about.

Very well, this was the question, and he might have three guesses at it ; what was she thinking of at that minute ?

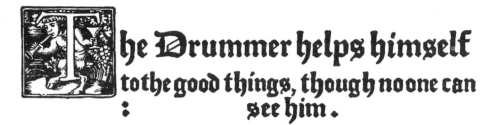

The Drummer helps himself
to the good things, though no one can
: see him.

Oh, it could be no hard thing to answer such a question as that, for lasses' heads all ran upon the same things more or less; was it a fine silk dress with glass buttons down the front that she was thinking of now?

No, it was not that.

Then, was it of a good stout lad like himself for a sweetheart, that she was thinking of?

No, it was not that.

No? Then it was the bad tooth that had been grumbling in the head of the one-eyed witch for a day or two past, perhaps.

Dear, dear! but you should have seen the princess's face when she heard this! Up she got and off she packed without a single word, and the king saw without the help of his spectacles that the drummer had guessed right. He was so glad that he jumped up and down and snapped his fingers for joy. Besides that he gave out that bonfires should be lighted all over the town, and that was a fine thing for the little boys.

The next night the princess flew away to the house of the one-eyed witch again, but there was the drummer close behind her just as he had been before.

"Uff!" said the one-eyed witch, "here is a smell of Christian blood, for sure and certain." But all the same, she saw no more of the drummer than if he had never been born.

"See, mother," said the princess, "that rogue of a drummer answered my question without winking over it."

"So," said the old witch, "we have missed for once, but the second time hits the mark; he will be asking you a question to-morrow, and here is a book that tells everything that has happened in the world, and if he asks you more than that he is a smart one and no mistake."

After that they sat down to supper again, but it was little the princess ate, for the drummer helped himself out of her plate just as he had done before.

After a while the princess flew away home, and the drummer with her.

"And, now, what will we ask her that she cannot answer?" said the drummer; so off he went back of the house, and blew a turn or two on his whistle, and there stood King Stork.

"And what will we ask the princess," said he, "when she has a book that tells her everything?"

King Stork was not long in telling him that; "Just ask her so and so and so and so," said he, "and she would not dare to answer the question."

Well, the next morning there was the drummer at the castle all in good time; and, had he come to ask her a question? that was what the princess wanted to know.

Oh, yes, he had come for that very thing.

Very well, then, just let him begin, for the princess was ready and waiting, and she wet her thumb, and began to turn over the leaves of her Book of Knowledge.

Oh, it was an easy question the drummer was going to ask, and it needed no big book like that to answer it. The other night he dreamed that he was in a castle all built of shining steel, where there lived a witch with one eye. There was a handsome bit of a lass there who was as great a witch as the old woman herself, but for the life of him he could not tell who she was; now perhaps the princess could make a guess at it.

There the drummer had her as tight as a fly in a bottle, for she did not dare to let folks know that she was a wicked witch like the one-eyed one; so all she could do was to sit there and gnaw her lip. As for the Book of Knowledge, it was no more use to her than a fifth wheel under a cart.

But if the king was glad when the drummer answered the princess's question, he was twice as glad when he found she could not answer his.

All the same, there is more to do yet, and many a slip betwixt the cup and the lip. "The bird I want is the one-eyed raven," said the princess; "Now bring her to me if you want to keep your head off of the wall yonder."

Yes; the drummer thought he might do that as well as another thing. So off he went back of the house to talk to King Stork of the matter.

"Look," said King Stork, and he drew a net out of his pocket as fine as a cobweb and as white as milk; "take this with you when you go with the princess to the one-eyed witch's house to-night, throw it over the witch's head, and then see what will happen; only when you catch the one-eyed raven you are to wring her neck as soon as you lay hands on her, for if you don't it will be the worse for you."

Well, that night off flew the princess just as she had done before, and off flew the drummer at her heels, until they came to the witch's house, both of them.

"And did you take his head this time?" said the witch.

No, the princess had not done that, for the drummer had asked such and such a question, and she could not answer it; all the same, she had him tight enough now, for she had set it as a task upon him that he should bring her the one-eyed raven, and it was not likely he would be up to doing that. After that the princess and the one-eyed witch sat down to supper together, and the drummer served the princess the same trick that he had done before, so that she got hardly a bite to eat.

"See," said the old witch when the princess was ready to go, "I will go home with you to-night, and see that you get there safe and sound." So she brought out a pair of wings, just like those the princess had, and set them on her shoulders, and away both of them flew with the drummer behind. So they came home without seeing a soul, for the drummer kept his cap of darkness tight upon his head all the while.

"Good-night," said the witch to the princess, and "Good-night" said the princess to the witch, and the one was for going one way and the other the other. But the drummer had his wits about him sharply enough, and before the old witch could get away he flung the net that King Stork had given him over her head.

"Hi!" but you should have been there to see what happened; for it was a great one-eyed raven, as black as the inside of the chimney, that he had in his net.

Dear, dear, how it flapped its wings and struck with its great beak! But that did no good, for the drummer just wrung its neck, and there was an end of it.

The next morning he wrapped it up in his pocket-handkerchief and off he started for the king's castle, and there was the princess waiting for him, looking as cool as butter in the well, for she felt sure the drummer was caught in the trap this time.

"And have you brought the one-eyed raven with you?" she said.

"Oh, yes," said the drummer, and here it was wrapped up in this handkerchief.

But when the princess saw the raven with its neck wrung, she gave a great shriek and fell to the floor. There she lay and they had to pick her up and carry her out of the room.

But everybody saw that the drummer had brought the bird she had asked for, and all were as glad as glad could be. The king gave orders that they should fire off the town cannon, just as they did on his birth-day, and all the little boys out in the street flung up their hats and caps and cried, "Hurrah! Hurrah!"

But the drummer went off back of the house. He blew a turn or two

The Drummer catches y̆ one=eyed raven ∴

on his whistle, and there stood King Stork. "Here is your dark-cap and your feather," says he, "and it is I who am thankful to you, for they have won me a real princess for a wife."

"Yes, good," says King Stork, "you have won her, sure enough, but the next thing is to keep her; for a lass is not cured of being a witch as quickly as you seem to think, and after one has found one's eggs one must roast them and butter them into the bargain. See now, the princess is just as wicked as ever she was before, and if you do not keep your eyes open she will trip you up after all. So listen to what I tell you. Just after you are married, get a great bowl of fresh milk and a good, stiff switch. Pour the milk over the princess when you are alone together, and after that hold tight to her and lay on the switch, no matter what happens, for that is the only way to save yourself and to save her."

Well, the drummer promised to do as King Stork told him, and by and by came the wedding-day. Off he went over to the dairy and got a fresh pan of milk, and out he went into the woods and cut a stout hazel switch, as thick as his finger.

As soon as he and the princess were alone together he emptied the milk all over her; then he caught hold of her and began laying on the switch for dear life.

It was well for him that he was a brave fellow and had been to the wars, for, instead of the princess, he held a great black cat that glared at him with her fiery eyes, and growled and spat like anything. But that did no good, for the drummer just shut his eyes and laid on the switch harder than ever.

Then—puff!—instead of a black cat it was like a great, savage wolf, that snarled and snapped at the drummer with its red jaws; but the drummer just held fast and made the switch fly, and the wolf scared him no more than the black cat had done.

So out it went, like a light of a candle, and there was a great snake that lashed its tail and shot out its forked tongue and spat fire. But no; the drummer was no more frightened at that than he had been at the wolf and the cat, and, dear, dear! how he dressed the snake with his hazel switch.

Last of all, there stood the princess herself. "Oh, dear husband!" she cried, "let me go, and I will promise to be good all the days of my life."

"Very well," says the drummer, "and that is the tune I like to hear."

That was the way he gained the best of her, whether it was the bowl of milk or the hazel switch, for afterwards she was as good a wife as ever churned butter; but what did it is a question that you will have to answer for yourself. All the same, she tried no more of her tricks with him, I can tell you. And so this story comes to an end, like everything else in the world.

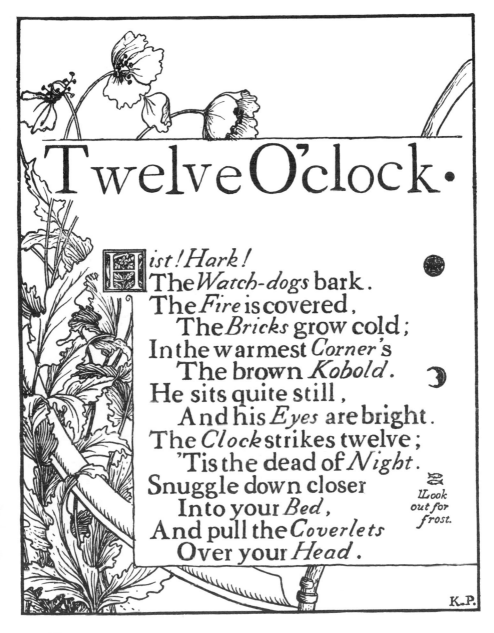

Twelve O'clock.

Hist! Hark!
The *Watch-dogs* bark.
The *Fire* is covered,
    The *Bricks* grow cold;
In the warmest *Corner's*
    The brown *Kobold.*
He sits quite still,
    And his *Eyes* are bright.
The *Clock* strikes twelve;
    'Tis the dead of *Night.*
Snuggle down closer
    Into your *Bed*,
And pull the *Coverlets*
    Over your *Head.*

Look out for frost.

K.P.

The Best that Life has to give ·

XXIV.

HERE was a blacksmith who lived near to a great, dark pine forest. He was as poor as charity soup; but dear knows whether that was his fault or not, for he laid his troubles upon the back of ill-luck, as everybody else does in our town.

One day the snow lay thick all over the ground, and hunger and cold sat in the blacksmith's house. "I'll go out into the forest," says he, "and see whether I cannot get a bagful of pine-cones to make a fire in the stove." So off he stumped, but could find no cones, because they were all covered up with white. On into the woods he went, farther and farther and deeper and deeper, until he came to a high hill, all of bare rock. There he found a clear place and more pine-cones scattered over the ground than a body could count. He filled his basket, and it did not take him long to do that.

But he was not to get his pine-cones for nothing: click! clack!—a great door opened in the side of the hill, and out stepped a little dwarf, as ugly as ugly could be, for his head was as big as a cabbage, his hair as red as carrots, and his eyes as green as a snake's.

"So," said he, "you are stealing my pine-cones, are you? And there are none in the world like them. Look your last on the sunlight, for now you shall die."

Down fell the blacksmith on his knees. "Alas!" said he, "I did not know that they were your pine-cones. I will empty them out of my sack and find some elsewhere."

"No," said the dwarf, "it is too late to do that now. But listen, you might hunt the world over, and find no such pine-cones as these; so we will strike a bit of a bargain between us. You shall go in peace with your pine-cones if you will give me what lies in the bread - trough at home."

"Oh, yes," said the blacksmith, "I will do that gladly."

"Very well," said the dwarf, "I will come for my pay at the end of seven days," and back he went into the hill again, and the door shut to behind him.

Off went the blacksmith, chuckling to himself. "It is the right end of the bargain that I have this time," said he.

But, bless you! he talked of that horse before he had looked into its mouth, as my Uncle Peter used to say. For, listen: while his wife sat at home spinning, she wrapped the baby in a blanket and laid it in the bread-trough, because it was empty and as good as a cradle. And that was what the dwarf spoke of, for he knew what had been done over at the black-smith's house.

But the blacksmith was as happy as a cricket under the hearth; on he plodded, kicking up the soft snow with his toes; but all the time the basket of pine-cones kept growing heavier and heavier.

"Come," said he, at last, "I can carry this load no farther, some of the pine-cones must be left behind." So he opened the basket to throw a parcel of them out. But—

Hi! how he did stare! for every one of those pine-cones had turned to pure silver as white as the frost on the window-pane. After that he was for throwing none of them away, but for carrying all of them home, if he broke his back at it, and upon that you may depend.

"And I had them all for nothing," said he to his wife; "for the dwarf gave them to me for what was in the bread-trough, and I knew very well that there was nothing there."

"Alas," said she, "what have you done! the baby is sleeping there, and has been sleeping there all the morning."

When the blacksmith heard this he scratched his head, and looked up and looked down, for he had burned his fingers with the hot end of the bargain after all. All the same, there was nothing left but to make the best that he could of it. So he took two or three of the silver pine-cones to the town and bought plenty to eat, and plenty to drink, and warm things to wear into the bargain.

The blacksmith takes ẏ dwarf's pine-cones.

At the end of seven days up came the dwarf and knocked at the black-smith's house.

"Well, and is the baby ready?" said he, "for I have come to fetch it."

But the blacksmith's wife begged and prayed and prayed and begged that the baby might be spared to her. "Let us keep it for seven years at least," said she, "for what can you want with a young baby in the house?"

Yes, that was very true. Young babies were troublesome things to have about the house, and the woman might keep it for seven years since she was anxious to do so. So off went the dwarf, and the woman had what she wanted, for seven years is a long time to put off our troubles.

But at the end of that time up came the dwarf a second time.

"Well, is the boy ready now?" said he, "for I have come to take him."

"Yes, yes," says the woman, "the boy is yours, but why not leave him for another seven years, for he is very young to be out in the world yet?"

Yes, that was true, and so the dwarf put off taking him for seven years longer.

But when it had passed, back he came again, and this time it did no good for his mother and father to beg and pray, for he had put off his bargain long enough, and now he was for having what was his.

"All the same," says he to the blacksmith, "if you will come after five years to the place in the woods where you saw me, you shall have your son, if you choose to take him." And off he went with the lad at his heels.

Well, after five years had passed, the blacksmith went into the forest to find the dwarf and to bring back his son again.

There was the dwarf waiting for him, and in his hand he held a basket. "Well, neighbor," says he, "and have you come to fetch your son again?"

Yes, that was what the blacksmith wanted.

"Very well," says the dwarf, "here he is, and all that you have to do is to take him." He opened the basket, and inside was a wren, a thrush, and a dove.

"But which of the three is the lad?" says the blacksmith.

"That is for you to tell, neighbor," says the dwarf.

The blacksmith looked and looked, and first he thought it might be the wren, and then he thought it might be the thrush, and then he thought it might be the dove. But he was afraid to choose any one of the three, lest he should not be right in the choosing. So he shook his head and sighed, and was forced at last to go away with empty hands.

Out by the edge of the forest sat an old woman spinning flax from a distaff.

"Whither away, friend?" said she, "and why do you wear such a sorrowful face?"

The blacksmith stopped and told her the whole story from beginning to end. "Tut!" said the old woman, "you should have chosen the dove, for that was your son for sure and certain."

"There!" said the blacksmith, "if I had only known that in the first place it would have saved me so much leg wear," and back he went, hotfoot, to find the dwarf and to get his son again.

There was the dwarf waiting for him with a basket on his arm, but this time it was a sparrow and a magpie and a lark that were in it, and the

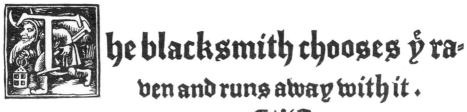

The blacksmith chooses ẏ raven and runs away with it.

⟨)∶(⟩

blacksmith might take which of the three he liked, for one of them was his own son.

The man looked and looked, and could make nothing of it, so all that he could do was to shake his head and turn away again with empty hands.

Out by the edge of the forest sat the old woman spinning. " Prut!" says she, "you should have chosen the lark, for it was your son for sure and certain. But listen; go back and try again; look each bird in the eyes, and choose where you find tears; for nothing but the human soul weeps."

Back went the man into the forest for the third time, and there was the dwarf just as before, only this time it was a sparrow and a jackdaw and a raven that he had in his basket.

The man looked at each of the three in turn, and there were tears in the raven's eyes.

"This is the one I choose," said he, and he snatched it and ran. And it was his son and none other whom he held.

As for the dwarf, he stood and stamped his feet and tore his hair, but that was all he could do, for one must abide by one's bargain, no matter what happens.

You can guess how glad the father and the mother were to have their son back home again. But the lad just sat back of the stove and warmed his shins, and stared into the Land of Nowhere, without doing a stroke of work from morning till night. At last the father could stand it no longer, for, though one is glad to have one's own safe under the roof at home, it is another thing to have one's own doing nothing the livelong day but sit back of the stove and eat good bread and meat; for the silver pine-cones were gone by this time, and good things were no more plentiful in the blacksmith's house than they had been before.

" Come !" says he to lazy-boots one day, " is there nothing at all that you can do to earn the salt you eat ?"

"Oh, yes," said the lad, " I have learned many things, and one over at the dwarf's house yonder, for the dwarf is a famous blacksmith." So out he came from behind the stove, and brushed the ashes from his hair, and went out into the forge.

" Give me a piece of iron," says he, " and I will show you a trick or two worth the knowing."

"Yes," says the blacksmith, " you shall have the iron; all the same I know that it is little or nothing that you know about the hammer and the tongs."

But the young fellow answered nothing. He made a bed of hot coals, and laid the iron in it.

"Here," said he to his father, "do you blow the bellows till I come back, and be sure that you do not stop for so much as a wink, or else all will be spoiled." So he gave the handle into the blacksmith's hand and off he went.

The old man blew the bellows and blew the bellows, but the dwarf over in the forest knew what was being done as well as though he stood in the forge. He was not for letting the lad steal his tricks if he could help it. So he changed himself into a great fly, and came and lit on the blacksmith's neck, and bit him till the blood ran; but the blacksmith just shut his eyes tight, and grinned and bore it, and blew the bellows and blew the bellows.

By and by the lad came in, and the fly flew away. He drew the iron out of the fire, and dipped it in the water, and what do you think it was? Why, a golden tree with a little golden bird sitting in the branches, with bright jewels for its eyes.

The lad drew a little silver wand from his pocket, and gave the tree a tap, and the bird began to hop from branch to branch, and to sing so sweetly that it made one's heart stand still to listen to it.

As for the blacksmith, he just stood and gaped and stared, with his mouth and eyes as wide open as if they never would shut again.

Now there was no king in that country, but a queen who lived in a grand castle on a high hill, and was as handsome a one as ever a body's eyes looked upon.

"Here," says the lad to his father, "take this up to the queen at the castle yonder, and she will pay you well for it." Then he went and sat down back of the stove again, and toasted his shins and stared at nothing at all.

Up went the blacksmith to the queen's castle with the golden bird and the golden tree wrapped up in his pocket-handkerchief. Dear, dear, how the queen did look and listen and wonder, when she saw how pretty it was, and heard how sweetly the little golden bird sang. She called her steward and bade him give the blacksmith a whole bag of gold and silver money for it, and off went the man as pleased as pleased could be.

And now they lived upon the very best of good things over at the blacksmith's house; but good things cost money, and by and by the last penny was spent of what the queen had given him, and nothing would do but for the lad to go out and work a little while at the forge. So up he got from back of the stove, and out he went into the forge. He made a bed of coals and laid the iron upon it.

"Now," says he to his father, "do you blow the bellows till I come back," and off he went.

Well, the old man took the handle and blew and blew, but the dwarf knew what was going on this time, just as well as he had done before. He changed himself into a fly, and came and lit on the blacksmith's neck, and dear, dear, how he did bite! The blacksmith shut his eyes and grinned, but at last he could bear it no longer. He raised his hand and slapped at the fly, but away it flew with never a hair hurt.

In came the lad and drew the iron out of the fire and plunged it into the water, and there it was a beautiful golden comb that shone like fire. But the lad was not satisfied with that. "You should have done as I told you," said he, "and have stopped at nothing; for now the work is spoiled."

The blacksmith vowed and declared that he had not stopped from blowing the bellows, but the lad knew better than that; for there should have been a golden looking-glass as well as the comb. The one was of no use without the other, for when one looked in the golden looking-glass, and combed one's hair with the golden comb, one grew handsomer every day, and the lad had intended both for the queen.

"All the same," said the old man, "I will take the golden comb up to the castle;" and it did no good for the lad to shake his head and say no. "For," says the father, "old heads are wise heads; and the queen will like this as well as the other." So up to the castle he would go, and up to the castle he went.

But when the queen saw the golden comb her brows grew as black as a thunder-storm. "Where is the looking-glass?" said she; and though the old man vowed and declared that no looking-glass belonged with the comb, she knew a great deal better. So, now, the blacksmith might have his choice; he should either bring her the looking-glass that belonged to the golden comb or bring her that which was the best in all the world. If he did neither of these he should be thrown into a deep pit full of toads and vipers.

Back went the old man home again and told the lad all that had happened from beginning to end. And then he wanted to know what he should do to get himself out of his pickle.

The blacksmith brings y̆ wonderful little bird and tree to y̆ Queen.

Well, it was no easy task to make what the queen wanted; all the same, the lad would try what he could do. So he rolled up his sleeves and out he went into the forge and laid a piece of iron upon the bed of hot coals.

This time he would not trust the old man to blow the bellows for him, but took the handle into his own hand and blew and blew.

The dwarf knew what was happening this time as well as before. He changed himself into a fly and came and sat on the lad's forehead, and bit until the blood ran down into his eyes and blinded him; but the lad blew the bellows and blew the bellows.

First the fire burned red, and then it burned white, and then it burned blue, and after that the work was done.

Then the young man raised his hand and struck the fly and killed it, and that was an end of the dwarf for good and all.

What he had made he dipped into the water and it was a gold ring, nothing less nor more. He took a sharp knife and drew charms upon it, and inside of the circle he wrote these words:

> "WHO WEARS THIS SHALL HAVE THE BEST
> THAT THE WORLD HAS TO GIVE."

"Here," said the lad to his father, "take this up to the queen, for it is what she wants, and there is nothing better in the world."

Off marched the old man and gave the ring to the queen, and she slipped it on her finger.

That was how the blacksmith saved his own skin; but the poor queen did nothing but just sit and look out of the window, and sigh and sigh.

After a while she called her steward to her and bade him go over and tell the blacksmith's son to come to her.

There sat the lad back of the stove. "Prut!" said he, "she must send a better than you if she would have me come to her." So the steward had just to go back to the castle again and tell the queen what the lad had said.

Then the queen called her chief minister to her. "Do you go," said she, "and bid the lad come to me."

There sat the lad back of the stove. "Prut!" said he, "she must send a better than you if she would have me come to her."

Off went the minister and told the queen what he had said, and the

he Young Smith forges the best that Life has to give.

queen saw as plain as the nose on her face that she must go herself if she would have the lad come at her bidding.

There sat the lad back of the stove. And would he come with her now?

Yes, indeed, that he would. So he slipped from behind the stove and took her by the hand, and they walked out of the house and up to her castle on the high hill, for that was where he belonged now. There they were married, and ruled the land far and near. For it is one thing to be a blacksmith of one kind, and another thing to be a blacksmith of another kind, and that is the truth, whether you believe it or not.

And did the queen really get the best in the world? Bless your heart, my dear, wait until you are as old as I am, and have been married as long, and you will be able to answer that question without the asking.

The End.

HIC LIBER CAPITE NOSTRO FACTUS EST MANUQUE NOSTRA.

RIDEANT HOMINUM STULTITIAS STULTI, SED
NE, QUOD IN STULTITIIS HOMINUM
HOMINIS ALIQUID EST,
OMNIA IN LEVI
HABEAMUS

*